RACE TO THE DEATH

It was getting dark. I found the street and paused at the corner.

Last chance to change your mind, Jess, I told myself. I pictured Judge Molloy ordering me jailed if she found out I'd talked to a juror. But then I thought of the housewife, Juror Number Seven, being run down by the hit-and-run driver just two days earlier, and of my conversation with her family that revealed she did not believe Billy Brannigan had murdered his older brother. My resolve returned. No backing down now.

I looked up the one-way street. A car slowly approached. Plenty of time for me to cross. But as I stepped off the curb, the roar of its engine froze me in my tracks. I turned. It was bearing down on me at racetrack speed. . . .

D1009015

MORE MURDER SHE WROTE
MYSTERIES

☐ **A DEADLY JUDGMENT by Jessica Fletcher & Donald Bain.** Jessica Fletcher is off to Boston to help her eccentric lawyer friend defend a tycoon accused of fratricide. But when the jurors become victims of deadly accidents—there's even more to ponder as she must find the real culprit before the killer finds her. (187717—$5.99)

☐ **A PALETTE FOR MURDER by Jessica Fletcher & Donald Bain.** Escaping to the Hamptons for a spell in the sun and a chance to paint, Jessica finds herself under the gun to solve a murder mystery where a piece of art, a mountain of money, a mourning millionare, and a slightly mad painter lead her down a twisting trail of illusion and confusion. And watching her every move is an artist of evil who is eager to color Jessica blood-red. (188209—$5.99)

☐ **THE HIGHLAND FLING MURDERS by Jessica Fletcher & Donald Bain. Created by Peter S. Fischer, Richard Levinson & William Link.** Jessica Fletcher and a group of her friends from Cabot Cove, Maine, take off for the British Isles and end up at a castle in Scotland. It would be a great vacation—except for the ghost. And the murders. . . . (188519—$5.99)

*Prices slightly higher in Canada

Buy them at your local bookstore or use this convenient coupon for ordering.

PENGUIN USA
P.O. Box 999 — Dept. #17109
Bergenfield, New Jersey 07621

Please send me the books I have checked above.
I am enclosing $_____ (please add $2.00 to cover postage and handling). Send check or money order (no cash or C.O.D.'s) or charge by Mastercard or VISA (with a $15.00 minimum). Prices and numbers are subject to change without notice.

Card #_____ Exp. Date _____
Signature_____
Name_____
Address_____
City _____ State _____ Zip Code _____

For faster service when ordering by credit card call **1-800-253-6476**

Allow a minimum of 4-6 weeks for delivery. This offer is subject to change without notice.

A DEADLY JUDGMENT

A *Murder, She Wrote* Mystery

A Novel by Jessica Fletcher
and Donald Bain
based on the
Universal television series
created by Peter S. Fischer,
Richard Levinson & William Link

A SIGNET BOOK

SIGNET
Published by the Penguin Group
Penguin Books USA Inc., 375 Hudson Street,
New York, New York 10014, U.S.A.
Penguin Books Ltd, 27 Wrights Lane,
London W8 5TZ, England
Penguin Books Australia Ltd, Ringwood,
Victoria, Australia
Penguin Books Canada Ltd, 10 Alcorn Avenue,
Toronto, Ontario, Canada M4V 3B2
Penguin Books (N.Z.) Ltd, 182–190 Wairau Road,
Auckland 10, New Zealand

Penguin Books Ltd, Registered Offices:
Harmondsworth, Middlesex, England

First published by Signet, an imprint of Dutton Signet,
a division of Penguin Books USA Inc.

First Printing, April, 1996
10   9   8   7   6   5

Copyright © MCA Publishing Rights, a Division of MCA Inc., 1996
All rights reserved

 REGISTERED TRADEMARK—MARCA REGISTRADA

Printed in the United States of America

Without limiting the rights under copyright reserved above, no part of
this publication may be reproduced, stored in or introduced into a re-
trieval system, or transmitted, in any form, or by any means (electronic,
mechanical, photocopying, recording, or otherwise), without the prior
written permission of both the copyright owner and the above publisher
of this book.

PUBLISHER'S NOTE
This is a work of fiction. Names, characters, places, and incidents either
are the product of the author's imagination or are used fictitiously, and
any resemblance to actual persons, living or dead, events, or locales is
entirely coincidental.

BOOKS ARE AVAILABLE AT QUANTITY DISCOUNTS WHEN USED TO PROMOTE
PRODUCTS OR SERVICES. FOR INFORMATION PLEASE WRITE TO PREMIUM MAR-
KETING DIVISION, PENGUIN BOOKS USA INC., 375 HUDSON STREET, NEW YORK,
NEW YORK 10014.

If you purchased this book without a cover you should be aware that
this book is stolen property. It was reported as "unsold and destroyed"
to the publisher and neither the author nor the publisher has received
any payment for this "stripped book."

For Sandy, Bernadette, and all the wonderful people at The Animal Inn. If their love of and care for four-legged animals were applied to the human species, what a lovely world this would be.

Chapter One

I saw it as a speck on the distant horizon, a tiny insect hovering in the hot haze of the day. It came closer, growing larger, and I could see how the earth's heated thermals caught it, bounced it about a bit, then allowed it to stabilize before the next updraft took hold.

"Oh, dear," I said to myself as I watched Jed Richardson maneuver to keep his small single-engine plane on an even keel as it approached Cabot Cove's airport, such as it is. I'd flown with Jed on a number of occasions, never completely comfortable—there's something to be said for the large wings and powerful engines of commercial jet aircraft—although I knew Jed was an excellent pilot, his skills honed over twenty years with a major airline until he retired and started Jed's Flying Service, ferrying Cabot Covers to Bangor and Boston to catch flights elsewhere, taking tourists on airborne sightseeing trips, and operating a flying ambulance service when someone was critically ill and in need of a major hospital center. A consummate professional.

If only his planes were bigger.

Jed had turned into his downwind pattern in preparation for landing the Cessna 182; I knew from him that you always landed a plane into the wind to provide maximum lift under the wings. He banked left until it was time to turn into the wind, which was blowing pretty hard, then slowly descended to the runway, the wings on both sides moving high and low to compensate for shifts of wind as he maintained control until the moment of touchdown, smooth as silk, flaring out and killing power to the engine as the wheels touched with a tiny puff of smoke, came up, then stayed down for good.

I waved as Jed taxied the aircraft to where I stood next to the small one-story white Quonset hut that served as Cabot Cove's terminal. The window on the passenger side opened and an arm reached out to return my greeting. I was glad to see them on the ground. I would have hated to lose my publisher, Vaughan Buckley, to an airline accident.

Jed killed the engine and the single prop came to a jerky standstill. He jumped out and came around to open the passenger door. Vaughan stepped onto a strut and then down to terra firma. He was as trim as always, looking especially cosmopolitan in his navy sports jacket, pressed tan chinos, argyle socks, and Windexed brown loafers. He and his wife, Olga, always turn heads on the street. She's a former model—tall, svelte, and sophisticated. And with a heart to rival Mother Teresa.

As he approached, I detected a slight limp. No, on second observation he walked like someone who'd just come off a rough sea voyage and was trying to find his land legs.

"Jessica," he said, extending his hand.

"My goodness, Vaughan, you look as if you've seen a ghost. Turbulent ride?"

He looked back to where Jed was tying down the Cessna, lowered his voice, and said, " 'Turbulent' is a gross understatement. Glad to be on solid ground again." His smile was weak. "Sorry to keep you waiting, Jess. We sat on the runway at Logan for quite a spell waiting for a long line of real planes—*big* planes to take off. But Jed had enough flying stories to help pass the time. Interesting man. Maybe has a book in him."

"Which I've been telling him for years. Anyway, it's wonderful to see you. Welcome to Cabot Cove."

This marked the first time Vaughan had visited me on my turf. I'd originally suggested he fly to Bangor and have a limo drive him to Cabot Cove. But, surprisingly, at least to me, he asked whether the small airline I'd mentioned in a scene in one of my books, operated by a crusty Maine native named Jed Richardson, would pick him up in Boston. I was tempted to talk him out of that plan. Somehow, I couldn't see my erudite publisher enjoying a couple of hours in one of Jed's puddle jumpers. He's strictly a first-class traveler, not the roughing-it type. He, Olga, and their two dogs, Sadie and Rose, live in a spacious, exquisite apartment in the Dakota, an elegant building on the Upper West Side of Manhattan that overlooks Central Park, the same building where John Lennon and Yoko lived until Lennon was shot to death outside the main gate.

But he'd opted for Jed's Flying Service, and here he was, safe and sound, if not a little shaky.

Jed drove us into town in his Plymouth Voyager.

"Hungry?" I asked as we entered town.

"Believe it or not, I am, Jess."

Jed laughed. "Gave your stomach a bit of a tumble," he said.

"Not at all," Vaughan said. "It's made of cast iron. I grabbed a muffin at LaGuardia before I caught the early shuttle. It's time for dinner according to my internal clock."

"Then I would say a second breakfast is very much in order," I said. "Mind dropping us at Mara's?"

"Not a problem," Jed said.

"Mara's is a local institution," I told Vaughan. "Good solid food and plenty of local color." I was pleased to see that some color of a different sort had returned to his cheeks.

"Join us?" I asked Jed.

"Nice of you, Jessica, but can't. Got to pick up a compass I had serviced over to Wiggins's shop, put 'er in one 'a the aircraft. See you later, Mr.

Buckley. Catchin' a four o'clock shuttle back to New York?"

"That's the plan."

"We'd best leave here 'bout two. I'm plannin' to use a bigger bird, twin engine 310H Cessna, just out 'a her regular inspection. Give you a more comfortable and faster ride back. She'll cruise at two-twenty, two-thirty."

"Sounds good to me," Vaughan said, unfolding his lanky frame from the minivan. "And thanks for a nice ride here. Think about doing a book, Mr. Richardson. I'd be interested."

"Good afternoon, good morning, whatever," Mara said from behind the counter in her postage-stamp size restaurant. "And good day to you, Mr. Buckley," she said without having been introduced to him. She wiped her arthritic right hand on her stained apron and extended it to him.

"I'm pleased to meet you," Vaughan said.

"I suppose I've talked a lot about your visit, Vaughan," I said. "Cabot Cove isn't like New York. Everyone in town knows my esteemed publisher is visiting me today."

"I'm flattered."

"Up here," Mara said, "you're a pretty big fish in a wee little pond."

"And in New York I'm just one fish in a school of millions of minnows."

"No offense," Mara said.

"None taken. You're right. And I'm delighted to be here."

"Are we having breakfast or lunch?" Mara asked.

Vaughan and I looked at each other. "Heard a lot about you from Ms. Fletcher, Mr. Buckley," said Mara. "Seems to me you're the blueberry pancake sort 'a fella."

Vaughan's smile was broad and genuine. "Sounds wonderful," he said. "And, please call me Vaughan."

As Mara led us to a small table covered in a red-and-white check plastic tablecloth, she asked, "Usual low-calorie special for you, Jess?"

"Not today, Mara. I think I'll join Vaughan. Make it two stacks of blueberry pancakes."

"You have quite an influence on our town's first lady," she said to Vaughan.

"I certainly hope so," he replied, holding out my chair.

After settling down at the table and taking in his surroundings—there were a few fishermen who'd just returned from a run, and some tourists—Vaughan said, "Cabot Cove is delightful, Jess, as I knew it would be. As magical as you'd painted it. Picturesque seaside town, quaint, friendly but with enough hustle and bustle to make even a Manhattanite like me feel at home."

"You're here during the tourist season," I said. "Come back in the dead of winter. Not much hustle and bustle then."

We sipped our coffee while I waxed a little more poetic about my town. He listened intently; Vaughan Buckley was a good listener, one of his many endearing qualities.

"You know, Jess, Olga and I have been looking for a country home. A real getaway place, and I mean *away*. Of course, we have the house in the Hamptons. It's nice there, but it seems like the entire publishing world feels the same way. Hard to escape in the real sense of the word. I'm thinking that Cabot Cove would be the perfect place to have a retreat. You know, come up and hibernate for weeks at a time. Sadie and Rose would love it." He chuckled softly. "I'm not sure Olga would want to become a regular passenger of Jed Richardson, though. She gets motion sick on elevators."

I laughed. "It looked to me as though you might have been a little queasy yourself when you got out of the plane this morning."

"No, not at all."

He finished his coffee. Why is it men can't admit to something like motion sickness? I wondered. I know few who can. Like not asking for directions when lost.

I fielded Vaughan's questions about fishing in the area, shopping, hospitals, and theater, sounding very much like a real estate agent. It would be wonderful if he and Olga had a home here. They're two of my favorite people.

On the other hand, one of the reasons I still

live in Cabot Cove is because, although you can make the trip in half a day, this sleepy town is a million miles from New York. Here I can be someone other than the famed mystery writer, the role I'm forced to play when in New York and other cities promoting my books. I like living in two separate worlds—Jessica Fletcher Number One: decent fisherwoman, maker of homemade jams and to-die-for iced tea, and wearer of thick, woolly, cable-knit sweaters. And Jessica Fletcher Number Two: famed mystery writer, Chanel earrings, silk chemise blouses, expert at making reservations, savvy shopper, and as-good-as-the-next-guy at finding a cab at rush hour. If I had to give up one for the other, I'd opt for Jessica Number One, the Cabot Cove version. It's the real me. As my mother always said, "Be true to your colors, Jessica."

Although Vaughan raved about the pancakes, he went easy, leaving half a stack on his plate before calling it quits, which Mara would probably take personally.

"Well, Jess, I suppose it's time we get down to business," Vaughan said after the plates had been cleared (Mara's expression confirmed what I'd expected), and our cups had been refilled with her signature strong, aromatic coffee.

I was glad to get to the real reason for Vaughan's trip to Cabot Cove. He'd never visited me before, and the fragile, paranoid ego of a writer—any writer—this writer was working overtime. Not that I was concerned that my long-standing relationship with Buckley House was in jeopardy. The sales of my books ranked me high on the publisher's bottom line. But I hadn't come up with an idea for my next work because, frankly, I didn't have a clue as to what it would be. I'd toyed with myriad plots, none of which stood up to scrutiny upon reflection. Was Vaughan Buckley about to prod me to come up with my next book, even chastise me for having become—well, lazy, perhaps? Or had he brought worse news? No matter how successful my books had been, it was always possible—my insecurity level seemed to increase with each passing minute—for any publisher to decide that an author's string had run, that her books no longer appealed to that large baby-boomer population, that her . . .

"Okay," I said, "time to talk business. You didn't come all the way to Cabot Cove for pancakes."

"But not a bad idea," he said, laughing. "Jess, I came here today to discuss your next book. I think the next J. D. Fletcher best-seller should revolve around a murder trial."

"Oh?"

"It's the hottest genre in publishing. The O.J. Simpson trial. Susan Smith. Grisham. Turow. One best-selling novel after another set during a trial. I think it's time you tapped into that interest."

"I don't know," I said. "I understand what you're saying, but although it may be the hot genre right now, it isn't *my* genre. I haven't the foggiest idea about murder trials other than what I follow in the papers. For me to write a book with a plot that relies heavily on trial procedure, I'd have to dedicate an awful lot of time to research. Maybe even sit through an entire trial to pick up the nuances, soak up the mood, study the judge, the jurors. And believe me, Vaughan, murder trials in Cabot Cove are few and far between. We haven't had anyone tried for murder here in years. I'd like to keep it that way. So should you if you're serious about buying a home here."

Vaughan laughed. "Not a high crime rate, I take it."

"An occasional stolen chicken. Graffiti on the bridge."

"I love it. Look, you know what a fan you have in me. I would never insist that you heed my suggestion about what sort of plot to use in your next book. You're the expert in that area, not me. All I ask is that you think about it."

"Of course I will. I just don't think—"

"Not now." He checked his watch. "How about a walking tour of Cabot Cove?"

"Sure. We can stroll toward my house, stop there for some iced tea for which I've achieved a modicum of local fame, and lunch if the walk spikes your appetite."

We said good-bye to Mara—"You didn't like the pancakes, Mr. Buckley?" "They were wonderful, just so filling"—and started walking.

Later, over iced tea on my patio, he said, "Looks like it's time to hook up with Mr. Richardson for the flight back."

"He'll be by in fifteen minutes to pick you up. It's been such a pleasure having you here, Vaughan."

"And it's been a pleasure to be here, see your town, sample your iced tea which, I agree, deserves a prize. Great to get away for a day."

"I imagine."

Jed arrived, and Vaughan climbed into his minivan.

"We'll talk soon," he said to me.

"Count on it. Safe home. Best to Olga. And to Sadie and Rose."

I watched them pull away, went to the patio to pick up the empty glasses, settled in front of the computer in my office, and started working on a plot for my next book, which had nothing to do with murder trials and the law. Fact was, I didn't want to devote months to sitting through a trial in order to gain knowledge of how it works despite Vaughan's urging me to do it. Besides, how would I arrange to attend such a trial?

No, not for me, I decided as I tried to concoct a plot based upon what are basically six standard approaches for a murder mystery—a hard-boiled private eye? A spy this time, or a rogue cop? A flat-out tale of horror? Maybe something in a Gothic setting. No cozy mystery this time around; my last two had been small-scale with all the suspects ending up together in a house with failed electricity.

A murder trial?

I gave up at midnight, climbed into bed, and thought about Vaughan's visit and his idea for my next book.

A trial?

No.

Sorry, Vaughan.

Lights out.

Chapter Two

I'm an early riser, but was awake even earlier than usual the following morning. I followed my usual routine: put on a robe and picked up the *New York Times* and the Cabot Cove *Spotlight* from the foot of my driveway. The *Spotlight* was a weekly, published on Thursday. This was Friday, its delivery day. I turned on the drip coffeemaker I'd set up the night before, got the fans going to draw in the cool morning air, and went to the patio to inspect my dozens of potted red geraniums. They didn't look too good to me, wilted, less than radiant, weak. I'd been delinquent in my watering, and rectified that immediately. Geraniums represent a passion of mine. I'd actually wanted to hold a pot of them at my wedding, but was told by friends and family that it would have been inappropriate. I shouldn't have listened to them. My dear husband, now deceased, knew my love of the red flower and showered me on every anniversary with pots of them.

As I was pouring coffee into an insulated carafe

to keep it from steeping longer than necessary, the phone rang. I picked it up in the kitchen. "Hello," I said.

"Hello there, dear Jessica. Have I caught you at a bad moment?"

"No. Who is this?" The laugh was deep and rumbling, a laugh I now recognized. "Malcolm? Malcolm McLoon?"

"Of course. It hasn't been *that* long, has it?" he asked in his characteristic loud, deep, stentorian voice that mirrored his physical presence.

"Five years?" I said.

"Oh, my, Jessica, if it's that long, we're both growing older at a rate faster than we wish."

Malcolm McLoon was in his late sixties, and everything about him was grandiose—long, flowing white hair, huge potbelly—a frustrated Shakespearean actor, fond of limp, floppy multicolored bow ties and whimsical suits, usually white or cream-colored, summer or winter. His reputation for being fond of the bottle rivaled his fame as one of the most successful, and controversial criminal defense attorneys in America. He'd handled dozens of high-profile cases since leaving Cabot Cove twenty years ago, and had won the majority of them, despite what critics pointed to as a gratingly pompous and obnoxiously flagrant style. They were right, of course. But there was another side of him that I'd gotten to know, a gentle charm, a man who would give you the shirt off his back provided you wore shirts with a collar size of twenty, and a size sixty suit.

"How are you, Malcolm?"

"Couldn't be better, Jessica. Tip-top. And how are you, young lady?"

"Just fine. I enjoyed the glorious spring we had, and so far the summer's been kind to me. Even getting in a little fishing. How do you like that?"

"I like it very much, indeed," he said. "Working on anything these days? A new book?"

"Funny you should ask," I said. "I had breakfast with my publisher yesterday to discuss what's next. Nothing decided yet. He wants me to—"

A murder trial? Malcolm McLoon? Interesting timing.

"I call with a proposition, dear lady."

"A decent one, I trust."

"Am I capable of any other kind? How would you like to work with me on my next case?"

Was this what they meant by serendipity?

"I don't understand," I said.

"Allow me to explain. I've been retained by the Brannigan family of Boston. You've heard of them, of course. Brannigan's Bean Pot? The best baked beans this side of the Charles River. Hmmm, hmm good."

"Of course I'm familiar with the name and the product. And I agree. They are the best baked beans—in a can. But you haven't tasted baked beans until you've tasted mine. I've perfected a wonderful recipe."

"Perhaps you'll do me the honor of cooking up a batch in my kitchen while you're here."

"While I'm there?"

"Yes." He said it as though I should have known all along why I would be in Boston. "Unfortunately, Jessica, it seems the Brannigan family troubles have gained notoriety in more these days than their baked beans."

I understood what he was saying. I'd followed recent media coverage of the murder of Jack Brannigan by his brother, William. "I can't think of anything more tragic than one family member killing another," I said.

"Billy Brannigan is an innocent man, Jessica. Being accused of murdering his brother, and being convicted of it, are two very different things. Truth is, he didn't do it. As his defense counsel, I'm confident I will successfully make that point to a jury of his peers."

"Congratulations on being chosen to defend him, Malcolm. From what I've read, it will be a difficult case to try."

"Not for this lawyer," he said. I smiled as he continued. "You are your usual gracious self to offer your congratulations, but I didn't call to elicit them, although there are those who label me a braggart and wouldn't put it past me to do just such a thing. But you know the real Malcolm, don't you?"

"Yes, I do," I said, my grin widening. "What can I do for you?"

"I want you to come to Boston for the summer . . . ," he sang. It was a line from a popular song I hear while waiting in my dentist's office, or flipping through the light FM channels on the radio.

"You're in good voice," I said. "But maybe I'd understand better if you talked, rather than sang."

"I wish to hire you as my jury consultant, to help me choose a jury I can count on to see things my way."

That's one way of putting it, I thought. As much as I believe in our system of jurisprudence and its advocacy system—certainly better and fairer than any other system in the world—I always cringe when I think of how attorneys from both sides try to stack a jury with men and women with a predisposition to lean in one direction or the other. Jury consultants had become, from what I'd read, integral parts of major cases, applying psychological insight and demographic patterns to choosing who serves on a jury, and who doesn't. They're professionals with special skills, and command large fees.

So why was he asking me *to be a jury consultant?*

"Why would you want *me* to be a jury consultant?" I asked. "I have no experience in such things."

"Oh, but you do, dear Jessica. You have great insight into people. All the reviews of your books pick up on that. You create characters like none other. What you have is every defense lawyer's dream, an intuitive feel for people, what they really think and feel, their hidden prejudices, dark secrets, and—say you'll do it."

"Malcolm, I am sincerely flattered by your offer and high opinion of me. But I really don't think that—"

I thought about blueberry pancakes with Vaughan.

"Let me sleep on it, Malcolm. Can I give you a call tomorrow?"

"I knew you'd do it."

"I didn't say—"

"Call collect. First thing in the morning. I've virtually been sleeping in my office getting ready for this trial. How wonderful it will be to have you on the case. Name your price. First-class all the way. The best suite at the Ritz-Carlton. A limousine. Caviar and champagne along with the morning paper each day. A new wardrobe if you wish. Nothing will be too good for my—"

"Jury consultant?"

"Yes. My jury consultant. I'll have all arrangements made when you call in the morning."

"I didn't say I would, Malcolm."

"Legal Sea Food."

"Pardon?"

"Dinner at Legal Sea Food in Cambridge. A splendid restaurant. Let me see, the second night we can—"

"I'll call in the morning. Give me your office number in case I've misplaced it."

After he did, I asked, "How long do you esti-
mate I would have to be in Boston?"

"Five, six weeks. I intend to push the defense
case along quickly, although you never know with
the prosecution. If they move as slowly as they
did in the Simpson case, it might be even longer."

"That's a long time for me to be away. I have
to start my next novel."

*A murder trial. Jury consultant. An insider learn-
ing how it works.*

"You'll hear from me in the morning. Tomorrow's Saturday, you know."

"Eight days a week when I'm into a trial, Jessica. I can't tell you how delighted I am that
you've agreed to be one of my jury consultants."

" 'One of'?"

"I'll explain when you're here."

"I didn't say I—"

"Enjoy your day, Jessica. Start packing. McLoon
and Fletcher are about to turn the Boston legal
system on its ear. Has a nice ring to it. McLoon
and Fletcher. You should consider law school.
You'd make a good attorney."

After a restless night, I took a chance and called
the number Malcolm had given me at seven Saturday morning. He answered on the first ring.

"When do I start?" I asked cheerfully.

"Tomorrow too soon?"

"Yes."

"Monday?"

"All right."

"Good. Monday morning at my office. I've already made your reservation at the Ritz starting tomorrow. Come a day early if you change your mind. Relax. Sightsee."

"I'll see you on Monday. Nine o'clock?"

"I'll have a driver pick you up at the Ritz at eight-thirty."

"All right," I said. "Are you still in the same office in Government Center?"

"Same one. See you then."

The contemplation of staying at the Ritz-Carlton was delicious. It's always been my hotel of choice when in Boston, my hotel of choice in many other cities.

I'd considered mentioning to Malcolm that the real reason I'd accepted his proposition was to soak up the atmosphere of a murder trial in preparation for my next murder mystery for Buckley House, but I didn't know how he'd respond to that. If there's one thing I abhor, it's when someone takes advantage of another under false pretenses.

I decided not to call Vaughan Buckley in New York to tell him of my plans. I wrote a short note informing him that I'd be in Boston for a shopping and theater spree, and would be in touch when I returned, adding,

"The more I think about your suggestion to set my next book during a murder trial, the more appealing it becomes. More later. Hope your flight back with Jed was smooth and pleasant. Jess."

"In case you haven't noticed," I said as I stirred an oversized pot of baked beans that had been simmering all morning on my stove, "I am a big, grown-up girl. I know precisely what I'm getting into, and have decided to do it after careful consideration."

"Sorry," Cabot Cove's sheriff, Morton Metzger, said from my kitchen table, "but it just don't seem like something you'd do, Jess."

"Why? Because I've never been a jury consultant before? I've never been lots of things before, but that doesn't mean I'm not willing to try them."

"But this is different," he said, spearing a piece of melon. "This involves that crazy coot, Malcolm McLoon." He chuckled. "Aptly named, I'd say. McLoon. Crazy as one."

"Oh, Mort, Malcolm is just—well, he's just different. You have to admit he's a brilliant trial attorney."

"And a drunk and womanizer. I read the papers."

The supermarket checkout papers, I thought, not voicing it.

"I remember back to when he was trying cases right here in Cabot Cove. Damn fool got Judge Mallory so mad one day he threw McLoon in jail himself. Remember?"

"Yes, I do. He's been jailed by other judges, too, for contempt."

"There you go. Take my advice, call the fat buf-

foon back and tell him to get another jury consultant." He guffawed. "Jury consultant. Just a fancy
name for somebody paid lots 'a money to help get
guilty people off."

"Taste?" I held out a wooden spoon with beans
on it.

"Good as usual," he said, "but could use a mite
more garlic."

"I already have two cloves in," I said. Our sheriff was known for his love of garlic. "Is it true you
put garlic on cornflakes?" I asked.

"Not true," he said, finishing the melon. "Sure
you won't reconsider?" he asked.

"About going to Boston. No. I'm going."

"Maybe Seth'll have better luck talkin' sense
to you."

"I doubt it."

I wiped my hands on my apron, turned, and
leaned against the counter. "There's more to my
going to Boston than I've told you."

"Really? And what might that be?"

"Don't make me sound like a criminal. When
my publisher, Vaughan Buckley, visited me Thursday, he told me he wants my next book to be
based upon a murder trial. I said I didn't agree
because I don't know how they work. Then, Malcolm called the next day and offered me this role
as his—one of his jury consultants. How about
that for timing? Serendipitous, wouldn't you say?"

"Sounds more like a coincidence to me."

"That, too."

"Hot as heck in here, Jess," he said, wiping his brow. "Why on earth you slavin' over a hot stove in the middle 'a summer?"

"Thinking of Brannigan's canned beans whetted my appetite for the real thing. Can you stay for lunch? Seth will be here shortly."

"Does he know about this silly trip you're taking to Boston?"

"Yes. I called him this morning to renew some prescriptions to bring with me. Told him the news. He was delighted." I smiled and transferred the beans into a glazed ceramic pot I reserve exclusively for them.

"Smells good, Jess. How 'bout some iced tea?"

"Brewing on the back patio. Ready in a minute."

"Got to call the station house and tell 'em I'll be back after lunch. Set another place at the table for me. Maybe Seth'll get through to you. He knows McLoon and his reputation."

"I'll be delighted to hear whatever he has to say."

Which wasn't much.

Seth Hazlitt, my very good friend and Cabot Cove's leading physician, mentioned Malcolm McLoon's unsavory personal reputation, and questioned whether I could afford to be away from Cabot Cove for so long. I explained how the trial would serve as research for my next book.

"Makes sense to me, Jessica," he said. "Please pass the beans and the corn bread. Beans are excellent, 'though there's a touch too much garlic in 'em."

Chapter Three

The moment Seth and Mort left, I went into high gear to prepare for my extended stay in Boston. I didn't know how I would manage it in the brief time available to me between that afternoon and Monday, but whenever my energy level flagged, the thought of being in Boston injected a shot of adrenalin.

I'm an unabashed Boston lover. To me, it's the closest thing America has to a European city, which is how I usually describe it to people who've never been there. It's the most civil of cities, quaint, charming, superb food, plenty of culture and intellectually stimulating.

Each September, the city's population swells by a quarter of a million—students and professors. Harvard University, Boston University, Boston College, Simmons, Northeast, Massachusetts Institute of Technology—they're all here. And if you love politics and sports, look no further. Heated conversation about either can be found virtually everywhere; Bostonians not only love to talk about

their elected officials and athletic heroes or scape-
goats, they have strong opinions, and are willing
to give them to you at the drop of a lobster. Bostonians love to talk. Period. About anything.

Of course, I have ties to Boston beyond those
of a tourist, including fond memories of having
been a student at Boston University where I studied English, and of living there as a young adult
while working for a fine publishing house as an
entry-level editor. Nothing but pleasant thoughts
to fuel my preparation for a month or more in
what many call Beantown.

Jed Richardson flew me to Logan Airport in his
Cessna 310H twin-engine aircraft, the same one
he'd used to ferry Vaughan Buckley back home.
Much of the smooth, quick flight that crystal-
clear early Monday morning was taken up with
Jed's questions about whether he should consider
writing a book for Buckley House. I certainly en-
couraged him, and offered ongoing advice if he
decided to do it.

As I left the general aviation building where Jed
had let me off and walked in the direction of waiting cabs, my heavy luggage on a rolling cart provided by the airport, a young woman in a black
uniform approached. She carried a sign that
read FLETCHER.

"Are you looking for me?" I asked.

"Mrs. Fletcher?"

"Yes."

"I'm here to drive you to the hotel."

"But I thought I was being picked up *at* the hotel."

"Mr. McLoon changed his mind when he learned you'd be flying in this morning. My name's Cathie. Let me help you with your luggage."

As she loaded my bags into the Lincoln Town Car's trunk, she said, "I'm really honored to be driving you, Mrs. Fletcher. My mom has read every one of your books."

"How nice to hear."

"I'm hoping to be assigned as your steady daytime driver while you're here."

" 'Steady *daytime* driver'?"

"Yes. There'll be a nighttime driver, too."

"Two full-time drivers?" I said. "For me?"

"Order of Mr. McLoon, Mrs. Fletcher."

"I'll have to speak with him about it," I said, settling into the comfortable leather rear seat.

One pleasant aspect of flying to Boston is the airport's close proximity to the city, much like Washington, D.C.'s National Airport. We stayed left coming out of the airport and followed signs to Sumner Tunnel where Cathie paid the dollar toll. We then took the Central Artery and, shortly thereafter, pulled up in front of the Ritz-Carlton, at Arlington and Newbury in Boston's historic Back Bay area. The ride, as short as it was, reminded me why I don't drive, especially in Boston. Lanes don't seem to mean much there, intersections are the scene of one driver challenging another, and entrance ramps onto parkways and expressways are more like takeoff ramps. But Cathie drove sensibly, for which I was grateful.

I checked my watch. Eight o'clock. I was due at Malcolm's office at nine.

Cathie unloaded my bags beneath the fluttering blue awnings and they were taken by a young man in a snappy uniform. "They'll be brought to your room, Mrs. Fletcher," he said. I hadn't introduced myself and was impressed he knew who I was.

I checked in. A few minutes later an assistant manager escorted me into an elevator operated by a young woman in uniform and wearing white gloves. At the end of a corridor on the top floor was my "room"—a large, lovely suite furnished in European style, and with a wonderful view of the Public Garden.

"It's absolutely beautiful," I said, taking it in. "But much too fancy for me, I'm afraid. And expensive."

The manager laughed. "Mrs. Fletcher, we are delighted to have you as our guest. I understand you'll be staying as long as a month, which makes it that much more important that you feel at home, have plenty of space, and be surrounded with nice things. Besides, Mr. McLoon's instruction to us is that you are to be spared nothing in the way of comfort."

"That's very kind of him," I said. Evidently the fee Malcolm was being paid by the Brannigan family was big enough to support this sort of unnecessary indulgence. Vaughan Buckley was lucky. It wouldn't cost him a cent for me to research my next novel.

"I'll leave you to settle in," the manager said.

"I'm afraid I don't have much time for that," I said. "I'm due at Mr. McLoon's office in a few minutes."

"Of course. The Ritz-Carlton's services are at your disposal, Mrs. Fletcher. And I've left my office and home numbers in case you need something special. We stand ready to provide our guests anything—as long as it's legal."

I laughed, and he left me alone in the sumptuous suite.

I'd been to the Boston Ritz-Carlton on many occasions, mostly for cocktails, dinner, and an occasional overnight stay. It's one of the world's premiere hotels, the oldest of all the Ritz-Carltons. That I'd be there for a month or more was both exciting and off-putting.

I quickly freshened up, then took a fast tour of the suite before going downstairs to where Cathie waited. The furniture was mahogany—king-sized bed, elegant desk, and towering armoire. Furniture and decor defined simple European elegance. A fireplace in the living room was inviting despite the time of year. I could always crank up the air-conditioning and enjoy a fire, I decided.

As I headed for the large window overlooking the Public Garden, I noticed a copy of that day's *Boston Globe* on a coffee table in front of a couch.

A front-page headline caught my eye: BAKED BEANS MURDER TRIAL TO BEGIN. I picked it up and read the first paragraph, which in the best journalistic tradition of telling readers the who, what, why, when, and where of a story, mentioned that Jack Brannigan had been murdered in that idyllic Garden. How tragic, I thought, to be brutally killed in such beautiful surroundings.

I checked myself in a full-length mirror, took a deep breath, and headed out the door to become—to become a jury consultant, of all things.

That's what's wonderful about being alive, I thought. You never know what's around the corner.

Jessica Fletcher—Jury Consultant.

It made me laugh.

Chapter Four

Flanked by Faneuil Hall and the Financial District, Government Center has never been one of my favorite sections of Boston. Sure, it has a history: the Freedom Trail, the Old State House, and the Custom House Tower are a stone's throw away.

But Government Center, with its skyscrapers and nondescript streets lacks the quaintness that characterizes the rest of Boston, most of which is comprised of neighborhoods—the Italian North End; the predominantly Irish neighborhood called Southie; Back Bay, the fashionable part of town; and Beacon Hill, reminiscent of London with its pubs and narrow, brick streets. Newbury Street's cafés and boutiques have always been high on my list of favorite areas. But I love Harvard Square, too, its coffeehouses, street musicians, and the university's old brick buildings magical to me. Come to think of it, I can never seem to make up my mind which part of Boston I like best.

But I do know it isn't Government Center.

Boston's business hub was bustling that Monday morning with thousands of people on their way to work, sharply dressed yuppies hurrying to their offices, cappuccinos and café lattes in hand (why anyone would spend that much money for a cup of coffee is beyond my comprehension), incongruous white Nikes on their feet beneath suits and dresses, a spring in their step as they mounted another day and week in their careers. But it struck me as I stepped out of the Town Car that as busy as Government Center was that morning, everything seemed more civil than in New York. There was a certain unstated order to it, as opposed to the usual mayhem accompanying New York's pedestrian's rush hour.

Malcolm's office was located in one of the district's skyscrapers, tall for Boston but not by New York standards. The elevator ascended quickly to the twenty-third floor where I easily found the suite, identified by an oversized brass nameplate. I opened the door, stepped into the reception area, and approached a desk. Seated behind it was an attractive middle-aged woman. The moment she saw me she jumped up, came around the desk, and extended her hand. "Mrs. Fletcher? I'm Linda, Mr. McLoon's receptionist. We've been waiting for you."

"Am I late?"

"Oh, no," she replied, her smile lighting up the room. "I'm personally excited about meeting you. When Mr. McLoon said you'd agreed to join the defense team, I was—well, I was tickled. I'm a fan."

"That's very kind."

"Are you working on a new book?"

"Well, not exactly. I—"

"LINDA!!!"

The bellowing male voice rattled the speaker on her desk.

"LINDA!!! Is Mrs. Fletcher here yet?"

"Oh, my," she said, scurrying behind her desk, pushing a button on the intercom, and saying, "She's here, Mr. McLoon."

"Well, send her in, for gracious sake."

Linda managed a small smile. "Follow me," she said.

We walked down a long, narrow hallway to the last door on the left. Linda knocked. "Come in," Malcolm's voice said through the heavy wooden door.

Malcolm was perched on the edge of his desk, his large head in a cloud of dense smoke from a long, fat black cigar clenched between his teeth. He wore a rumpled white shirt, a red-and-yellow bow tie, wrinkled gray pants, black sneakers with white socks peeking over the tops, and a green-and-blue tartan plaid jacket that made me think of my dear friend and quintessential Scotsman, Scotland Yard Inspector George Sutherland, who I immediately wished was there at my side.

"Our guest of honah has arrived," Malcolm said, coming off the desk with arms open wide, fly wide open. He wrapped me in an all-encompassing, sweaty embrace, the cigar still billowing smoke. Would the smell ever come out of my suit? I wondered.

"Guest of honor?" I said, disengaging. "I'm the one who's honored."

"Nonsense. Sit down, Jessica. I want to introduce you to some good people." He gestured to a chair in front of his desk. I nodded at the others in the room, who sat closely grouped on chairs in one corner, and took the seat Malcolm had indicated.

"LINDA!!!" McLoon shouted into his intercom. "We need more coffee." To me: "Still prefer tea?"

"Yes. It doesn't matter."

"Tea for Mrs. Fletcher. And rustle up some donuts. Jelly ones. Where the hell are my cigars? Did you hide 'em again?"

"No, sir. You put them—"

"I know, I know." He waddled to a closet and pulled a box of cigars down from a shelf. With the one he'd been smoking still smoldering in the ashtray, he lighted another.

I took advantage of the lull to take in his office. Obviously, an interior decorator's hand hadn't been utilized. The room was pure Malcolm in all his brilliant disarray. A hodgepodge of not-so-interesting art of the sort bought at flea markets to match the color of furniture hung crookedly on the walls, along with photographs of Malcolm with celebrities and politicians, also crooked—the pictures, not necessarily the politicians. A burnt-orange shag rug, decorated with multiple burn holes and reminiscent of every Holiday Inn hotel room in the 1970s, took up a portion of the floor in front of his desk. Bookcases lining one wall looked like a housing project, the books on them haphazardly stacked. The windows needed cleaning, undoubtedly because of a film of nicotine. A blue haze hung over everything.

"Jessica, you look mahvelous," Malcolm said, his Boston accent shining through as he plopped in his high-backed leather chair and propped his black sneakers on the desk. "Haven't aged a day since I last saw you."

I indicated with my eyes that the others in the room were waiting to be introduced to me. Malcolm struggled to his feet and stood between us. "Like you to meet the other fine folks on the team, Jessica."

A woman went to Malcolm and whispered something in his ear, causing the corpulent attorney to pull up the zipper of his pants, never missing a verbal beat. "Jessica Fletcher, meet Rachel Cohen, my cocounsel on this case, and soon-to-be-household-name in every court of this land."

I took Ms. Cohen's extended hand. She was dressed the part of the successful attorney—navy pinstripe suit with fashionable above-the-knee skirt, tailored white blouse, navy heels, expensive haircut.

"And I present Ritchie Fleigler, the best private

investigator this side of the Charles River. Maybe even beyond." McLoon's private investigator, Ritchie Fleigler, had ink-black hair that matched the color of his T-shirt, and that he wore shoulder length. His tight jeans were blue, his high-top sneakers white. He was well over six feet tall, which helped him carry off the look.

"And this is my better half, Miss Georgia Bobley, my loyal and long-suffering administrative assistant." Ms. Bobley was a short, attractive young woman with chestnut-brown hair, nervous green eyes, a cinematic smile, and a trim figure. Her clothing that day consisted of a lightweight salmon V-neck sweater over a brown blouse, pleated tan skirt, and clogs.

I exchanged greetings with them.

There was another person in the room, a handsome young man seated in a black vinyl chair wedged into the corner. He sat quietly, one leg crossed over the other, his attention seemingly directed to a chipped marble bust of Winston Churchill.

"Jessica, meet William Brannigan," McLoon said.

The defendant.

For some reason, having him there startled me. I assumed he was in prison. He stood, looked at me without expression, and extended his hand, which I took.

"Hello, Mr. Brannigan," I said. "I'm pleased to meet you."

"Likewise," he said softly. "Please call me Bill."

"All right—Bill."

"Very good, then," said Malcolm. "Everyone's been introduced. We'll all be spending a lot of time together over the next few months"—he glanced at me for a reaction—"and I think we're going to make one hell of a team. We'll be putting in long hours and late nights. But it will be justified when our efforts result in justice being served, when this fine young man, from a fine and distinguished family, unfairly accused of the dastardly act of murdering his own flesh and blood, is judged to be innocent by a jury of his peers." He delivered his message with great dramatic flourish, drawing from his experience as an actor before becoming an attorney. I'd never seen him in action in court before, but I was getting a glimpse now. He spoke as though delivering a Shakespearean speech. Eloquent. Flowery. And loud.

"Now, let's get down to work," he said. "Tomorrow, we start interviewing prospective jurors. I don't need to remind everyone in this room how important this phase of the trial will be, certainly the most critical step of the case so fah. Jessica, I'll explain more about the actual process over lunch."

"I'd appreciate that," I said, indulging in understatement. I knew nothing abut what had become a critical part of the justice system—the selection of jurors.

"Ritchie," McLoon said to his investigator, "I know you've got to run. Keep digging and call me this afternoon."

"No problem," Ritchie said, exiting the room.

"Rachel?" Malcolm said, thumbing through an agenda book the thickness of *War and Peace*.

"Yes, Malcolm?" his assistant defense counsel said, smiling at me.

"Let's talk. What's the latest with you?"

"Well, I found a tick on the dog this morning. My son, Josh, is performing in a middle school concert tonight. And my husband, Joe, is on call tonight at the hospital."

I was the only person in the room to laugh. I glanced at the defendant, Bill Brannigan, who was immersed in the contents of a thick manila file folder. He didn't look up.

"Perhaps you'd be kind enough, Rachel, to include the Brannigan case in your comments." Malcolm said it without any hint of annoyance. "Any headway on the Cape Cod front?"

"I'll know more by the end of the day," she said.

"Then I suggest you get to work on it right now and fill us in at lunch."

"I'd love to join you, Malcolm, but can't," she said. "I'll have to work through lunch if I'm to get out of here tonight in time to attend Josh's concert."

"Of course," said Malcolm. "Tell that little fellow of yours that if he doesn't sing good, he'll answer to me."

Now, everyone laughed, with the exception of Brannigan. It was good to see that a pleasant relationship existed between Malcolm and his assistant counsel, between everyone on McLoon's team for that matter.

Malcolm's personal assistant, Georgia Bobley, left the room as Linda arrived with tea, coffee, and a dozen jelly donuts in a box, which she placed on the small conference table. Once she was gone, it left McLoon, Billy Brannigan, and me in the office.

"All right, now, Jessica, let us spend the few hours before lunch reviewing the case for your benefit, and to give you a chance to get to know the reason for our being here, the defendant, Mr. William Brannigan."

"Fine," I said, feeling very much out of my element.

"As I've told you, Willie, Mrs. Fletchah is a real people person, the best I've ever known. She creates believable characters in her bestselling novels because she knows what makes people tick, what causes them to do things, make decisions. I've coaxed her to help us make sure that everyone on the jury is a people person, too. Not a police person. Not a prosecutor person. But a people person."

He took a long, deep drag on his cigar before continuing. "With that understood, let us proceed. Billy Brannigan has been charged with having murdered his brother, Jack. The prosecution bases its case against our client (it felt strangely good to be included in "our client") on William, here, having been threatened with being cut out of a family trust by the trust's trustee, his older brother, Jack. Jack threatened that action based upon a ridiculous clause in the trust allowing William to be cut out if he was ever charged with a crime involving moral turpitude. Ever *charged with*! Not even convicted. An abominable perversion of everything precious about our system of justice. William Brannigan was falsely accused of attempting to rape a young woman on Cape Cod. Based upon that—and it was only her word that was taken—Jack was about to take from his younger brother the source of income that their father had wanted him to enjoy. William Brannigan is not a little bit innocent, Jessica. That is like being a little bit pregnant. You're either pregnant or you're not. You're either innocent or you're not. He is *completely* innocent, and the jury will not only come to realize this when I am through presenting our case, that same jury will actually feel sorry for this exemplary young man whose life is now in my hands. In *our* hands!"

I wanted to applaud.

He wasn't finished. He came behind Brannigan, placed ham-hock hands on the young man's shoulders, and intoned, "This is a well-respected man, Jessica, hard-worker, a family man."

"Yes, I'm—I'm certain he is."

It's been my experience that people living off

trusts generally aren't "hard working." Nor was I aware that Brannigan was married. But it wasn't the time or place for me to raise those issues.

"Bill, do you want to say anything to Mrs. Fletcher?" McLoon asked. "Naturally, I'll go over the case with her in detail, step by step. But do you have anything to offer at this moment?"

"Yes," he said.

His smile was wide and winning. What a handsome young man, I thought. Chiseled features, brilliant blue eyes, thick black hair.

"First, I want to say I love your books, Mrs. Fletcher."

"Thank you."

"And, I'd like to tell you a story, a chapter from my life. One day, I woke up just like you and millions of other people. Just an ordinary early spring day in Hingham, Massachusetts. Hingham's about half an hour from Boston, Mrs. Fletcher, right on the water, a picturesque waterfront village a lot like where you come from in Maine.

"I hit the snooze button three times before getting out of bed that morning, got into the shower, and was out the door pretty quick. I drove to the Cape and worked hard all day, ate lunch like everybody else."

I was wrong, I thought. The trust hadn't stripped him of a work ethic as trusts often do.

"But then the routine of my day changed. Of my life. I learned my brother had been killed. I jumped in my car the next morning and was heading for his home—the radio had news about his murder, which was really upsetting; I wasn't sure I was capable of driving safely—when several police cars pulled alongside me and I was arrested for Jack's murder."

"As Malcolm knows," I said, "I'm not a lawyer, and don't know very much about the law aside from what I've had to learn for my books. But my understanding is that when you're indicted for murder, bail is out of the question. Yet, you're sitting here."

Malcolm laughed. "I can be very persuasive, Jessica. Perhaps you remember that from my younger days."

"Oh, yes, I certainly do. Still—"

"My family's name helped," Brannigan said, looking down as though embarrassed. "Bail was a million dollars."

"Wow," was all I could say.

"I just wanted to humanize the circumstances for you, Mrs. Fletcher. And I appreciate any help you can give to clear my name, and hopefully to find Jack's real killer."

"I'm here to help, Bill," I replied. "I'll do my best. And my name is Jessica, or Jess if you prefer."

The intercom buzzed. "WHAT?" McLoon bellowed.

"Court TV is on the phone, Mr. McLoon,"

Georgia Bobley said. "He said you told him to call at ten."

Malcolm checked his watch. "Punctual, isn't he? Put him through."

"Court TV?" I asked.

Malcolm ignored me and picked up the phone. "McLoon here. Yes. Of course. Yes. She's sitting here as we speak. Right. My pleasure. That will be fine. Thank you."

He hung up.

"Court TV?" I repeated.

"These damn journalists think they're bigger than God, Jessica. They want to have a camera crew live in my house for a few days to record my comings and goings." He laughed loudly. "Here's McLoon throwing his alarm clock across the room. Here he is drinking his fourth cup of good scotch whiskey. Here he is brushing his dentures. Give them an inch, Jessica, they'll take a mile. Where were we?"

"Malcolm, does the press—does Court TV know by any chance that I'm a jury consultant on this case?" I asked.

"Know? About you? What were we talking about?"

"I'm talking about Court TV," I said. "I heard you say that 'she's sitting here as we speak.' As far as I can see, I'm the only *she* in this room."

"Yes. How they got wind of it I'll never know."

"Did you tell them?" I asked.

"Might have. No matter. Cameras in the courtroom won't bother me. Shouldn't bother you, either."

"Are you allowing the camera crew into your home, Malcolm?"

"Had to. No choice."

I looked at my nails and smiled. No doubt about it. Malcolm McLoon had treaded upon my dubious fame to help entice Court TV to cover the Brannigan trial.

I felt distinctly used.

I thought of walking out of the office.

On the other hand, I was using him. I agreed to become a jury consultant only to learn how a murder trial works to accommodate Vaughan Buckley.

"There'll be cameras following us everywhere, Jessica. Hanging outside the courtroom three deep. But I know you're a trouper, an old pro when it comes to media attention."

"I'll manage," I said.

"Damn, it's coming up on ten-fifteen," he said, getting up from his chair. "Must run, dear lady. Have an appointment to get fitted for a couple of new suits. Georgia says this outfit has to go."

I silently agreed with her.

"Know where Seaside Restaurant is, Jessica? In Faneuil Hall?"

"No, but I certainly know how to get to Faneuil Hall."

"I'll have Georgia contact your driver to meet you downstairs at quarter of twelve."

"That's not necessary, Malcolm. It's only five minutes from here, and it's a beautiful day."

"Seaside's a fine little eating establishment. Good food, not a media hangout. Meet you there at noon. In the meantime, stay right here. Here's a list of the names of the prospective jurors we'll be questioning tomorrow. All two-hundred twenty-five of them."

He handed me a neon-orange folder. "Get a feel for them, Jess. Willie, you come with me. I need your advice on buying suits. Relax, Jessica. And welcome to Boston. You have the town at your disposal. Whatever you want. Name the restaurant to Georgia and she'll make the reservation. Of course, a car will be at your disposal. How was your ride over here this morning?"

"Fine," I said.

"Courteous driver?"

"Very."

"Remember his name?"

"Yes. *Her* name is Cathie. Can't remember her last name, but I'll bet it's Irish. Pretty girl."

Into the intercom: "GEORGIA! Call the limo company. Tell them we want Cathie what's-her-name to drive Mrs. Fletcher for the duration."

"During the day," I said.

"What?"

"Cathie told me I have a daytime driver, and a nighttime driver."

"That's right. Nothing too good for my favorite jury consultant." He kissed me on the cheek.

"Glad to have you on board, Jessica. Damn, you look good. I'd propose if I didn't already have a few former wives on the payroll."

To Brannigan: "Don't you worry about a thing, Willie. With Malcolm McLoon and Jessica Fletcher on your side, it won't be long before the world knows that you are an innocent man. Till lunch, Jessica."

"Till lunch, Malcolm."

Chapter Five

I left McLoon's office a few minutes before noon and rode the elevator to the lobby. Waiting there were two TV camera crews and a few print reporters. My initial reaction was that they were standing by for the arrival of some big-shot political or business leader. Then I realized they were waiting for me.

"Mrs. Fletcher," they said in unison, encircling me. I suppose my puzzled expression made the point that I didn't know why they wanted to talk to me.

"Mrs. Fletcher, Hap Gormley from the *Herald*. Ready to begin jury selection tomorrow?"

I started to reply, then realized not only would it be inappropriate to comment about a murder case, I didn't know enough to say anything intelligent.

"Regina Wells, Court TV, Mrs. Fletcher. Can I set up an interview with you later today?"

"Well, I—"

"Peg Johnson, the *Globe*. Why did Mr. McLoon

ask *you* to be one of his jury consultants? You're a writer. Have you ever taken part in jury selection before?"

I thought of what Malcolm had told me: *I created good characters because I was intuitive about people.*

But I kept that to myself. "Excuse me," I said, heading for the building's front door.

I made it to the street and had taken a few steps in the direction of Faneuil Hall when Ms. Wells from Court TV caught up. "Please, Mrs. Fletcher, a pretrial interview. Mr. McLoon's been very cooperative. We'll be living in his house for a few days."

"Ms. Wells, I really don't think I'm free to comment to the press."

"We're not 'the press,' " she said. "We're Court TV. We cover the trial from gavel to gavel. We always do interviews with the major players. You're certainly one of them."

"Maybe another time," I said.

She kept pace with me. I stopped again, looked at her, and said, "Did Court TV plan to cover the Brannigan trial from gavel to gavel *before* I agreed to help Mr. McLoon select a jury?"

"Honestly? No. There are two other high-profile trials starting tomorrow—one in California, one in Florida. It was a toss-up between the three until we were informed you'd be taking part in the Brannigan trial."

"I see."

"Mr. McLoon lobbied hard to have us cover it. What do you think of him?"

"Malcolm McLoon? A delightful man and good friend. I hate to be rude, but I'm running late for lunch with him."

"At Seaside?"

"Yes."

"There's a TV crew already in there."

"In the restaurant?"

"Yes. They're covering it."

" 'Covering it'? Covering *lunch*?"

She laughed. "The Brannigan trial is big news in Boston, Mrs. Fletcher. Big news nationwide because we're carrying it." She handed me a business card and said, "We'll be seeing lots of each other over the next few months. This is all new to you. Once you're in the swing, you'll have time for interviews. Won't hurt the sale of your books, either. Enjoy lunch."

"Sorry I'm late," I told Malcolm after I'd joined him at a large corner table.

"Not to worry, dear lady," he said. A pretty young waitress waited for our orders. "The usual for me, Heather," Malcolm said. "You, Jessica?"

"May I see a menu?" I asked.

"No drink? You're with Mr. McLoon," Heather said.

Our waitress, who I now knew was Heather, smiled and cocked her head.

"Club soda and lime, please," I said.

I looked across the room to a raised platform on which a television camera manned by two young men was positioned. "You're quite the celebrity these days," I said.

"Damn vultures," McLoon said, nodding in the direction of the camera.

"I'd say you're enjoying it." I kept my tone pleasant.

"Goes with the territory."

Heather delivered our drinks; Malcolm's glass was oversized and filled with a potent-looking brown liquid. He raised it to me. "Here's to a successful defense of Billy Brannigan."

As I touched my rim to his, a strobe light went off. We both turned to face a photographer, who immediately knocked off another shot.

"Malcolm, I think we have to talk," I said into his ear.

Another flash from the strobe.

"Could we have some privacy?" I said to the photographer.

I was answered by a woman carrying a pad and pen, who stepped from behind the photographer. "Just a few questions," she said.

"Not now," McLoon said, waving a fat hand at her.

"Please, the press section is over there," the manager of the restaurant said to the reporter and photographer, guiding them in the direction of the TV camera.

"Good publicity for the restaurant," Malcolm said. "The owner's a friend of mine."

"I'm not sure I'm up to all this media attention, Malcolm."

"Ignore 'em, Jessica. Let's get down to business."

"Maybe we should get down to business in your office. Have a sandwich sent up and—"

Malcolm indicated why that wasn't a good idea by motioning for Heather to replenish his empty drink. She already had it in hand, immediately set in front of him, and handed me a menu. I said after a quick perusal, "I'll have a cup of lobster bisque and a spinach salad."

Malcolm downed half of his second drink, wiped his fleshy mouth with a cloth napkin tucked into his shirt collar, and asked in a low, gravelly voice, "Did you go over the list of jurors?"

"Yes."

"Based upon what I've seen, I'd say we've got a good pool to select from. Agree?"

"I don't know. As I told you, I've never been involved in selecting a jury. Maybe this was a mistake, asking me to help you."

"Nonsense. Besides, you'll be working with one of the best jury selection experts in the country."

"I will?"

"Jill Farkas. Know her?"

"No."

"You'll meet her this afternoon. Good thing Brannigan has plenty of money. She costs a bloody fortune."

Heather served me a steaming bowl of lobster bisque with huge chunks of half-submerged lobster, and a salad of fresh greens covered with real bacon bits. She placed Malcolm's third drink in front of him. The momentary lull in the conversation gave me a few seconds to further evaluate my reason for being there. If Malcolm had hired a high-priced professional jury consultant, and had lobbied to have Court TV cover the trial, then my presence was solely to add name appeal. I wasn't America's most famous writer, but I had enjoyed considerable media exposure over the years. Besides, I was a writer of murder mysteries, which undoubtedly added a certain additional appeal.

"Malcolm," I said, "I—"

"How's the soup?"

"I haven't tasted it yet."

"Better do so before it gets cold. While you enjoy it, let me give you a fast course in picking juries, Malcolm McLoon style. The first thing—"

"Malcolm, could we first talk about my role here?"

"That's what I'm doing. Here's the way I want you to approach it."

"Malcolm—"

"I've got this high-priced pro on the team, but I trust gut instincts more. *Your* gut instincts. I want you to watch closely, Jessica, take everything in, even the smallest details. Pay attention to their body language while they're being interviewed. Their facial expressions. Whether they wince at something I ask them, or smile, or frown. I'll worry about *what* they say. You worry about *how* they say it. Together, maybe we can get a useful handle on what they're really all about, their general background, prejudices, myths, beliefs, hates, and loves—just like the characters in your books. Three-dimensional characters."

"But these are real people, not characters," I said.

"Exactly. I need a jury of *real* people, men and women who didn't finish college, better yet, who never stepped foot in a university. No more education than a two-year community college. Lower middle class. Irish if possible." He laughed. "And, of course, loving baked beans, preferably the Brannigan Bean Pot style."

The bisque had cooled but was delicious. I realized Malcolm was not about to discuss what was really on my mind—why I was there in Boston—so I asked, "How does jury selection work?"

"Starts tomorrow, Jessica. The lawyers from both sides will be in the courtroom to ask questions of each prospective juror. They come in in bunches, a dozen or so at a time."

"What kind of questions will you ask?"

"The best are open-ended," he said. "Gets 'em to talk freely about themselves. While they do that, you and Jill Farkas and others on the team interpret what they say. We already know where they live, their phone numbers, what they do for a living from the questionnaires. What I really need, Jessica, is for you to be my cab driver."

"Your *what*?" I swallowed a spoonful of soup and laughed. "I don't even drive."

"I know that, Jessica. Philip Corboy, the famous trial attorney, once told me how he goes about picking a jury. He had this cab driver friend who'd been driving for thirty-five years. Knew every street, every neighborhood. Knew the city like nobody else. You drive a cab for thirty-five years, or tend bar that long, you develop a damn good insight into what makes people tick. Corboy would go over the juror questionnaires with his cabbie friend, who'd say, 'Drop this one. Half the people living on that street are cops.' Or, he'd tell Corboy, 'Lots of prejudice against Hispanics in that neighborhood. Your client's Hispanic, right? Don't pick anybody from that neighborhood.'

"See? This cab driver added another dimension to what little information Corboy already had about the prospective jurors. Now, I know you don't live in Boston, and don't know what a cab driver would know. But you've been creating characters for as many years as he'd been driving a cab. And you solve puzzles in every one of your books. That's what I want you to do for me. Solve the puzzle of which twelve people will give us the best shake."

"Be your cab driver."

"Yup. Be my cab driver. They say all great authors are great observers. Take it all in, their ap-

pearance, mannerisms, idiosyncrasies, choice of
clothes. Listen closely, but don't take notes. If
you're busy taking notes, you might miss something. Jot things down between panels."

"All right. I should tell you, Malcolm, that I
have a reason for being here besides wanting to
help you select a jury. You see, my publisher visited me in Cabot Cove and—"

"Well, well, look who's here," he said.

I looked toward the restaurant's entrance where
a half-dozen people waited to be seated. "Who?"
I asked.

"See that elegant lady in the pink-and-white
suit?"

"Yes."

"That's Whitney James, the DA prosecuting the
Brannigan case."

"She's beautiful," I said.

"Cold as ice. Good litigator."

We watched as the TV camera turned in Whitney James's direction, and the reporter and photographer made their way to her. Malcolm
guffawed. "Looks like Ms. James doesn't mind a
little publicity herself. Only reason she's here. Not
her kind of place for lunch." To Heather, who
stood at Malcolm's side: "Corned beef hash on
top 'a greens, my dear. And do this again." He
pointed to his empty glass.

"White wine," a male voice said.

Standing behind Malcolm was a tall, handsome
sixty-something gentleman whose weather-beaten

face contrasted with his wardrobe—double-breasted blue blazer with gold buttons, white shirt, and bright red tie dotted with tiny blue sailboats. His salt-and-pepper beard and mustache were neatly trimmed. I had the immediate impression that his deeply tanned and creased face had been fashioned sipping cocktails on long sailboats and yachts, not clamming at dusk from a small Boston whaler off Cape Cod.

"Hello, Malcolm. How do you do it? Always a pretty woman at your side." The man's voice came through his nose, making it sound as though speaking was an unpleasant chore; I felt that if he were able to hire someone to speak for him, he'd do it.

"Hello, Warren," said Malcolm, reaching up to shake a limp hand. "Join us?"

"Thank you, no. But you can introduce me to Mrs. Fletcher."

"Sure. Jessica, meet Warren Parker, man-about-town, friend to the rich and famous, one of Boston's most prominent socialites."

"Nice to meet you, Mr. Parker," I said.

"My wife is your biggest fan, Mrs. Fletcher."

"That's very nice to hear."

"How did my favorite barrister, here, coax you into abandoning your word processor for the life of jury consultant?"

"Malcolm is, among other things, extremely persuasive," I answered.

The small laugh that came through his lank lips

was as strained as his voice. "So I've noticed," he said. "Whitney found it fascinating when she heard."

"She's over there being interviewed," Malcolm said.

"I know," said Parker.

"Poisoning the public about Billy Brannigan," Malcolm said grumpily, sounding for the first time as though the alcohol he'd consumed had had an effect on him. He finished what was in his glass.

"I'd better rescue her," Parker said. "A pleasure meeting you, Mrs. Fletcher. My wife will be thrilled that I did." He made his way in Whitney James's direction, his gait casual, one shoulder dropped slightly lower than the other in what I describe as socialite slouch.

"What does Mr. Warren Parker do for a living?" I asked Malcolm.

"Dates rich, attractive, powerful women—when his wife is at their summer place on the Cape, which is most of the year. He's good at it."

"Interesting way to make a living," I said.

"Actually, he's a financier. With two character flaws."

"Oh? What are they?"

"Dating Whitney James?"

"That's only one," I said.

"And he hates baked beans. Where the hell is my corned beef? You'd think all they serve in this establishment is whiskey."

Chapter Six

I was apprehensive about meeting Malcolm's paid professional jury consultant, Jill Farkas. She was a professional; I was a rank amateur treading on her turf.

But my fears were unfounded, at least initially. Ms. Farkas was a handsome, gracious woman partial to tailored brown suits. Her blond hair, streaked with silver, was carefully coiffed. She spoke in modulated tones. My reading of our first meeting said she didn't resent my presence. Of course, I knew that could change once we disagreed on prospective jurors. But no sense worrying about it now. Tomorrow, when jury selection was to start, was time enough.

Billy Brannigan's defense team gathered around the small conference table in Malcolm's office. Brannigan chose to sit in a chair apart from the group.

"Okay," Malcolm said, having removed his plaid jacket and loosened his tie. "What do we have?" He directed this to his assistant defense counsel, Rachel Cohen.

"I tried all morning to get hold of Cynthia Warren, but no luck."

"Cynthia Warren?" I asked.

"Billy's alibi," Malcolm said, looking at his client. Brannigan didn't react.

"Where do you think she's gone?" Malcolm asked.

"Probably hasn't gone anywhere, Malcolm," Rachel replied. "She knows she isn't scheduled to testify for at least a week, so there's no reason for her to be on tap. Maybe it would make sense if we—"

She was interrupted by the sound of the receptionist's voice over the intercom. "For you, Rachel," Linda said. "Your baby-sitter."

"Damn," Rachel said, jumping up and fairly running from the room.

I couldn't help but smile. Her dual role as attorney and mother certainly kept her hopping.

"Everybody had a chance to go over the juror questionnaires?" McLoon asked.

We nodded.

McLoon looked at his investigator, Ritchie Fleigler. "What have you dug up on the detectives?" he asked.

Fleigler chuckled. "Detective John Sullivan isn't going to be happy with what I've come up with," he said.

"Why?" McLoon asked.

"Seems he once worked as a Chippendale dancer in New York."

"What in hell is a Chippendale dancer?" McLoon asked.

"Like female strippers, only the men strip and dance for women."

"That so?" McLoon said, leaning back, a wicked grin on his face. "One of Boston's homicide detectives used to take his clothes off in public?"

"Just for a couple of months," Fleigler said.

"One day is enough," said McLoon. "What else?"

"Here's the best part," said Fleigler. "It seems John Sullivan, now Detective John Sullivan, got fired from his gig as a dancer for allegedly fondling one of his female customers."

"Music to my ears," McLoon said. "It's all documented?"

"I have it right here," Ritchie said, patting a file folder.

McLoon now turned his attention to his personal assistant, Georgia Bobley. "Are all the logistics in place?" he asked.

"Excuse me," said Fleigler, "but I have more."

"Okay, shoot."

"I have a friend over at the coroner's office."

"A female friend, I presume," said McLoon.

Fleigler smiled. "Of course. Anyway, she tells me they've lost some paperwork. Or maybe I should say they've lost *the* paperwork."

"On this case?" McLoon asked.

"Yup. The original of the coroner's report seems to have disappeared."

McLoon, who'd been making notes on a yellow legal pad, grunted, "Good."

Rachel Cohen returned, looking as though

she'd been crying. "Malcolm, I have to go," she said. "Ashley needs stitches. She took a fall, tripped on the stairs at school. The teacher says it's a pretty bad cut. I'll have to get her to a plastic surgeon."

I looked at Malcolm to see whether yet another intrusion into his assistant counsel's workday had annoyed him. It evidently hadn't because he smiled and said, "Do what you have to do for that pretty little thing, and give her a big kiss. Tell her Uncle Malcolm says she's got bad timing."

"Thanks, Malcolm," Rachel said. "You're a sweetheart. Sorry about this. I'll be back as soon as I get things squared away with the doctor."

McLoon consulted something he'd written on a second pad. Before he could verbalize it, Billy Brannigan spoke. "I remember once when I fell at the playground," he said softly. "I must have been around seven but I'll never forget it. It wasn't so bad, the cut that is, but nobody could find my mother, so a teacher's aide and my brother took me to the hospital. I didn't see my mom until that night and could never understand where she'd been. I was lucky to have my brother, Jack, to take care of me that day. We were real tight growing up, and he's always been there for me. That's why I couldn't understand when he wanted to cut me out of the trust."

"I don't want to hear that kind of talk from you again," Malcolm said, slapping his beefy hands on the table with such force that it caused everyone to sit up straight. "The prosecution claims that's your motive for killing your brother. Let's not have anybody in this room even *think* it, let alone talk about it."

Billy slumped in his chair like a child who'd been scolded by a parent, and turned away.

I wished Billy Brannigan had said more because I was curious about his growing up in a very rich family. I said, "Sometimes it's the mental things that leave bigger scars than all the cuts and bruises."

McLoon ignored my comment. "Okay," he said, "where were we? I figure jury selection to take about a week. Ritchie, I want you to—"

"Don't forget the TV interview, Malcolm," Georgia Bobley interrupted.

"What time is that?" Malcolm asked.

"Five," she replied.

Malcolm said to me, "I want you with me on this interview, Jessica. Sort of your coming-out party. Don't worry, you won't have to say much. I'll do most of the talking."

We all chuckled. Malcolm wasn't telling us anything we didn't already know.

I started to protest being part of the interview, but he immediately went on to give Ritchie Fleigler a series of instructions about how to investigate the background of certain jurors culled from the list.

He then turned to Jill Farkas: "Anybody get the ax so far?" he asked.

"Yes," she said, explaining why she wanted to dismiss seven people from the prospective juror list, all having to do with their employment. In two cases, they worked for companies that had failed business dealings with Brannigan's Bean Pot. One of them worked for the district attorney's brother's law firm. The rest were connected in some tangential way with law enforcement.

When Jill finished her report, she looked up, smiled, and said, "That's the easy part. Tomorrow is another story."

Malcolm ended the meeting: "Time for Jessica and me to get to the interview. I'm sure I'll be up all night, as usual, but I want you to get some sleep. It's like the advice I gave my daughter when she was pregnant: 'Get some sleep during those nine months because after that, you'll never sleep again.' See you all in court."

As Jill Farkas was leaving, she stopped and said to me, "I want you to know, Jessica, how pleased I am that we'll be working together. Malcolm explained his reasoning for asking you to join the team, and I was in complete agreement. We probably should get together a little earlier tomorrow so I can show you how I work, and to coordinate our efforts."

"I'm free tonight," I said. "I mean, after this television interview."

She smiled brightly. "I think that's a wonderful idea. Dinner?"

"I'd love it."

I walked out of the building with Malcolm feeling very excited, like a player on a team the night before the big game. Any annoyance at having been coaxed to Boston under false pretenses had disappeared, and I looked forward to learning about jury selection that night from Jill Farkas.

Following the television interview, Malcolm's driver dropped me at the hotel. "Don't stay up too late with Jill," he said. "It gets tough starting tomorrow. Welcome to the team, Jessica. Anything you want, anything you need, you call me, day or night."

He then did something that surprised me. He kissed me on the cheek.

I stood on the sidewalk and watched him drive away. A remarkable man, I thought, so filled with energy despite being so grossly overweight, and consuming so much alcohol. Was he now heading for dinner and another round of drinks? I shuddered at the thought.

As I entered the hotel to get ready for dinner, I thought again of being on a team, of getting ready for the big game the following day. That's when it struck me. When it's a game, the winner gets a trophy.

In this "game," the winner doesn't get a trophy. In this game, the winner gets his life back.

Some game.

Chapter Seven

The courthouse in which the Brannigan trial was held was one of two massive buildings on a piazza behind the Center Plaza Building. I stopped to read plaques on each: the older one was erected in 1895; the newer, taller annex went up in 1936. I entered the older building.

It occurred to me as a security guard checked my name against a list that I hadn't been in a courthouse in years, which could be viewed as strange considering that I make my living writing about crime, particularly murder. But in my books, as in most murder mysteries, the crime is solved long before it gets to a courtroom. Of course, if I followed through on Vaughan Buckley's suggestion to set my next novel during a trial, I'd be breaking that tradition.

A long table had been set up on either side of the room for the defense and the prosecution. When I arrived, all the other members of the defense team were present, with the exception of Malcolm McLoon. I sat next to Jill Farkas. "I can't tell you how much I learned last night," I said, referring to the three-hour dinner we'd enjoyed beneath the cobalt-blue Venetian crystal chandeliers and gold-filigree ceiling of the Ritz-Carlton Dining Room, surrounded by regal draperies and huge picture windows overlooking the Public Garden. With live piano music playing softly in the background, Jill Farkas and I dined on rack of lamb for two, topped off with reckless abandon by enjoying a sinful slice of Boston cream pie. She gave me a primer during dinner on the *science* of jury selection, how she depended entirely upon computers into which information was fed concerning demographics, neighborhood pattern of behavior, and other telltale indications of how people might react to evidence presented during a trial. I was certainly impressed, although I wondered whether all that high-tech really did a better job than the cab driver Malcolm had told me about.

"Where's Malcolm?" Rachel Cohen asked, nervously looking around the spartan and severe room.

"I don't know," Georgia Bobley replied. "I tried him this morning, but he didn't answer at home or the office."

A bailiff ordered everyone to rise for the judge's entrance. As I stood, I noticed for the first time the presence of two Court TV cameras.

The judge, whose name was Walter Wilson,

struck me as being surprisingly young. I've always pictured judges as being older. I pegged Wilson at forty, give or take a year or two. He was very pale, and had what is commonly called a baby face. He'd prematurely lost a great deal of hair, and took considerable pains to distribute what was left by bringing it up and over the curvature of his bald pate. His face was pleasant, his mouth curving upward into the hint of a perpetual grin. From a distance, I thought his eyes were green. I was surprised by how short he was, again dealing from a stereotype of judges being tall and imposing. All I could envision for a fleeting moment was Judge Wilson batting for his college baseball team.

When everyone was seated, I glanced over at the prosecution table where District Attorney Whitney James sat with her assistant, Cliff Cecil. I then looked to where spectators would sit. That section was empty. I commented on this to Jill Farkas.

"Never during jury selection," she replied. "Just counsel, the defendant, and the judge. And, of course the prospective jurors."

"But what about the TV cameras?" I asked.

"Set up and ready to go once the trial starts, but there will be no filming during this phase. By the way, the judge has ruled that the jury will not be sequestered."

"Isn't that unusual in a murder case?" I asked, thinking of the O.J. Simpson trial.

"It's the judge's call," Jill replied. "I always prefer a sequestered jury."

Rachel Cohen and Georgia Bobley kept looking around in search of Malcolm McLoon. "Where is he?" Georgia muttered to herself.

"Is counsel ready on both sides?" Judge Wilson asked.

Rachel Cohen stood. "Your Honor, we're waiting for Mr. McLoon."

The judge smiled. "Ah, yes, Mr. McLoon. Do you have any idea where he might be?"

"I'm sure he's in the building, Your Honor. If we could just have a few moments—"

"The court system runs slow enough without having these kinds of delays," said the judge. "We'll proceed without him. You're a lawyer, Ms. Cohen. Handle it."

Wilson instructed the bailiff to bring in the first twenty prospective jurors.

Because they sat in order of numbers they'd been assigned, those of us at counsel tables were able to match individuals with their questionnaires. The twenty men and women seemed to be a cross-section of the population, black and white, male and female, some dressed as though going to work or a party, others dressed down as though they were about to play a softball game. Judge Wilson welcomed them and then gave a short speech that we would hear over and over that day, repeated for each successive group of twenty:

"Good morning, ladies and gentlemen. Let me

tell you something about this case before we begin. It is a murder case involving a young man from a wealthy family, charged with killing his older brother. Those chosen to sit on this jury will not be sequestered, but will be escorted to and from this courtroom each day by members of the sheriff's department. There will be many admonitions and restrictions placed upon jurors in this case, which must be followed to the letter. Anyone breaching these rules will be subject to criminal prosecution.

"Because of the extensive media coverage of this case, I do not expect any of you to not know something about it. That, in my opinion, does not rule out any of you from serving on this jury, provided what knowledge you do possess can be put aside, and that you can come to this trial with an open mind as to the guilt or innocence of the accused."

Wilson pointed to Billy Brannigan. "This is the accused in the case, Mr. William Brannigan. He is charged with having killed his older brother, having to do with a family trust for which his older brother was trustee. There will be a great deal of conflicting testimony and evidence, some of it complex where it involves the trust itself. But I'm certain those of you chosen to serve will have no problem in sorting out fact from fiction, and in coming to a fair and just verdict.

"Now, based upon what I have told you, and based upon what you already know about this case, is there anyone here who believes they would have a personal problem serving on this jury?"

One woman raised her hand. She started to say something but Judge Wilson cut her off. "All right, you're excused," he said.

Just like that. No questions asked.

"Anyone else?" Wilson asked.

Two more hands went up, and they were dismissed without comment or question.

Seventeen prospective jurors remained seated, which surprised me. It was my assumption that most people tried to get out of jury duty, something I've always found dismaying. But here the judge had given them an easy out, and most elected to stay. Either they were especially conscientious—or intimidated.

The judge asked a series of generic questions of the remaining prospects. Satisfied with the responses he received, he turned the questioning over to the district attorney, Whitney James, who stood and issued her own greeting. As she spoke, I took the opportunity to get a better look at her. She was certainly pretty, but not beautiful, her features interesting as opposed to classic. Her demeanor was soothing rather than strident. Of course, I knew that this was her first opportunity to impress prospective jurors. Malcolm had said she was cold as ice, but that wasn't coming through this morning. She had chosen a neatly tailored suit the color of cranberries; a simple blouse and scarf coordinated with it nicely. A cameo pin adorned a lapel; classic black pumps completed her wardrobe. She'd put her thick brunette hair up into a chignon, and her makeup had been tastefully applied.

Using a prepared list of questions based upon each prospective juror's questionnaire, Ms. James asked a series of probing questions. When her allotted time was up, Judge Wilson turned to us and said, "You're up, Ms. Cohen."

Rachel had no sooner stood and was about to approach the jurors when the courtroom doors opened and Malcolm McLoon blustered through them. By this time, I wondered whether he'd suffered such a massive hangover that he would be incapable of conducting an examination of the jurors. But as he approached the table, I was taken with the bright look in his eyes, and the obvious energy he was feeling. He wore a double-breasted buff suit, pale blue shirt, and a colorful tie of red and green. His arms were laden with file folders.

"Good morning, Mr. McLoon," said Judge Wilson, the pique in his voice evident.

"Good morning, Your Honor," Malcolm boomed, dropping the files on the table with great flourish. "My profound apologies to the court, sir, for my late arrival. I was unavoidably detained, the reason for it of little or no interest to this court."

Judge Wilson leaned forward, narrowed his eyes, and said, "I'll be the judge of that Mr.

McLoon. I intend for this court to start on time each day. Please be advised of that."

"Of course, Your Honor," Malcolm said, adding a throaty chuckle. "It shan't happen again, I assure."

"No, I'm sure it won't," replied Wilson, sighing deeply and sitting back in his high-backed leather chair.

Rachel Cohen quickly handed Malcolm her list of questions. He scanned it quickly, cleared his throat, went to where the prospective jurors sat, and issued a loud, "Good morning, ladies and gentlemen."

There were muttered responses.

As Malcolm proceeded to question the men and women, I was impressed with his mental acumen, style, and manner. He seemed to establish an immediate rapport with whatever person he was questioning. At one point, he narrowed in on a woman who'd captured my attention, too, Elizabeth Woo. I'd naturally assumed she was Oriental, as did Malcolm. But she was the picture of Ireland; her wedding ring solved the mystery. Obviously, this freckled-face, green-eyed redhead was married to a gentleman named Woo. Malcolm joked with her about that, which brought a mild rebuke from Judge Wilson: "Could we move on to more substantive matters, Mr. McLoon," he said.

"Of course, Your Honor."

Which he did, probing their attitudes and feelings about a variety of subjects. Although he'd told me not to take notes, I couldn't help it, and noticed that Jill Farkas was doing the same.

Malcolm spent what I considered an inordinate amount of time with a young man named Thomas McEnroe, who'd listed his occupation as pottery maker.

"An interesting line of work," Malcolm said, a big smile across his broad face. "I always admire people who are able to make a living in the arts."

"Yes," McEnroe replied. He was a slender, gentle person with soft brown eyes. He wore a T-shirt, blue sports jacket, jeans, and Birkenstock sandals. "I'm one of those fortunate people who is able to make a living doing what he loves most."

"Fortunate indeed," said Malcolm. He faced the judge. "Unfortunately, most of us in this room are unable to make the same claim." Whitney James rolled her eyes. Judge Wilson closed his.

I glanced to my left and saw Jill Farkas write a note next to McEnroe's name: "Probably resents the rich."

I looked up just as Malcolm turned and stared at me. He gave an almost imperceptible nod of his head and smiled. I smiled in return. We were on the same wavelength—we liked the pottery maker, Tom McEnroe.

And so it went for the rest of the morning. By lunch, my notes indicated that only two of the remaining seventeen impressed me as possible jury candidates, at least from the defense perspective.

By day's end, I had come up with five jurors who had my stamp of approval, including the pottery maker, an unemployed construction foreman, a businessman who owned a company that manufactured scissors and tweezers, a housewife whose two children were grown and living on their own, and who'd actually mentioned that she liked baked beans. That comment came about when Malcolm asked her what she enjoyed doing on weekends: "I enjoy being with my husband, friends, barbecuing in the backyard, hot dogs, hamburgers, baked beans, watermelon." This time, when Malcolm looked at me, his smile was considerably broader. I had to stifle a laugh.

The fifth acceptable juror was a young woman who was an actress turned waitress. She indicated it was her dream to complete the circle and become an actress again.

Toward the end of the afternoon, Judge Wilson summoned Malcolm and Whitney James into his chambers. Before he did, he informed the rest of us that court was in recess until nine the following morning.

Rachel Cohen left the courthouse immediately—something to do with a problem at home. Georgia Bobley said she was heading back to the office to take care of some administrative problems. I didn't know where Billy Brannigan was; he seemed to have disappeared once court was let out.

I sat outside in the marble hallway and waited

for Malcolm to emerge. When he did, he came through the large leather doors with such force that I thought they might come off their hinges. He was obviously angry. I got up and said, "What's next?"

"What's next is a drink. Come on."

"The press is waiting outside," I said, falling in step with him. "You promised them a press conference."

"The hell with them," he said. "I have nothing to say."

With Malcolm parting the press like Moses parting the Red Sea, I followed him down to where our chauffeur-driven car waited. "You seem upset," I said.

"You bet I am. That damn Whitney James is showing her true colors already." He fell silent for the rest of the ride, and I didn't intrude upon it.

We pulled up in front of the Union Oyster House, the oldest continuous service restaurant in the United States. I'd been there before, but it had been a while ago. By the time we entered, Malcolm seemed to have regained some of his good nature. He greeted people as we proceeded to a table in the corner on which a card had been placed: RESERVED. "My table," Malcolm said, holding out a chair for me. "My own little corner of the world."

"You seem to have little corners of your own all over town," I said.

"Makes me happy," he said, calling for a waiter.

"A couple of dozen oysters, and my usual. You, Jess?"

"Mineral water with lime," I said.

The place was filling up, a series of old small rooms now bustling with businessmen and women, and tourists enjoying freshly shucked oysters and beer or cocktails.

With our drinks served, I asked Malcolm what had upset him.

"Whitney is using her preemptive rights to dismiss four out of the five jurors you and I agree on."

"What a shame. Which one will she accept?"

"The pottery maker, McEnroe."

"I noticed Jill Farkas write a note about him," I said. "She thinks he might harbor resentment for the rich."

Malcolm shook his large, leonine head. "I like him. You like him. That's enough for me."

Chapter Eight

If time does, indeed, go by quickly when you're having fun, the week of jury selection should have progressed at a snail's pace. It was hard work, attempting to look into the minds and hearts of a couple of hundred men and women in whose hands Billy Brannigan's life would be placed.

But the week did go by quickly. There was spirited debate between defense and prosecution over some of the individuals, but in most cases the prospective jurors came and went until, at some time Friday afternoon, a panel of twelve acceptable to both sides had been chosen, along with six alternates. The trial itself would commence at nine Monday morning.

The strengths and weaknesses of Billy Brannigan's defense team, headed by the flamboyant and larger-than-life Malcolm McLoon, came to the surface during that week. As brilliant an attorney as Malcolm was—and that was evident during his questioning of the prospective jurors—he would never win any awards for organization. He shot from the hip at every turn, which brought a series of objections from Whitney James, as well as from Judge Wilson. None of this fazed Malcolm. Instead, it seemed to spur him on to greater eloquence, obviously reveling in the combat, something all successful trial attorneys must enjoy if they are to face the battle day after day, year after year, case after case.

But it made me uncomfortable as I went about my chore of evaluating responses to questions from Malcolm and Whitney James. What began to bother me was that the whole process of jury selection was not, it seemed to this layperson, predicated upon finding twelve open-minded, fair, and impartial men and women. Instead, the game was to pick as many jurors who might have a predisposition to favor acquittal. Whitney James, of course, was looking for twelve men and women who would come into the court wanting to hang Billy Brannigan.

But that was too esoteric for me to deal with. Great legal scholars, I suppose, have debated that aspect of our legal system for centuries.

The only tangible conflict I experienced began to emerge the second day of jury selection, and it came from a not unexpected source, Malcolm's highly-paid professional consultant, Jill Farkas. I certainly was willing, even anxious to defer to her expertise. But there were a few times when I genuinely and fervently disagreed with her. Because I was there at Malcolm's behest, I felt it was my duty to present my opinions to him, which didn't always set well with Ms. Farkas. Although she tried to present a quiet, reasoned, and professional demeanor, I could sense her growing irritation when we debated our respective views.

I tried to leave behind the pressures and intensity of each court day, to compartmentalize it. Once I left the courtroom, I was free to do what I wished, and made it a point to avoid anything having to do with the trial. That is, when Malcolm and the press allowed me to do that.

Reporters were everywhere. Malcolm complained a great deal about them, but also seemed to bask in their harsh lights. He also seemed determined to include me in his life, night and day. I managed to avoid accompanying him on most of his nightly sojourns, taking every opportunity to slip away to my sumptuous suite in the Ritz to soak in a hot tub, read a good book, and get to bed early.

But I couldn't do it every night without seeming rude.

Malcolm's evenings were spent at tables reserved for him in favored watering holes where he held court with friends and cronies, well-wishers, critics, reporters, detractors, politicians, and cab drivers.

Judging from Malcolm's schedule during the week, I assumed we'd be working right through the weekend. But to my surprise when court ended Friday afternoon, he announced that our only weekend commitment was a meeting on Saturday afternoon in his office, which he promised wouldn't last more than an hour. Aside from that, Malcolm urged us to enjoy Saturday and Sunday in order to be fresh on Monday morning.

The major source of concern at the Saturday meeting was the whereabouts of Cynthia Warren, the young lady from Cape Cod who, according to Billy Brannigan, could provide an alibi for him the night his brother, Jack, was murdered. Ritchie Fleigler, Malcolm's investigator, said he'd gone to the Cape in search of Ms. Warren but found no one at home.

"Probably off on a brief vacation," Rachel Cohen offered.

"Hell of a time to take a vacation," Malcolm said. "The faster we get her on the stand once we start our case, the quicker this thing can be wrapped up. Keep after her, Ritchie," he said. "Unless the prosecution throws us a curve, I don't see their case going more than a week. I want her ready the minute we take over."

I returned to the Ritz-Carlton immediately after the meeting and called Mort Metzger and Seth Hazlitt in Cabot Cove. They'd been reading newspaper articles about the trial and my role in it, and Seth had subscribed to Court TV just to see me on television.

"I don't think you'll see much of me," I said.

" 'Course I will. They always show the defendant's reactions. You'll be sittin' right there with him, won't you?"

"I suppose so."

"*Boston Globe* says you and this professional consultant, Farkas is her name, aren't getting along too good," Seth said.

"That's not true, Seth. She's a very nice woman, and knows a great deal."

"Well, all I can say, Jessica, is that it still doesn't make any sense to me to have you selectin' jurors in a murder case. That's a big burden."

"I'm well aware of that," I said, feeling the weight of it. "I have to go. Mort says I should try to use my influence to keep cameras out of courtrooms."

"Did he now? How do you feel about it?"

"Too early to have an opinion. I suppose I'll develop one as the trial progresses. Good talking to you, Seth. I'll stay in touch."

I spent the rest of Saturday playing tourist, strolling the crazy-quilt, bumpy brick sidewalks of Beacon Hill, stopping to admire the few remaining authentic "purple panes," a fluke that occurred when manganese oxide reacted with the sun on glass shipped to Boston in the early nineteenth century to create an unusual lavender color.

After a stop at Caffe Bella Vita where I sat outside, sipped an espresso, and watched the world go by, I headed to the Isabella Stewart Gardner Museum in the Kenmore Square/Fenway section

and feasted on the works of Botticelli, Manet, and
Matisse. My timing was perfect; a classical music
concert featuring a local string quartet started at
five, and I took it in, allowing the music to wash
away the cares of the week.

The markets of the Italian North End were still
open when I arrived, and I ate dinner on the
move, a little something from this vendor, something else from another. By the time I returned
to the hotel, I felt completely rested and at ease.
There was no trial, no jury, no matters of life and
death. Just me, Boston, and the contemplation of
yet another day at my leisure.

I slept late Sunday morning, at least by my standards, and took a croissant and coffee from Cafe
de Paris to the Public Garden. It was a "fat morning," as Seth Hazlitt liked to say, a cobalt-blue
sky, refreshing breeze, and abundant sunshine. I
found a bench near the famed Swan Boats and
enjoyed my breakfast. It was one of those special
moments in which everything seemed in balance,
the Swan Boats gliding by on pedal power as they
have for more than a century since an English
immigrant and shipbuilder first introduced them
to the Public Garden's lagoon. Children waved to
me as they passed, and I waved back.

A special moment.

Until I realized I was sitting at the scene of
Jack Brannigan's murder. How could I have forgotten that? He'd been knifed to death while in
one of the boats as it sat moored that night with

its five sister vessels. What had Jack Brannigan been doing there? I wondered. Did he routinely go to the lagoon at night for solitude, or was he meeting someone? Meeting his younger brother, Billy? Not according to Billy and his alibi, Cynthia Warren.

The intrusion of murder into my idyllic scene covered it with a blanket of suspicion and dread. I tossed the remains of my breakfast into a trash can and returned to the hotel where I spent the afternoon making notes for my next novel. Unfortunately, reality had settled in again.

Malcolm called me at six to invite me to join him for dinner, which I declined.

"Ready for tomorrow?" he asked.

"I suppose so."

"As I've told you, Jessica, your role is just beginning. I want you there keeping your eyes trained on the men and women in that jury box. I want to know at the end of every day who's falling asleep, who's nodding at what Whitney is saying, and who's screwing up their face every time she opens her mouth. Jury consultants just don't choose a jury, Jess. They're a lawyer's eyes and ears throughout the trial."

"I understand," I said.

"You sound down," Malcolm said.

"I was at the Swan Boats this morning," I said. "Where Jack Brannigan was killed. I suppose it sobered me."

"Well, don't dwell on it," he said. "Get yourself a good night's sleep. See you tomorrow."

I had dinner in my room, and went to bed at ten after finishing *Dirty Story* by Eric Ambler, a wonderful mystery I'd never gotten around to reading. It took a long time to fall asleep. Each time I was close to it, a picture appeared on an imaginary screen in front of me. I'd open my eyes and peer at it. Jack Brannigan was arguing with someone in the Swan Boat. I could see him clearly; I'd seen photographs of him in Malcolm's office. But his assailant was in shadows. And then, just before the screen and the picture disappeared, I saw Billy Brannigan ram a knife into his brother's chest.

"Please, don't let him be guilty," I said aloud after one of the screenings. "Let it be a demented, warped, sadistic stranger with a knife."

Finally, sleep came, but not soon enough, or with enough peace to refresh me. I woke up Monday morning feeling dreadfully hung over, not from alcohol, but from a system that hadn't sufficiently shut down.

The trial was about to begin.

Chapter Nine

"All rise!"

Judge Wilson, resplendent in his black robe, entered the courtroom at precisely nine o'clock Monday morning. He took his seat behind the bench and said, "Good morning, ladies and gentlemen."

"Good morning, Your Honor," we responded, along with the twelve jury members and six alternates. Wilson glanced up at the television cameras at the rear of the room and made what I considered to be a face of displeasure. He then turned his attention to a sheaf of papers before him.

Our entire team was present, including Malcolm, whose new blue suit served to trim him a little, at least perceptually. As usual, he looked bright, rested, and ready for a vigorous day despite what I was sure had been a late night. Billy Brannigan was dressed in a conservative gray suit, white shirt, and red-white-and-blue tie. Jury consultant Jill Farkas, Rachel Cohen, and Malcolm's personal assistant, Georgia Bobley, all looked as though they might have chosen their clothing from the same shop—tailored suits, muted blouses, and sensible shoes.

While Judge Wilson continued to peruse the papers on the bench, I took the opportunity to focus on each member of the jury. The twelve who would make the ultimate decision—providing none of them dropped out during the course of the trial—consisted of eight women and four men. There was a housewife, an art collector, the actress-turned-waitress, a high school teacher, an auto mechanic, a secretary, a single mother of a college-aged child, an advertising executive, an accountant at a city hospital, a chef, fireman, and a real estate broker. Three were Irish-American. Two Italian-Americans had been to Ireland; one liked it, one didn't. Four were black, one was Hispanic, one had been born in the old Soviet Union, and the twelfth had been born in Israel but raised in Boston.

The six alternates consisted of the pottery maker, a weatherman for a local radio station, an elementary school teacher, a retired travel editor, an airline pilot, and the owner of the tweezer business.

"I have a little business to take care of before we get underway," Judge Wilson said in a voice deeper than one would anticipate from someone with such a boyish face. "I'm certain everyone in this room is aware of the television cameras, which will record these proceedings and transmit them to a national television audience. Frankly, I would prefer that they weren't here, but I was persuaded by others that by bringing the American public into the courtroom, we serve a higher purpose. It has been arranged that the cameras will never show the faces of our jury. That may strike some as an unnecessary restriction considering the fact that the jury will not be sequestered. But I think a basic sense of decency dictates not allowing these television cameras, or any other cameras, to intrude upon each juror's privacy. As a result, I have instructed all media to not photograph the jurors as they come and go.

"I see that we have a full house this morning, including a number of reporters. I will not tolerate interruptions during the course of the trial, and anyone who interrupts shall be summarily dismissed. I expect nothing short of your upmost respect for the judicial process that is about to take place."

I'd read in one of myriad news stories about the Brannigan case that Judge Wilson's avocation was the piano. As I looked at him on the bench, I pictured him seated at the piano playing Chopin, a pleasant contrast to the life-and-death atmosphere of the courtroom over which he presided.

"All right, are the people ready with their opening argument?"

District Attorney Whitney James stood and said, "They are, Your Honor."

"Then let's get on with it."

Whitney James placed her hands on the lectern, drew a deep breath, and exhibited a wide smile as she greeted the jury. She thanked them for being there, and complimented them on their heightened sense of civic duty. As she spoke, I sensed an accent I hadn't been aware of during the previous week's questioning. It had a hint of Great Britain, although not quite. South African? Australian? Or, since I hadn't heard it before, maybe a carefully calculated accent she used whenever addressing a jury.

She shifted position, crossing her arms and shifting her weight onto her right leg, her left foot out to one side. "This is the unfortunate story, ladies and gentlemen, of death within a family, of brother killing brother in cold blood." She looked at Billy Brannigan before continuing.

"In the defendant's mind, he had good reason for killing his older brother, Jack. Of course, everyone who kills another person has what they consider a good reason at the time. In William Brannigan's case, he killed his brother to avenge the threat of being cut out of a trust fund left him by their father, now deceased, the founder of a company we all know and respect, Brannigan's Bean Pot. Because that company was extremely successful, their father had placed a great deal of money in trust for each of his sons. Millions of dollars in each of those trust funds. And as we all know, money—or the fear of losing it—can be a powerful motive for murder."

This time, she looked directly at me, perhaps expecting me to nod in agreement because, as a writer of murder mysteries, I was well aware of motives for murder. Receiving no response from me, she turned away and continued her statement.

"Knowing that his son, William, would probably not amount to much in life—"

"Objection, Your Honor," Malcolm said, now on his feet. "This is a trial about murder, not the defendant's future earning power."

"Overruled," Judge Wilson said. "Continue, Ms. James."

"The father provided for William Brannigan through the trust. And because he had infinite faith in his older son, Jack, who was an important member of the management team of Brannigan's Bean Pot—and, I might add, the younger son, William, has never had anything to do with the company—"

"Objection. Irrelevant."

"I'll allow fairly wide latitude during opening statements, Mr. McLoon. You'll benefit from it, too, and I have no doubt you'll take full advantage of my generosity. Go on, Ms. James."

"The father made Jack the trustee," she said. "It was a wise choice. Jack Brannigan managed the trust with skill and care.

"But James Brannigan, who not only was a successful businessman but was also a man of high moral principle, included a clause in the trust that stipulated that should his younger son, William, ever be charged with a crime involving moral turpitude, the trust was to be dissolved, with all remaining funds going to his older son, Jack. By the way, six months before he was murdered, Jack Brannigan was named president of Brannigan's Bean Pot. He was obviously a young man with considerable talents and ability."

"Your Honor," Malcolm said.

"Overruled."

Whitney James cleared her throat, took a sip of water from a cup on the lectern, and said to the jury, "The defendant is no stranger to horrific crimes. A year ago he was charged with the rape of a young woman on Cape Cod. Even though the rape victim eventually decided to drop charges— we will present evidence that a tremendous amount of pressure was put on her to do that by the defendant—having been charged met the condition of the stipulation in the trust that it be dissolved, and that the money go to Jack Brannigan. This placed Jack Brannigan in an extremely difficult position, as I'm sure you can understand. On the one hand, as trustee, it was his responsibility to carry out his father's wishes. On the other hand, he knew how devastating this would be to his younger brother, whom he loved very much. Had he not felt this conflict of loyalty, he would have dissolved the trust immediately, and had the legal right to do so. Instead, he told the defendant that he would eventually have to follow the terms laid down by their late father, but tried to work things out, even offering the defendant an opportunity to work for the company, to earn an honest living, to no longer simply live off the work and sweat of other family members.

"Instead of responding with gratitude, William Brannigan was angry. We will present witnesses who will testify to that anger. He threatened his brother on more than one occasion."

Now, her accent became more pronounced, and she spoke with deliberate slowness. "Eventually, on a fateful spring night, with no moon to illuminate his murderous act, the defendant confronted his brother on one of the Swan Boats in Boston Garden, until then a source of simple pleasure for thousands of children and their families. That night he—he rammed a knife into his older brother's chest."

There was a slight hitch to Whitney James's voice as she spoke those final words. Genuine emotion, or calculated to elicit sympathy from the jury?

No matter. She left the lectern and took her seat behind the prosecution's table. Her assistant nodded enthusiastically; I lip-read him: "Beautiful job, Whitney. Beautiful."

"Is that all, Ms. James?" Judge Wilson asked, surprised as we all were, at the brevity of her opening argument.

She stood: "Yes, Your Honor."

Wilson looked over at Malcolm McLoon. "You're up, Mr. McLoon."

Malcolm stood, slowly came around the table, and headed for the lectern. Whispering could be heard in the courtroom. The judge adopted a stern expression as he looked into the faces of the audience and press. The whispering stopped.

Malcolm took his position at the lectern. Unlike Whitney James, who'd worked from notes, Malcolm had nothing with him. He slowly took in each juror's face before saying, "Good morning, ladies and gentlemen. You have just heard the people's opening statement, and I assure you that Ms. James is absolutely correct—about *one* thing. There was no moon the night Jack Brannigan was killed."

A few of the jurors smiled. Whitney James stood. "I object, Your Honor. Counsel does not have the right in opening argument to impugn opposing counsel."

"Overruled," Wilson said. But then he said to Malcolm, "Don't make me have to rule on this again, Mr. McLoon."

Malcolm looked at the judge with an expression of abject surprise. He raised his hand and said, "I assure Your Honor the last thing I wish to do is place him in a position of having to make such rulings. It will not happen again."

The judge said nothing, and Malcolm continued.

"William Brannigan, seated here with his life in

your hands, is as innocent as a baby's breath. You don't have to take my word for it, although I would be delighted if you did. I will *prove* it to you, not with sweeping conjectures but with the facts. And bear in mind that it is not our obligation to prove anything. That's the prosecution's job, to prove their flimsy case beyond a reasonable doubt. But we're willing to take on the burden of proof, too. You will see through a totally credible witness that William Brannigan could not have killed his brother because he wasn't in Boston that night. He was on Cape Cod. You will hear this from Ms. Cynthia Warren, the defendant's good friend. William Brannigan and Cynthia Warren were together on the Cape the night Jack Brannigan was killed. It was an unusually warm evening, and they decided to get some lobsters and celebrate the onset of summer. Billy bought two, two-pound lobsters and they cooked them in a pot on Cynthia Warren's patio. Cynthia husked ears of salt-and-pepper corn, and Billy Brannigan drew the butter."

Whitney James stood and objected again.

"What is the basis of your objection, Ms. James?" Malcolm asked.

"I ask the questions, Mr. McLoon," Judge Wilson said sharply.

"Irrelevancy," James said.

"Sustained," Judge Wilson said.

Malcolm sighed and faced the jury. "The fact that the defendant and Ms. Warren cooked lobsters is not irrelevant," he said, "no matter what my learned colleague claims."

James was on her feet again objecting.

Before Judge Wilson could rule, Malcolm added, "You will hear from the clerk of the fish market where Billy Brannigan bought the lobsters that day, and you will see the receipt."

"Overruled," Wilson said.

It was obvious from the grin on Malcolm's face that he was delighted how that exchange had gone.

"Oh, by the way, it's interesting—and I might add, highly unusual—that you will not hear any DNA evidence presented by the prosecution during this trial. On second thought 'unusual' is a gross understatement. 'Incredible' is more like it. The reason you will not hear any witnesses presented by the prosecution concerning blood is that the blood found at the scene did not match the young man's sitting over there, William Brannigan." Malcolm pointed at Billy. "And no blood was ever found in Billy's home or car, or on any item of clothing. Nor can the prosecution present to you the murder weapon because that has never been found.

"And so what you will be presented with by the people, whose sacred duty it is to *prove* William Brannigan's guilt beyond a reasonable doubt, is what they claim is a motive. Just that. A motive. People are not convicted of murder simply because the prosecution dreams up a motive."

Malcolm now went into a history of the Brannigan family: "James Brannigan, the defendant's father, founded Brannigan's Bean Pot over half a century ago. The company went on to market its baked beans nationally, and is today the second leading seller of baked beans. Perhaps you've enjoyed some yourself. The Brannigan family is a big Irish-Catholic family, seven children in all. Billy is the youngest at twenty-five. He chose not to work for the company, but that did not make him unusual. Of the seven children, only three are active in the management of Brannigan's Bean Pot. Jack Brannigan was one of those three. Of course, they all enjoy tasting new recipes." There were smiles in the jury box, and a few chuckles.

"No one misses Jack Brannigan more than Billy Brannigan," Malcolm said, sadness in his deep voice. "The day before Jack was murdered, Billy called Jack to give him some good news. He'd planned to ask Cynthia to marry him, and Jack was the first person with whom Billy wanted to share that exciting news. He also wanted advice from his big brother on the best way to propose. At the Red Sox game they planned to attend that weekend? At a cookout? Perhaps a boat ride? But the most important thing Billy asked his brother, Jack, was whether he would agree to be his best man."

Malcolm paused for effect.

"What was Jack's answer? 'Only if you will let me throw your bachelor party in the tree house.'

He was referring to a tree house the two brothers had built in the backyard of the home in which they grew up."

Malcolm now leaned on the lectern—please don't let it collapse under his weight I thought—and said, "I have been defending the innocent for my entire adult life. I have fought tooth-and-nail for men and women accused of heinous crimes, but who had not committed those crimes. And I can tell you without hesitation or reservation, ladies and gentlemen of the jury, that I have never defended a client in whose innocence I so strongly believe. William Brannigan, the young man whose life you will determine, loved his brother, Jack, more than any other person in this world. He is sickened and saddened at the loss of his brother. To even suggest that he was responsible for his brother's death is blaspheme. And I am confident that when presented with the facts, you will waste little time in allowing this fine young man to get on with his life. I trust you to do that, and so does he. Thank you."

As Malcolm waddled back to the defense table, I saw two women members of the jury dab at tears with their handkerchiefs, and made a note of that next to their names in my notebook.

No doubt about it. Malcolm McLoon with all his personal excesses, was good. If I ever ended up being accused of murder, I knew who to call.

Chapter Ten

"You did? Good news, Ritchie. Bring her in."

We were in Malcolm's office. It was nine o'clock, and we'd just returned from dinner after the end of the first day of trial. Malcolm had received the call from his investigator, Ritchie Fleigler, the moment we'd walked through the door. Judging from Malcolm's side of the conversation, it sounded like good news.

Then it sounded like bad news. "Why the hell can't you?" Malcolm shouted into the phone. "She's upset? All the more reason to get her here to Boston. Put her up in a hotel, keep her close."

Malcolm frowned as he heard what Fleigler said next. "All right, Ritchie, but I want you down there first thing in the morning."

He slammed down the phone, tugged at his collar to loosen it with his left hand, and ran the fingers of his right hand between his collar and thick neck. "Well, what do you think, Jessica?" he growled.

"About what?"

"About today. First day of a trial is always problematic."

"I suppose I was so busy focusing on the jurors that I really didn't pay much attention to anything else. Your opening statement was eloquent."

"Thank you. You can win a case with your opening statement. Lose it, too." He pointed to the phone. "That was Ritchie. He finally made contact with Cynthia Warren down on the Cape. She said she'd gotten away from the pressure. Glad she decided to come back. Ritchie says she's upset about testifying. A basket case, he says."

"Which I can certainly understand," I said.

"All she has to do is tell the truth, that she was with Billy the night his brother was murdered."

"Still, Malcolm, it must be traumatic having to testify in a murder trial. I certainly wouldn't want to be a witness."

"That damn Judge Wilson," he said. "I never did much like him, although I suppose he's trying to be fair. I just wish he were older. I like older judges, even the cantankerous and short-tempered ones."

Like you, I thought, smiling. I knew why Malcolm was upset with the judge. District Attorney Whitney James had managed to win two points during hearings held with the jury outside the courtroom.

One involved Malcolm's request that two DWI convictions of Billy Brannigan be excluded on the basis of a lack of materiality and relevance. The judge allowed it because the most recent had been the week before the murder.

The second was Malcolm's request that the court recess at noon on Friday to accommodate some personal commitments of his staff. He meant, of course, his assistant counsel, Rachel Cohen, who had to be somewhere with her youngsters. But Malcolm didn't explain that to the judge. He left it vague; the judge was not vague when he said, "Motion denied."

Malcolm shuffled through a mountain of papers piled on his desk. As he did, his frown deepened. He sighed and shook his head. I wondered whether it was time for me to leave, which would not have displeased me. I was exhausted, and wanted to get back to the comfort of my suite at the Ritz-Carlton. I was about to suggest that I leave him alone when he looked up and said, "You might as well know that I'm worried about Cynthia Warren's testimony."

"Why?" I asked. "As you said, if she was with Billy that night, all she has to do is tell the truth. Do you question whether she's being truthful?"

He sat back, laced his fingers on top of his sizable belly, and said, "No, it's not that. The problem is she seems like a fragile little flower, not the most solidly grounded of women. You never know about people like that. Sometimes they become so fearful that they fly away, like a bird escaping a cat."

"But Ritchie said she's returned home. That's a good sign, isn't it?"

"The best sign would be if she were holed up in a room next to you at the Ritz-Carlton. That's what I wanted Ritchie to do, bring her back to Boston tonight. He said he tried to convince her of that, but she refused. Said she'd come tomorrow."

I didn't relish the thought of having Ms. Warren in a room next to me. I wasn't anxious to become caretaker to a star witness in a murder trial.

"There's something you can do for me, Jessica. I'd like you to go to the Cape with Ritchie tomorrow morning and escort Ms. Warren back here. Ritchie knows how to dig up things, how to find people, but he tends to be brusque. I'm afraid he'll scare her off even more. You, on the other hand, are a woman."

"Thank you," I said.

"And Cynthia Warren is a woman. More important, you know people, know how to handle them, know what gets them upset and what calms them down."

"I'm flattered, but I'm afraid I'm not that astute."

Malcolm sat up and slapped his hands on the desk. "I don't need modesty from you, Jessica. What I need is for you to go with Ritchie tomorrow morning and make sure Cynthia Warren gets back here." He smiled. "Besides, I'll treat you to lunch at Thompson's Clam Bar, in Harwichport. Close to where Ms. Warren lives, right on the water." He laughed. "The more I talk about it, the more I'd like to skip court tomorrow and go with you."

"I know Thompson's," I said. "But you don't have to offer lunch. It would be better if we headed straight back to Boston with Ms. Warren and had lunch here."

He stood and went to the window, looked out over Boston at night. For some reason—maybe it was the way his large body seemed to have settled, the way he held his head, or the expression on his face as he left the desk—that caused me to think he was, at that moment, suffering a great sadness. But he didn't say that. He turned to me and said, "Use your best judgment, Jessica. That's why I'm sending you. I need people with good judgment."

"Of course I'll go," I said, standing and straightening my skirt as a signal I was about to leave. "I suppose I really don't have any function now that the trial has started."

He held up his hand. "Nonsense. I've told you that the most important phase of your responsibilities has just started. I need you to read those jurors. But I figure I can get along without you for one day. Getting Ms. Warren here is our top priority."

"Then I'll be off to the Cape in the morning."

The sadness I discerned earlier was still very much evident on his round face.

"Anything wrong, Malcolm?" I asked.

For a moment, I thought he might cry. But he forced a smile and said, "A few problems, Jessica. Maybe when this is over, you and I can sit down, have a couple of stiff drinks, and I'll explain them to you."

Before leaving, I said, "I want you to know, Malcolm, what a wonderful experience this is for me. I'm learning a great deal about how our justice system works." I thought of George Plimpton, the author known for actually living the roles and occupations of those he writes about. What fun that must be for him. It also crossed my mind that maybe I should set my next book in outer space, and see if I could hitch a ride on a space shuttle. But I immediately dismissed that notion. I could never survive on Tang and dehydrated beef jerky.

"Mind an early start tomorrow?" Malcolm asked.

"Oh, no. I'm an early riser."

"Fine. I'll have Ritchie pick you up at seven."

"I'll be waiting."

Chapter Eleven

We barreled along in Ritchie's Olds 88, his radio crooning Charlie Parker, Miles Davis, Benny Goodman, and other jazz greats being played by a Boston FM station.

We reached the Bourne Bridge, which crosses the man-made Cape Cod Canal and links the rest of the world to the Cape. The smell of salt water, and memories of innocent, good old-fashioned summer fun brought a smile to my lips. I've always found Cape Cod and its landscape, atmosphere, and attitudes to be a step back in time, despite its increasing commercialization.

As we made our way to Cynthia Warren's house in Harwichport, I took in the long stretch of pine trees that line Route Six. Because most trees on the Cape are pines, the look doesn't change much from winter to summer, a comforting sameness that renders the arm-shaped peninsula timeless.

"We'll avoid Suicide Alley," Ritchie said, turning off the main highway onto a smaller road. "Unless I'm in a real hurry I stay clear of it."

"Suicide Alley?" I asked.

He laughed. "Yeah. The right name for it." He explained that it was the name given to a stretch of the two-lane highway that has been the scene of countless accidents as drivers attempt to pass one another, too often into oncoming traffic. "We'll take the back roads," he said.

"Ever been to her house before?" I asked as we passed quaint cottages lined with white picket fences, salmon-colored roses climbing trellises, an occasional American flag flying, and through picturesque towns with tiny shops.

"Sure. I've been on this case a couple of months now. I've been out here twice to interview her. A very nice young woman. Beautiful, too. Brannigan has good taste in women.

"There's Tip O'Neill's house," he said as we passed an unassuming weathered shingle home with pink shutters. "*Was* his house, I guess. His widow still lives there."

We eventually turned into a crushed seashell driveway leading to a home I would use if I were scouting locations for a film about Cape Cod. It was an old, rambling white house with navy-blue shutters and a wraparound porch adorned with dozens of hanging pots of red geraniums. An Irish setter slept on the front steps. He was no watchdog. He didn't raise his head as we pulled in.

The yard was well-kept, the lawn stretching down to a serene ocean inlet with a small, postage-stamp-size patch of sand. Water lapped quietly against the pilings of a dock; a Sunfish with a red sail rested against a willow tree, the tree's branches gently arching out over the water.

We got out of the car and walked up the front steps to the house. The dog finally raised its head, wagged its tail halfheartedly, stretched its legs, and went back to sleep. He was obviously old, and probably deaf. Although time wasn't on his side, he acted as though it were.

Ritchie knocked.

"Beautiful home," I said, admiring the white wicker furniture on the porch. A planter housed a healthy crop of pansies. A seashell collection and weathered beach glass in a large glass bowl created a beautiful centerpiece on a white wicker table. "I could spend the rest of my life sitting on this porch," I said.

"That'd be nice, huh?" Ritchie said. He knocked again.

"Does she live here alone?" I asked.

"Uh-huh," Ritchie replied, knocking again. He peered through a small row of windows in the front door.

"Doesn't look like she's home," I said.

"Her car's here," he said, pointing to a white BMW convertible in front of an old barn that served as a garage. Its license plate read, SUMRLOVN.

Ritchie knocked, louder this time. When there was no response, he went to a picture window and looked inside. "Jesus," he said.

"What is it?" I asked, coming to his side.

He responded by pulling a small cellular flip phone from his shirt pocket and dialing 911.

I pressed my nose to the glass and looked inside. A woman in a bathrobe was sprawled on the floor, a white couch next to her soaked in blood. "Oh, my God," I said softly.

"We need somebody over at Four Snow Lane right away," Ritchie said into the phone. "We've got a dead woman here." He signed off, pulled a cigarette from his shirt pocket, and sat on a white wicker chair. "I know one thing," he said.

"What's that?" I asked.

"Malcolm sure isn't going to be happy."

The initial contingent of police that arrived were so young that if it weren't for their uniforms, I'd have mistaken them for Boy Scouts. They were soon joined by two older detectives in plain-clothes, a crime laboratory technician in a white lab frock, and a police photographer. The criminalist dusted for fingerprints while the detectives examined the body. The uniformed police draped a yellow CRIME SCENE tape across the driveway and front walk.

While I waited for a detective to take a statement from me, I stood in a far corner of the living room and watched the police go about their crime scene investigation. It wasn't easy looking at Ms. Warren's body. She'd shed a great deal of blood from the wound in the center of her chest. The knife, which was on the floor beside her, had undoubtedly pierced her heart. Death would surely have been immediate.

I thought of Jack Brannigan's murder. From the reports I'd read, he, too, had died from a single knife wound to the chest.

I gave my statement, and was left alone after that to casually wander about the living room, wondering when someone would tell me to leave. No one did. Ritchie Fleigler was chain smoking on the front porch and talking into his cellular phone.

I scrutinized a row of framed pictures on the fireplace mantel. Cynthia was in all of them, Billy Brannigan in some. There were photographs on tables and on the wall, which I also took in. There's something especially powerful about pictures of someone who has just died, especially if that death was sudden and unexpected. How tragic, I thought. Cynthia Warren had been a beautiful young woman, her smile worthy of Hollywood. Tan and blond, she had a girl-next-door freshness about her. So did some of her friends in the photos. One girl appeared in a number of shots. She caught my eye because her dark Mediterranean sensuousness was in stark contrast to Cynthia's fairness. Another beautiful young woman. The world was full of them.

I paid special attention to the pictures that included Billy Brannigan. He looked happy enough, although I could sense a strain in his expression.

Probably uncomfortable having his picture taken, I thought, like many people, me included.

Aware that no one seemed interested in me, I strolled into the kitchen. A pale blue gingham tablecloth hung neatly over a small table, surrounded by four hand-painted wooden chairs with cushions that matched the cloth. Delicate white lace valance curtains graced the windows. Yesterday's newspaper, open to the entertainment section, sat on a white countertop. An open box of SnackWell's devil food cookies was next to it. Two of the cookies were missing. A thoroughly rinsed single glass and plate were in the sink.

I almost leaned on the counter but caught myself in time. The last thing I wanted to do was compromise evidence with my palm or fingerprints.

My next stop was the den. Cynthia had wonderful decorator taste. This room, like the rest of the downstairs, was light, airy, and casual. Soft floral prints of red and yellow on an overstuffed couch and armchairs were inviting. Floor-to-ceiling bookcases lined one wall. Built into them was a huge projection television set and an elaborate stereo. Matching oversized forest-green leather recliners provided screening-room comfort for two.

What was especially appealing was the view from a large bay window, aptly named because it overlooked the bay.

The books in the bookcases didn't appear to have been placed in any particular order—alpha-

betically, or by size or topic. Like people who peek
into medicine cabinets when visiting others'
homes, I peruse books. While you may not be able
to judge a book by its cover, you can often judge a
person by his or her collection of books. Cynthia's
literary taste ran to Tom Wolfe's *Bonfire of the
Vanities*; Thoreau's *Cape Cod*; *Men Are from
Mars, Women Are from Venus*; Amy Tan's *The
Kitchen God's Wife*; *Paris Trout*; Shakespeare's
Twelfth Night; Agatha Christie's *The Man in the
Brown Suit*; *Sand and Foam* by Kahlil Gibran; and
Coffee, Tea or Me?, that frothy little tale of airline
stewardesses (they call them flight attendants
now) from twenty-five years ago. The entire bottom row of the shelves housed travel guides. Cynthia Warren was certainly eclectic in what she
chose to read.

I was drawn to a small wooden table with a
glass top on the other side of the room, on which
was displayed an unusual piece of pottery, pre-
Columbian in appearance, but modern at the
same time. The potter had made good use of metallic yellows and greens to create a stunning work
of art. I enjoy pottery, and began collecting it ten
years ago, picking up a piece wherever I travel to
remind me of the city, state, country, or island I'd
visited. Before that, it was miniature spoons, then
coffee mugs, and finally Christmas tree ornaments. It was when my display racks for the
spoons and mugs overflowed, and my Christmas
tree bowed unnaturally under the weight of too

many ornaments, that I turned to pottery. This was a beautiful piece, another example of Ms. Warren's good taste. A small, cherry writing desk sat in a corner in front of the large bay window, a perfect setting for creating a letter or note, or in my case if I lived here, a manuscript page. Unlike the rest of the downstairs, the desk was messy. Not dirty, but heavy with papers. I reached in my pocket for my half-glasses, put them on, and read the papers on top of various piles. A pink slip of paper caught my eye, and I leaned closer to read it. It was a Cape Cod Savings Bank deposit slip in the amount of ten thousand dollars. The account was in Cynthia Warren's name. She'd made the deposit yesterday. She evidently had a good job, or profession. The house testified to that.

The mood in Malcolm's office later that afternoon was grim. No surprise. A vibrant young woman had been brutally murdered, reason enough for the funereal atmosphere. But on top of it, a young man, Billy Brannigan, on trial for his life, had lost his only alibi.

We all sat there without saying anything, waiting for Malcolm to break the silence. The only sound was the incessant ringing of the telephone, which was being answered by an answering machine.

Malcolm was slumped in his chair behind his

desk, watery eyes fixed on the desktop, tie yanked open and hanging crookedly over his belly.

"Malcolm, maybe we should—"

He waved off Rachel Cohen's words.

"I just thought that—"

"Can't be," Malcolm muttered to himself.

"Where's Billy?" Georgia Bobley asked tentatively, as though her intrusion into the great attorney's thoughts might result in a spear through her heart.

"My house," Malcolm said. "Linda's with him."

"That's good," said Jill Farkas, never looking up from her laptop computer.

"Damn it!" Malcolm said with force. He got to his feet, went to the small bar, and poured himself a large glass of whiskey.

We looked at each other as our leader emptied the glass with one long swallow.

"Looks like the prosecution's got itself a guardian angel," he growled.

"The lobby's filled with reporters," Georgia Bobley said.

I winced when I thought he was about to pour himself another drink, but he didn't. The emptied glass seemed to have loosened him up, like oil freeing a rusty hinge. He was out of his reverie, wheels almost visible as they spun in his head. "What'd the DA say?" he asked Rachel Cohen.

"They want Judge Wilson to revoke Billy's bail."

Malcolm guffawed. "What the hell do they think, Billy went and killed his only alibi?"

"They've been chafing ever since he was given bail, Malcolm. You know that. The DA's up for reelection. He's making a case out of allowing accused murderers to walk around free on bail."

"If Ritchie calls in, put him through," he told Georgia, who sat next to the answering machine noting callers who'd identified themselves. Ritchie Fleigler had stayed on the Cape; I'd been brought back to Boston by my driver, Cathie, who'd been dispatched to pick me up the minute Malcolm learned about Cynthia Warren. Court had just broken for lunch when the call came through, and Judge Wilson had honored Malcolm's request for a recess until the following morning.

Malcolm paced, stopping at the bar but resisting the temptation to pour another. "They want to play that game," he said, "we can play games, too. Hell, who's to say that our esteemed district attorney isn't so anxious for a conviction in the Brannigan case that he had Ms. Warren killed?"

"That's pretty far-fetched," Rachel said.

"So's the notion that Billy might have killed his girlfriend, to say nothing of his ticket out of a life sentence."

"We should have a statement ready for the press," Georgia offered.

Malcolm looked at me. "How about it, Jessica?"

"Write a statement?"

"You're the only writer here."

"I write murder mysteries. Not press releases."

"Why not hold an impromptu press conference downstairs?" Rachel suggested. "They'll be hounding you for a statement anyway."

"Make sense?" Malcolm asked me.

I nodded.

"Rachel, start writing a motion for a mistrial," Malcolm said. "Georgia, go downstairs and tell the media vultures to expect a statement in an hour. Jill, can you run an analysis of how each member of the jury is likely to react to Ms. Warren's death?"

"I'm doing that now," she said, her eyes glued to the laptop's small screen, fingers flying over the keys.

Ritchie Fleigler called in frequently from the Cape, the last call after a conversation he'd had with the Harwich chief of police, an elderly gentleman named Steven McPartland who'd arrived at Cynthia Warren's house shortly before I was picked up by Cathie. McPartland was a kindly man. I pointed out the sleeping old dog on the porch, and asked what would happen to him.

"I'll take him home with me," McPartland said without hesitation. "Got an old-timer myself. They'll get along."

"Any leads?" Malcolm asked Ritchie. "Any suspects?"

His frown indicated that the answer to both questions was negative.

Rachel Cohen left at six to file the motion for a mistrial.

Georgia Bobley asked if she could leave, too. "I have a date," she said, "but I can—"

"No, you go enjoy your date, young lady. There's another pretty gal down in Harwichport who won't be going out on any more dates. Enjoy it while you can." She left under that ominous cloud.

Jill Farkas printed out a report on a small ink-jet printer attached to her laptop. Malcolm studied it. "Looks like we chose wrong in a few cases," he said.

"Not originally," she replied, obviously pricked by his criticism. "How could I have forecast the death of our star witness?"

"Of course you couldn't," Malcolm said. "This will be helpful. Go on, get on home. Should be an interesting day in court tomorrow."

She left without saying good-bye to me.

"So, Jessica, here we are."

I smiled. "Yes, Malcolm, here we are. I should be running, too. I know you want to get home to Billy and—"

"In due time. Frankly, as upsetting as this day has been, I'm in the mood for a good dinner. Like French food?"

"Almost as much as clambakes and corn on the cob. But I'm very tired. The impact of finding Ms. Warren's body this morning is starting to hit me."

"Good French food will help. Come on, there's an excellent place near here."

It was while riding down in the elevator that

Malcolm remembered he'd promised to make a statement to the waiting press. They were there in droves, and he talked for twenty minutes. When he was through, they turned to me and started firing questions.

"Sorry," Malcolm said. "Mrs. Fletcher has no statement at this time—nor do we *have* time for questions. Have a pleasant evening." He took me by the arm and led me through the lobby doors and to the street.

"Will Brannigan's bail be revoked?" a reporter yelled after us.

Malcolm's response was a wave of his hand.

"Mrs. Fletcher, you discovered the body this morning," another reporter shouted. "What was your reaction?"

Malcolm stopped, turned, and said, "She was obviously delighted and pleased to come upon an unfortunate young woman who'd been butchered. Made her day. Good God, man, where is your sense of decency?"

The reporters and television cameras followed us to Julien, a darling little French restaurant a few blocks from the office. We were seated in Queen Anne wingback chairs in the high-ceilinged room that had once been a bank's boardroom. Malcolm told me Boston's first French restaurant had been opened on this same site in 1794.

"Everything in Boston has history attached to

it," I said after ordering a glass of white wine; Malcolm had a martini, straight up.

"Here's to bad luck, Jessica," he said, holding his glass up to mine.

"I'd rather drink to Ms. Warren," I said. "And to Billy Brannigan. What are his chances now that she's no longer his alibi?"

"Not good. Then again, life's what happens while you're making other plans. I read that somewhere. But I've faced worse situations," he said. "You haven't had much to say since this morning, Jessica."

"Because I didn't know what to say. What words are there?"

"We have to remember one thing, Jessica. Cynthia Warren might be gone, but there's another life at stake. Billy Brannigan's."

"I know that," I said. "Life goes on. So does a trial."

"Exactly. When you were at her house this morning, did you see anything unusual?"

"No."

"I just thought with your track record solving crimes, you might have picked up on something others would miss."

"There was one thing," I said.

Malcolm put down his drink. "What was that?"

"A deposit slip."

"Ms. Warren's deposit slip?"

"Yes."

"For how much?" he asked.

"Ten thousand dollars."

"When was it deposited?"

"Yesterday."

"That's a lot of money."

"It certainly is."

"Any idea of the source of the money?"

"No."

"Interesting."

I ordered the ragout of New England scallops with puree of white beans and truffles, and Malcolm had a salmon souffle.

By the time I escorted Malcolm from the restaurant into the glare of TV lights and the blinding flash of still photographers' strobes, he was quite drunk. I was concerned I might have to support him as we made our way to the waiting limousine, but he managed on his own. The reporters fired a barrage of questions at us, which we ignored. As I was about to climb in the backseat with Malcolm, a young man asked, "Is he drunk?"

I turned, haughtily drew myself up to full height, and said, "Of course not. Mr. McLoon is very tired, as might be expected. Besides, he—he hasn't had a drink all day."

As the driver headed for the Ritz-Carlton to drop me off, two thoughts weighed heavily on me.

The first was that I'd run away from home and joined a circus: "Step right up and see the mystery writer-turned jury consultant and the alcoholic defense lawyer hang by their fingertips from the world's highest trapeze."

The second was how protective I'd become of Malcolm McLoon.

I suddenly missed Cabot Cove with a passion. My next novel be damned, I thought.

Sorry, Vaughan, but learning how our jury system works is becoming too painful.

I glanced over at Malcolm, who'd fallen asleep against the limo's door.

I wanted to go home.

Chapter Twelve

"Please rise. Court is in session. The honorable Judge Walter Wilson presiding."

The courtroom was crowded, and a long line of disappointed spectators lined the sidewalk outside. The section designated for the press was filled. There was a palpable tension in the air as Judge Wilson entered and took his place at the bench.

The jury was not present. The morning's agenda would be focused upon the death of Billy Brannigan's alibi, Cynthia Warren, and its impact upon the trial.

"Good morning," Wilson said gruffly.

"Good morning," we replied.

Wilson said, "The unfortunate event yesterday, the death of an important defense witness, has prompted a motion by the defense for a mistrial. Or, failing that, a two-week continuation. I'll hear oral arguments this morning on that motion."

"Here goes nothing," Malcolm whispered to me. That he was bristling with energy and resolve was remarkable, considering his condition last night.

I looked over at Billy Brannigan sitting next to Malcolm. His handsome young face was without expression. Georgia Bobley had told me early that morning that Billy had been on heavy-duty tranquilizers since learning of Cynthia's death. He'd slept at Malcolm's house. Linda, Malcolm's receptionist, had watched over him because he'd expressed suicidal thoughts. She hadn't dared sleep until Billy was showered, dressed, and in a limo heading for the courthouse that morning.

"Mr. McLoon?" the judge said, ready to hear Malcolm's argument in favor of the written motion delivered by Rachel Cohen the night before.

Malcolm went to the podium. "Good morning, Your Honor," he began, his voice matching the grave expression on his face. "Given yesterday's sad death of Cynthia Warren, a beautiful young woman who'd planned to marry the defendant, and who was with him on Cape Cod the night of his brother's unfortunate and distinctly premature demise, the defense's ability to fairly and effectively present his case has been terminally compromised. Cynthia Warren was a pivotal witness, Your Honor. That she was with the defendant the night of Jack Brannigan's murder isn't hearsay. It's a fact, and she would have stated that fact in this courtroom. Not only do I consider it patently unfair to be asked to defend William Brannigan without Cynthia Warren's testimony, there is the parallel dimension of how convenient her death is for the People. One might even—" Whitney James was on her feet.

"Your Honor, I was afraid Mr. McLoon would move in this direction. I—"

"You're interrupting me, Ms. James," Malcolm said.

"You bet I am, Mr. McLoon. I deeply resent the insinuation that the prosecution might view Ms. Warren's death as a benefit. How dare you?"

"You will admit, Ms. James, that the timing of Ms. Warren's death is convenient for you."

"Your Honor, Mr. McLoon should be held in contempt of this court. What he is saying surely—"

Judge Wilson wielded his gavel. "Order," he said loudly. "I will not tolerate this sort of bickering between counsel."

Malcolm said, "It was my understanding, Your Honor, that the defense and the prosecution would have equal opportunity to present its argument regarding this motion for a mistrial. Ms. James is treading on my time, something I find both bothersome, yet characteristically boring of her."

"Your Honor, I demand that you—"

"This is my time at this podium, Ms. James."

A series of sharp raps with the gavel restored order.

"I will allow counsel for each side to proceed with their arguments for and against this motion for a mistrial."

"I withdraw the motion for a mistrial, Your Honor," Malcolm said.

We all looked at each other.

"Never in my long legal career have I represented someone as innocent as Mr. William Brannigan. The People do not have one credible shred of evidence to link him to the murder of his brother. I am prepared to go forward with the defense after a continuance of two weeks, during which time we will be able to restructure the presentation of our case without the testimony of Cynthia Warren."

Malcolm returned to the table and sat heavily.

District Attorney James argued against continuance, basing her protest on the fact that the prosecution would be presenting its case for at least a week, possibly two, ample time for the defense to regroup.

Judge Wilson ruled: "I don't find any grounds for a mistrial based upon the death of a witness. Further, I find Ms. James to be correct in her reasoning. The defense will have plenty of time to alter its strategy. Bring in the jury."

Ms. James was on her feet again. "Your Honor, may I be allowed to bring up before the court another issue before the jury is brought in?"

"Yes, Ms. James?"

"The matter of the defendant's bail. Considering what has occurred, I feel it is inappropriate for him to be walking free."

Malcolm bellowed from where he sat, "Is Ms.

James suggesting that the defendant might have murdered his alibi?"

"You're out of order, Mr. McLoon," Wilson said.

Malcolm stood. "No, Your Honor, it is Ms. James who is out of order—and out of her mind."

"You're in contempt, Mr. McLoon."

"I am in shock rather than contempt, Your Honor."

"Sit down, Mr. McLoon."

"Her motion to revoke the defendant's bail is outrageous."

"And you are out of order, Mr. McLoon. Get out your checkbook. I'm fining you five-hundred dollars. I'll rule on the bail issue at another time. Bring in the jurors!"

A bailiff approached Malcolm and held out his hand. "Write a check," Malcolm groaned at Georgia Bobley. He then added loud enough for Judge Wilson to hear, "I'll sign it—*with pleasure!*"

"The people calls Detective John Sullivan," Whitney James said.

Detective Sullivan was tall, of medium build, and had a pleasant face and ready smile. As he took the oath, I realized that his credibility was established before he ever took the stand. The jury would like and believe him.

Malcolm was smiling. Whether Judge Wilson would allow us to present what Ritchie Fleigler had dug up on Sullivan—that he'd worked for a brief time as a male stripper—was conjecture. I also wondered whether it would even matter to the jury.

Guided by Ms. James, Detective Sullivan took the jury through the nighttime discovery of Jack Brannigan's body on a Swan Boat in the Public Garden. He was the first law enforcement officer to arrive on the gruesome scene: "It was," he said, "a clean killing."

"What do you mean by 'clean'?" Whitney asked.

"I don't mean soap-and-water clean," he replied, "but there was relatively little blood, despite a stab wound to the chest."

"How much blood was there?" asked the DA.

"As stabbings go, not a lot."

"Would you say a pint of blood?"

"Yes, about a pint. Maybe less."

"To what do you attribute the small amount of blood, Detective Sullivan?"

"I'd rather not attribute it to anything, Ms. James. I leave that up to the coroner, or a criminalist."

"Detective Sullivan," James said, "did you see anything unusual at the scene that night?"

"No," he answered.

"It was a quarter past twelve when you discovered the body. Is that correct?"

"Yes, that's correct."

"And how was it that a plainclothes detective was the first to arrive on the scene?"

"I was part of a new plainclothes task force patrol working the Public Garden. There've been a lot of kids hanging out there lately. Some vandalism on the Swam Boats. Drugs."

I saw that Malcolm wrote something down. Several jurors also made a note.

Whitney James conferred with her assistant for a moment before resuming her questioning. "What did you do when you first came upon the body, Detective?"

"I called for backup."

"On your radio?"

"Yes."

"Then what did you do?"

"I determined that the man was dead, and then the backup arrived."

"Who?"

"Detectives Wagner, O'Malley, and Lofgren, initially, and then a lot of other cars. It's not every night we find a dead body in the Public Garden."

"In what position did you find the body?"

"He was facedown."

"And you could see the wound?"

"No. But I could see the blood. It seemed to be coming from his stomach. It wasn't until later that I learned it was from a wound to his chest."

"Detective, one last question. Was there a moon the night of Jack Brannigan's death?"

"No. It was a particularly dark night."

"And there were no witnesses. Is that right?"

"At least none that came forward to the police, ma'am."

"Thank you, Detective."

Malcolm replaced Whitney behind the podium. "Good morning, Detective Sullivan."

"Good morning, Mr. McLoon."

"Detective, is it hard to see in the Public Garden on nights when there is no moon?"

"Yes."

"It is my understanding, Detective, that even before the death of Jack Brannigan, there had been some debate about putting better lighting in the Public Garden."

"Objection," snapped Whitney.

"Sustained. Counsel, rephrase."

"Detective, is it your belief the Garden isn't lighted—"

"Objection."

"Sustained. Counsel, rephrase again."

"Detective, you said that on a moonless night it is more difficult to see in the Public Garden than on nights with the moon full. Correct?"

"Yes."

"Okay. Are there a lot of lights around the Swan Boats at night?"

"No."

"How many? One? Two?"

"Yeah, but they aren't always working."

"I see. Sometimes they're broken. So there wouldn't be any light."

"Objection."

"Overruled."

"Usually, one of them is working," said the detective.

"Usually?" asked Malcolm. "That means not always?"

"That's right. On some nights none of them work."

"And you testified just a few minutes ago that you always make it a point to check the Swan Boats because kids hang out there. Is that correct?"

"Yes. It's become a favorite hangout spot."

"Detective, isn't it true that you've made arrests of some of these kids before, at the very spot Jack Brannigan's body was found?"

"Objection," Whitney exclaimed.

"Overruled."

"A few."

"A few, you say. Over what period of time? The last couple of years, months, weeks?"

"A couple of arrests over the past couple of years."

"Two arrests over the past two years?"

"Yes."

"What were those arrests for, Detective?"

"Drugs. Loitering."

"That's it?"

"The drug arrest also involved possession of a weapon."

"Oh? What sort of weapon?"

The detective paused. "A knife."

"When did this happen, Detective Sullivan?"

"About six months ago."

"Right around the time of Jack Brannigan's murder?"

"That's correct."

"Weeks before?"

"A couple of days before, sir."

"Where is that person now, the person arrested for possession of a knife?"

"I have no idea, sir," Sullivan answered. "I don't—I can't keep tabs on all the arrests I make."

"Why is that, Detective? Make a lot of them in Boston?"

"Yes. Unfortunately."

"To the best of your knowledge, Detective, would that person you arrested for possession of drugs, and a lethal weapon, be behind bars?"

"He's not." Sullivan shrugged.

"There's one more thing I'd like to ask you, Detective Sullivan. It's my understanding that you've been with the Boston Police Department for four years. Correct?"

"That's correct, Mr. McLoon."

"What did you do before becoming a police officer?"

"Various occupations," he answered, shifting position in the witness chair.

We held our collective breath at the defense table. Detective Sullivan proved to be a good witness for our side. There was nothing to be gained by attacking his moral character.

Malcolm obviously viewed it the same way. "No further questions," he said.

Chapter Thirteen

The first witness called after the lunch break was a criminalist, Dawn Kiss, a thoughtful and articulate middle-aged woman. I loved her name, perfect for a heroine in a historical romantic novel.

"Ms. Kiss, would you describe to members of this court the evidence you discovered and handled at the crime scene," Whitney James said.

"Certainly," said Kiss. "My findings, as far as the blood is concerned, corroborates with what Detective Sullivan testified earlier. I collected blood samplings from what appeared to be a pint or so of blood from the victim. I also collected fiber and hair samplings."

"And?"

"The Public Garden is a very public place. Its name serves it well. On any given summer afternoon you'll find hundreds or thousands of people enjoying the Garden and Swan Boats. Aside from the samplings that matched the victim, the remaining hair and fiber samples we found could belong to any of thousands of people."

"Thank you, Ms. Kiss. No further questions."

Malcolm conferred briefly with Rachel before taking his place behind the podium. "Good afternoon, Ms. Kiss. Nice to see you again."

"Thank you."

"Ms. Kiss, you say you collected a lot of hair and fiber samplings from the scene of the crime. Right?"

"That's correct."

"And, you say that some of the hair samples matched that of the victim, Jack Brannigan?"

"Correct."

"You also testified that some of the clothing fibers matched that of the victim, Jack Brannigan."

"Yes."

"And the other samplings, of which you said there were many, didn't belong to anyone who could be identified."

"Yes."

"Well, then, having established that, let me understand this correctly," Malcolm said. "The police department's forensics lab has a number of fiber and hair samplings that had been collected at the crime scene by you, but they have no idea to whom they belong. Do I understand that correctly?"

"Yes, you do."

"You're aware, aren't you, that samplings of the defendant's hair and clothing were taken the day of his arrest?"

"Of course. I took them."

"Ms. Kiss, the hair and clothing evidence you collected at the crime scene—did *any* of it match the defendant, Mr. Billy Brannigan, the gentleman sitting over there?"

"No, sir, it did not."

"Not one iota of hair, clothing, or unidentified fiber matches that of the young man who is on trial here for the murder of his brother?" Malcolm's voice was now thunder.

"Objection," said Whitney. "Argumentative."

"Overruled."

Kiss answered softly. "Yes, sir, that's correct."

Malcolm continued: "And let's talk about something we haven't yet touched upon. The blood you collected. Did any of the blood from the crime scene match Mr. Brannigan's DNA?"

"Yes."

Malcolm froze. We all did. He looked back at us, his expression one of confusion and concern.

"What, Ms. Kiss?"

"I said 'yes, sir.'"

"It is your testimony here today that DNA of the blood collected from the defendant matched the DNA blood taken from the crime scene?"

Ms. Kiss appeared to be cringing under Malcolm's questioning. Now, she drew a deep breath, smiled, and said, "Oh, no, sir. It didn't match the *defendant's* DNA. It matched the victim, Jack Brannigan. You said 'Mr. Brannigan.' I took that to mean the victim."

"Thank you, Ms. Kiss."

Judge Wilson interrupted. "Counsel, from now on, in order to avoid such confusion, let's refer to the defendant as William Brannigan, or Billy if you prefer, and the victim as Jack Brannigan."

"A good suggestion, Your Honor," Malcolm said. "Now, Ms. Kiss, Detective Sullivan testified that a few days before Jack Brannigan's murder, he'd made an arrest of a young man, name unknown at this juncture, at the very same place where Mr. Jack Brannigan lost his life. Are you aware of that testimony by Detective Sullivan?"

"Yes, I am."

"To your knowledge, Ms. Kiss, has any effort been made to match the DNA, and other evidence found at the crime scene, to such possible suspects as the young man arrested by Detective Sullivan; and who, by the way, was in possession of a lethal weapon, a knife?"

"Objection. Beyond the scope of the witness's knowledge."

"Sustained."

"Doesn't it make common sense, Ms. Kiss, to see if a person, arrested at the same spot as a vicious stabbing, and possessing a knife—and not in jail—just might be—"

"Objection."

"Rephrase the question, Mr. McLoon."

He did.

The criminalist replied, "No, I was not asked by the police to check evidence found at the Brannigan crime scene with others known to have been arrested in that area."

"You were never directed to examine evidence from an arrest made days earlier at the Public Garden that involved a knife?"

"That's correct, sir."

"Thank you, Ms. Kiss. I have no further questions for this *prosecution* witness."

District Attorney James conducted a half-hearted redirect examination of Ms. Kiss, then called two other witnesses from the police, neither of whom could offer anything to link Billy Brannigan to the murder of his brother. Malcolm worked quickly during cross-examination, reinforcing for the jury the lack of tangible evidence against Billy Brannigan.

"It's my understanding, Ms. James, that your next witnesses will testify regarding the trust fund," said the judge.

"That's correct, Your Honor."

"Then I think this is a good time to recess. Court will reconvene at nine in the morning. Have a pleasant evening."

Originally, we were to meet in Malcolm's office immediately following the end of the trial day. But as we gathered in the hallway and braced for the press that lined the steps, he announced, "My dear friends and colleagues, this day calls for a celebration."

Twenty minutes later we all sat at the boat-shaped bar at Jimmy Jr., the holding area for one of Boston's most famous seafood restaurants, Jimmy's Harborside, right on the fish pier. Malcolm was greeted with open arms by the owner, the son of the original Jimmy, and by the bartender who immediately asked, "The usual, counselor?"

Malcolm was in high spirits—without the drink. As we took stools at the bar, he remained standing, even did what can only be described as a little jig in place as he took the drink from the bartender, raised it to everyone in the room, and said loudly, "To justice. To freedom. To the loyal and hard-working members of the district attorney's office who must present a case—without *having* one. I love it!"

I took a sip of my ginger ale and looked around the bar. It was crowded, made more so by a dozen members of the press who'd followed us inside. I said to Rachel Cohen, "Maybe he shouldn't be so loud."

She raised her eyes and said, "I always tell him that. But when things go well, he's uncontrollable. He has this need to boast, to rub it in to the prosecution. Excuse me, Jessica, I have to call home. My son is sick."

"I'm sorry."

"Just a cold."

She threaded the crowd in search of a public phone. When she returned, she said, "Josh has a fever. I have to go."

"I'll go with you," I said. "Not home with you. I'll leave with you."

Malcolm wasn't happy when we told him we were leaving. He'd been building up a head of steam, his voice louder with each drink, his oratory more flowery and boastful. "Have you ever seen such a pathetic attempt to convict someone?" he roared. "That stream of the city's finest, taking the oath and then having nothing to swear to. My God, I love it!" He did another jig. "We don't need an alibi. We don't need Cynthia Warren, bless her soul. Billy Brannigan was acquitted today. This case is o-v-e-r!"

I saw that many of the press were making notes. Although there weren't any TV lights, I noticed a man pointing a small camcorder at Malcolm throughout his victory speech.

"Maybe we'd better get him out of here," I said to Rachel Cohen as we gathered up our purses and briefcases.

"Forget it," she said. "There's no stopping him now. This is just the beginning of a long night. One bar after another until he runs out of steam. I have to run. The sitter has to get home."

"Of course."

As I passed Malcolm, he grabbed my arm. "The party's just beginning, Jessica. The night is young, and so are we."

"Malcolm, maybe it's time for all of us to leave."

"Nonsense." He turned to Ritchie Fleigler, who was drinking a Boston mini-brew. "You won't abandon ship, will you, my lad?"

"Hell, no," the young investigator said.

"Tomorrow, Jessica, we'll strike at the hearts of the prosecution again, particularly the stone-cold heart of Ms. James."

"I still think you should—good night, Malcolm."

He hugged me and attempted a kiss, but I slipped his grasp and followed Rachel out the door to the parking lot.

"A ride?" she asked.

"No. You get on home to that sick boy." I then remembered that my nighttime driver wasn't there. We'd taken off from the courthouse in Malcolm's limo without telling the driver where we were going. "I'm fine," I said.

The moment Rachel drove off in her car, I climbed into a waiting cab. "The Ritz-Carlton, please," I told the driver.

"What's going on here?" he asked. "What's got all the newshounds out?"

"Nothing. Just some celebrity in Jimmy's."

It felt good to ride in a taxi, instead of a limo. It felt real. That was the problem, I realized. Being involved with Malcolm McLoon and the Brannigan case had become unreal to me, an impressionistic blur.

The moment I was in my suite, I undressed, showered, slipped into pajamas and a terry-cloth robe provided by the hotel, ordered up a sandwich from room service, and turned on the TV in the living room. A local newscast had just come on. After two stories about Boston politics, Cynthia

Warren's face filled the screen, a picture from her college yearbook. The newscaster said,

"The unsolved murder of Cynthia Warren in Harwichport, on the Cape, has thrown the outcome of the Billy Brannigan murder trial into doubt. As followers of the trial know, Ms. Warren was to testify that she and the defendant were together on the Cape the night his older brother, Jack Brannigan, was stabbed to death in a Swan Boat in the Public Garden. Although her sudden death leaves Brannigan without an alibi, his attorney, the flamboyant Malcolm McLoon, doesn't seem to think it matters, according to statements made this evening at a popular waterfront restaurant. Our reporter, Frank Carlucci, is on the phone from there now. Frank?"

"That's right, Steve. I'm here at Jimmy's Harborside where Malcolm McLoon has been discussing the case with—well, with whoever will listen. It's his contention—and he's celebrating it at the bar—that the prosecution has already lost the case despite losing Ms. Warren's alibi for his client. I sat through the trial today, Steve, and McLoon may be right. The prosecution presented nothing to link Brannigan to the murder of his brother. Tomorrow, they'll try to introduce details of the trust District Attorney Whitney James claims was the motive for the murder. But having a motive—and committing a murder—are two different things. By the way, famed murder mystery writer, Jessica Fletcher, who's working with McLoon as a jury consultant, was there at his side while he held court. Back to you."

It took me all of a minute to pick up the phone and call Malcolm's office. I assumed I'd reach the answering machine, but Georgia Bobley answered on the first ring.

"Georgia, Jessica Fletcher here. Look, since things are going so well, I thought I'd take a day or two off."

She laughed. "I don't blame you," she said. "Going home?"

"No. I thought a leisurely day on Cape Cod would renew my vigor, recharge the engine, so to speak. Think Malcolm will mind?"

"I don't know, but I wouldn't worry about it. God, Jessica, I couldn't wait to get out of Jimmy's. He was still going strong when I left."

"I'm sure he was. Well, please tell him I won't be in court tomorrow, but I'll check in."

"Great. Enjoy the day. You've earned it."

Knowing I wouldn't have to face the courtroom lifted a weight from my shoulders. I called the limo service and arranged for Cathie to pick me up at the hotel at eight, enjoyed my sandwich, read a few chapters from a book, and was about to climb into bed when the phone rang. It was Vaughan Buckley calling from New York. "Wake you?" he asked.

"Another ten minutes and you would have."

"I've been meaning to call, Jessica, ever since I heard you were in Boston for the Brannigan trial. What a marvelous opportunity to research your next novel."

"I'm not sure I share your enthusiasm, Vaughan. It's been a—well, let me just say it's been a trying experience."

"As I can certainly imagine, Jess. You found the body of Brannigan's alibi witness."

"Unfortunately, yes."

"Will that derail the defense case? Will there be a mistrial declared?"

"No to both questions."

"I assume the heroine in your next book will be a jury consultant."

"Maybe. I've really been too busy to think plot and characters."

"I love it. This bright and vibrant jury consultant to a murder case finds herself in jeopardy herself. Stalked, perhaps, by the real killer while an innocent man faces the electric chair."

The chill I suddenly felt had nothing to do with the temperature in the room.

"Are you there, Jess?" Vaughan asked.

"Yes, I'm here. That's a splendid idea, Vaughan. I'll keep it in mind."

"Need anything while you're there?"

"No. Malcolm McLoon is taking excellent care of me."

Vaughan laughed. "He's quite a character, isn't he?"

"That he is. Vaughan, I hate to cut this short, but I'm exhausted."

"Then get to bed, lady. I'd like to come back to

Cabot Cove after you get back, brainstorm a little about the next book, kick around some ideas."

"I'd like that. Thanks for calling, Vaughan. It was thoughtful of you."

Chapter Fourteen

The day's newspaper was at my door when I awoke. The lead story on the front page was the Brannigan trial. There were two pictures: the same yearbook photo of Cynthia Warren used on TV the night before; and one of me exiting Jimmy's Harborside.

The story dwelled on Malcolm's statements at the bar, that the trial was, for all intents and purposes, sewn up at least as far as the prosecution was concerned. From the approach the writer of the article took, she seemed to agree with the eminent defense counsel, pointing out more than once the complete lack of hard evidence linking Billy Brannigan to the crime.

I assumed the press would be camped on the Ritz-Carlton's doorstep when I came out to meet Cathie. But to my relief, there wasn't a scribe in sight. I got in the front of the Lincoln Town Car. Somehow, riding in the back of limousines strikes me as unnecessarily elite, especially with such a pleasant and verbal driver. I enjoyed Cathie's company, and we passed the drive to Cape Cod chatting about a variety of things—driving for a living, her eventual goal of owning her own limousine service, my writing routine, publishing, the Red Sox, gardening and, of course, the Brannigan trial.

Her take on the trial was simplistic: Once she heard that Jack Brannigan had wanted to be Billy Brannigan's best man, and wanted to host a party in his honor, she decided Billy couldn't have killed him.

Did juries make up their collective minds as simply and quickly as that? I wondered. If so, Billy Brannigan had nothing to worry about. Malcolm's seemingly premature celebration last night was warranted.

"Where are we heading on the Cape?" Cathie asked as we crossed the Bourne Bridge.

"Police headquarters, on Sisson Road."

As we drove into town, the image of Cynthia Warren's body lying in a pool of blood on her living room floor filled the windshield. I couldn't shake it, not because it was so gruesome and tragic—although Lord knows it was—but because there was something wrong with the picture. Something was askew, didn't jibe.

But what was it?

"I'll be here," Cathie said as I opened my door.

"Get yourself some coffee, a second breakfast," I said. "Take two hours. Even if I'm out before that, I'll enjoy a walk."

I entered the unassuming police department

and was immediately greeted by Steven McPartland, the chief of police who'd arrived at Cynthia's
house as I was leaving the day the body was discovered. "Hello, Mrs. Fletcher," he said pleasantly, a warm smile on his weather-beaten face.

"Good morning," I said. "I hope you don't mind
me barging in unannounced."

"Not at all. Not much doing around here this
morning. Having a famous writer stop in is
pretty exciting."

"Hardly that," I said. "I wonder if I could speak
with you about Ms. Warren's murder."

"Sure. Come on in the office."

The chief's office was typical Cape Cod—simple
wooden furniture, a large painting of a lobster
boat and fisherman framed over the desk, and a
horseshoe crab hanging upside down over the
door, a twist on hanging horseshoes upside down
for good luck.

"Well, what can I do for you, Mrs. Fletcher?"
McPartland asked. "Oh, how about some coffee?
Tea? I forgot my manners for a moment."

"A cup of tea would be appreciated," I said.

He opened the door and passed along my order,
including coffee for himself.

Once seated again, I asked, "Have you developed any leads on Ms. Warren's murder?"

He shook his head. Chief McPartland was a
handsome man, with a head of thick white hair,
clear blue eyes that appeared to be dancing, espe-

cially when he squinted, and an easy, deep-pitched laugh.

"Have you determined whether she was killed by someone robbing her house? Or was it someone who went there with the intention of murdering her?"

"Can't really tell that yet, Mrs. Fletcher. Could have been either way."

"Was anything missing from the house?"

"Not that we can tell."

"What about her family?"

"Her mother flew in from Ohio. Father's dead. We can't release the body until the autopsy is completed."

"Do you think it was someone she knew, or a stranger?"

"Now *that* I can answer. Judging from the look of the living room, my bet would be on someone she knew, probably knew real well."

"A boyfriend?"

"Maybe."

"Do you think that whomever murdered her is from the Cape, and might still be here?"

"I have no idea," said McPartland. "I suppose the attorneys for Mr. Brannigan are pretty upset over this."

He obviously hadn't read that morning's paper, in which Malcolm was crowing about how he'd won the case. I said, "Yes, they are. That's one of the reasons I'm here, Chief McPartland. As you know, I'm part of Mr. Brannigan's defense team."

"So I read, and see on Court TV."

"You're very gracious, Chief, allowing me in here this morning, and answering my questions."

"My pleasure. You ought to set one of your books down here on the Cape. We've had a few juicy murders."

"I'm sure you have. Chief McPartland, would it be possible for me to visit Ms. Warren's house again?"

"Why would you want to do that?"

"Oh, I don't know. I was very touched being there when the body was discovered. It's such a beautiful house, so welcoming, hardly a setting for murder."

He said nothing.

"Could I? Go there again? Just for a few minutes?"

"I see no problem with that, Mrs. Fletcher. But I'll have to accompany you. It's still an off-limits crime scene."

"Of course."

We walked outside to where Cathie and her Town Car were waiting. "She's my driver," I said.

"Afraid she can't come with you," he said. "Into the house."

"Of course not. But she can follow us there and wait outside, can't she?"

"That would be fine."

Cynthia's house looked even more lovely than I remembered. But there were the yellow plastic

CRIME SCENE tapes draped around the house that shrouded it in death's shadow.

How unfair, I thought, that an innocent young woman would no longer reap the benefits of the work she'd put into her home.

"Mrs. Fletcher, are you all right?" asked McPartland.

"Yes, I'm fine. Just saddened by her death, that's all."

"Did you know Ms. Warren?" he asked.

"No. Did you?"

"Saw her around. Here and there. She was a knockout. Knew her boyfriend better. He spent a lot of time down here, mostly with her. Had a run-in with him once. She called police to the house, domestic stuff. Never arrested him, though I thought she should have pressed charges."

"I wasn't aware of this. Was it ever in the newspapers? Have the lawyers for the prosecution looked into it?"

"Nope. Ms. Warren wouldn't file a complaint. Just wanted us to calm him down, which we did."

"May we go inside?"

"That's what we're here for."

We started up the steps to the porch, but Cathie's voice stopped us. "Mrs. Fletcher, a call for you."

I went to the car and took the cellular phone from her. "Jessica Fletcher here."

"Jessica, it's Georgia."

"Yes, Georgia?"

"I think you'd better get back right away."

"Why?"

"Juror Number Seven is gone."

"Gone? How? Why?"

"Dead."

"Dead?"

"Dead. Run over."

"I'll be there as soon as I can."

I returned to where McPartland stood. "Chief, something has come up. I have to return to Boston immediately."

"Thought you wanted to see the inside of the house."

"Oh, I do. A raincheck?"

"Anytime, Mrs. Fletcher."

"You've been very kind." We shook hands. "Thank you."

"Pleasure's all mine. Hurry back."

"A problem?" Cathie asked as we headed for the bridge.

"A big one. One of the jurors has died."

"That's terrible."

"Yes, it is. Run over, I was told."

"I don't wonder, the way people drive in Boston. We're kind of notorious for bad driving."

"I'll never question that again," I said.

Chapter Fifteen

I called Malcolm on the limo's cell phone on the way back to Boston and was surprised to find him in his office.

"Why aren't you in court?" I asked.

"Judge Wilson canceled today's session. Says he has to spend the day deciding whether to revoke Billy's bail. You heard?"

"About Ms. Montrone? Juror Number Seven? Yes. Georgia called. How horrible. Georgia said she was run over."

"That's right, Jessica. Hit-and-run, right in front of her house."

"When did it happen?" I asked.

"Last night. About midnight. Where are you now?"

"In the car heading back from the Cape."

"Sorry your day off was ruined."

"It really wasn't a day off, Malcolm. I hooked up with the police chief, McPartland. He took me to Cynthia Warren's house. I was about to go in when—"

"Why did you go there?"

"Simple curiosity. That's all. I should be at your office in an hour. Will you be there?"

"Yes."

I heard the click of the phone being lowered into its cradle. Malcolm was obviously upset, and who could blame him? His client might end up having his bail revoked, and we'd lost one of our handpicked jurors. Of course, one of the six alternates would replace Juror Number Seven, and we'd passed favorably on them, too. But you never knew. I'd learned from Jill Farkas that once a trial gets underway, jurors tend to bond into a somewhat cohesive unit, making it easier to reach a unanimous decision. Injecting a new person into the mix could be, according to our high-priced jury consultant, disruptive, no matter who that new person was.

I mentally went over the profiles of the six alternates. If I had the choice to make of who to replace Juror Number Seven, it would have been Thomas McEnroe, our pottery maker. But that choice wasn't mine to make, nor anyone else's on either side. Judge Wilson would pick a number out of a hat, so to speak, and the alternate juror bearing that number would replace Juror Number Seven.

When I reached Malcolm's office, everyone was there except Rachel Cohen, who'd taken advantage of the unexpected day off to catch up on things at home. Malcolm had ordered in enough

Italian food to feed us and everyone else in the building. It covered the conference table; the aroma of garlic competed with the sour smell of Malcolm's cigars, which were piling up in a foot-wide ashtray.

I passed on the food. The last thing on my mind was lasagna and spaghetti with white clam sauce.

In contrast to the festive food on the conference table, the mood was distinctly somber. Everyone, including Linda, the receptionist, was busy reading documents of one sort or another. Jill Farkas sat hunched over her laptop computer in a corner of the large office. I'd no sooner arrived and greeted everyone when she picked up a sheet of paper that had inched out of the ink-jet printer, scrutinized it for a moment, and handed it to Malcolm. He frowned as he read it, then passed it to me.

It was a printout of a computer analysis she'd run on the twelve jurors, including Juror Number Seven. In the analyses, Jill had come up with an evaluation of how each of the twelve jurors had been leaning, based upon her observations. The one juror she identified as being most likely to acquit Billy Brannigan was the dead housewife, Juror Number Seven.

"I agree completely," I said, handing the paper back to Malcolm. "If I had to choose one of the jurors who was seeing things our way, it would have been Ms. Montrone."

"Any word yet who'll replace her?" Georgia Bobley asked.

"No," Malcolm growled. "Wilson will pick a number at random tomorrow. That's who we'll get."

I asked Jill Farkas, "Have you run the same kind of analysis on the six alternates?"

"I can only do one thing at a time, Jessica," she said. "I intend to start that analysis this afternoon."

People eventually drifted out of the office over the next few hours. Investigator Ritchie Fleigler left to do some additional digging into the backgrounds of the six alternate jurors. Jill Farkas, who seemed to become increasingly agitated as the day wore on, announced she was going home to run the computer analysis on the alternates. Georgia Bobley became ill. After vomiting twice in the ladies' room, Malcolm told her to go home and get to bed.

That left Linda in the reception area, and Malcolm and me in his office. I hadn't had much to say since arriving. I busied myself going over previous evaluations of the jurors and alternates, but my mind really wasn't on that. What kept occurring to me was that two people who would have been helpful to Billy Brannigan had died under violent circumstances.

Certainly, if Cynthia Warren had provided an alibi under oath, there was little chance this jury, or any jury for that matter, would convict Billy.

And if my instincts, and Jill Farkas's computer analysis were correct, Marie Montrone, Juror Number Seven, would likely have voted for acquittal.

I voiced this to Malcolm, and it seemed to generate interest. "Do you see a correlation between these two deaths?" he asked.

"Goodness, no, Malcolm. That would be a stretch, even for this fiction writer. Then again, the reality is that both these people have been killed. We tend to view a pedestrian fatality as an accident. But according to what I've heard here today, Ms. Montrone was run down in front of her house—which I assume is in a quiet residential neighborhood—by a car traveling at excessive speed. And, the driver took off. It's possible, isn't it, that he deliberately hit her?"

Malcolm opened a file folder on his desk. "My preliminary information is that Ms. Montrone was already up on the sidewalk when she got hit."

My eyebrows went up. "That would lend even more credence to the possibility that the driver of that car deliberately went after her."

Malcolm pondered what I said before asking, "Are you sure this isn't your overactive imagination going into high gear?" He smiled to soften the question.

I smiled, too. "It could well be, Malcolm. I have a confession to make to you."

"Don't tell me I'm going to end up defending *you* for murder?"

"I certainly hope not, although if I'm ever charged with a serious offense, you'll be the first to know. No, I agreed to come to Boston to work as a jury consultant for you because my publisher in New York, Vaughan Buckley, has convinced me to use a murder trial as a setting for my next novel. I told Vaughan that I didn't know anything about how murder trials worked, and so he suggested I sit through one. Then, your call came inviting me to not only sit through a trial, but to be a part of it. I couldn't resist."

"Looks like you used me," Malcolm said, chuckling.

"I suppose you could view it that way," I said. "Of course, I have the feeling that inviting me to join your team had something to do with enticing Court TV to cover this trial."

"I wouldn't do a thing like that," he said, his right hand on his heart, an exaggerated expression of hurt on his face.

"Oh, yes you would, Malcolm, and it's all right with me. I don't mind being used, as long as I'm doing a little using myself."

"The perfect definition of a good deal, Jessica. Both parties benefiting."

"Exactly."

Malcolm gestured to the remains of the Italian takeout on the table. "You haven't eaten," he said.

"Not hungry," I said. "The trial is going to continue tomorrow morning?"

"Supposed to, although you never know with Judge Wilson."

I looked at a large clock on the wall. It was a little after one. "Would you mind if I used Cathie again this afternoon and went back to the Cape?"

"Of course not. As I said, I was sorry to ruin your day off."

"I'm not viewing it as a day off, Malcolm. I'd like to touch base with Chief McPartland again. He doesn't seem very busy, and I think he would welcome my visit."

"Sure. Go ahead. But why?"

"I keep thinking of that deposit slip I saw on Ms. Warren's desk, the one for ten thousand dollars. I'd like to follow up on that."

"Be my guest."

"And, Malcolm, would there be anything wrong in my visiting Ms. Montrone's family?"

Malcolm thought before responding. "Might be, Jessica. You remember Wilson's admonition to us."

I certainly did remember it:

"Under no circumstance is anyone involved in the case, from either the defense or prosecution, to have any contact, of any nature, written, oral or through third parties, with any member of the twelve-person jury or the six alternates. Because I have faith in each juror's integrity and honesty, and because the attorneys representing the people and the defendant are known to me to uphold the highest professional standards, I have decided against sequestering this jury. Its members are admonished to not read about the case or hear reports about it through radio or television, and are not to discuss the case with anyone until it has been submitted to them. And I reiterate—no person from either side is to have any personal contact with members of the jury."

"I suppose I shouldn't," I said.

"Based upon Judge Wilson's admonition, I'd be the last person to suggest you visit Ms. Montrone's family. An attorney is an officer of the court. Wouldn't think of violating the judge's word.

"Then again, Judge Wilson said we couldn't have contact with *members* of the jury. Ms. Montrone was alive when he made that ruling. Obviously, you wouldn't be making contact with her, now that she's dead. But tell me something. Why do you want to do it?"

"I might be able to confirm whether Jill's analysis is correct, that Ms. Montrone was leaning in our favor. If she was, that could make my speculation about a possible connection between the death of Ms. Warren and Ms. Montrone a little more credible."

Malcolm sat back, laced his fingers over his belly, and closed his eyes. I wasn't sure whether I should tiptoe out of the room, or sit and hold my breath. He opened his eyes and said, "Jessica, I haven't heard a word of this conversation. Have you?"

"No."

"Then I suggest you go off and enjoy the afternoon on Cape Cod. Breathe in that good fresh ocean air. Get yourself a lobster dinner. And do whatever else it is you want to do. Take an extra day if you want. I think we can do without you in court tomorrow."

I headed for the door, turned and said, "Thanks, boss. I'll be in touch."

Chapter Sixteen

My second trip to the Cape that day took longer than the first. There was more traffic, and a bottleneck had developed on the Bourne Bridge.

But eventually we pulled up in front of the police building. I went inside and was immediately greeted by Chief McPartland. "I had a feeling I'd see you again," he said pleasantly.

"Well, you knew more than I did," I said. "Coming back this afternoon was strictly a last-minute decision."

"I suppose you want to go back to Ms. Warren's house."

"If you wouldn't mind."

"Not at all. Nothing much happening here, except after you left we did investigate some stolen lobster pots."

I smiled. "Sounds like where I come from," I said. "Did you find the thief?"

He chuckled. "No, and probably won't, although you never know. Liable to turn up somewhere in a day or two. Chances are whoever took them wanted a souvenir. Never can figure tourists, 'specially those from New York. Come on, Mrs. Fletcher. Hope you get to stay this time."

I stifled a smile at his rush to judgment about who'd stolen the lobster pots and went with him in his marked car, Cathie following in the Town Car. The chief and I entered the house where the white couch and white rug stained with Ms. Warren's blood had been removed. Other than that, and aside from some residue of fingerprint dust, the house looked as though nothing unusual had taken place there.

"Anything special you're looking for, Mrs. Fletcher?" McPartland asked.

"Yes, as a matter of fact. Did you, or any of your men see a bank deposit slip on Ms. Warren's desk the day her body was discovered?"

"Can't say that I did. It wasn't in any of the reports."

"Mind if I take a look where I first saw it?"

"Please do."

I entered the den and went to the desk. There it was, in roughly the same position as when I'd first seen it. I pulled a small decorative handkerchief from the breast pocket of my blue blazer and used it to pick up the slip. Chief McPartland peered over my shoulder. "Ten thousand dollars," he muttered. "That's a pretty good sum of money."

"Yes, it is," I agreed. "I'm curious where she got such a sum."

"I'd be curious too, Mrs. Fletcher. As far as I know, Ms. Warren didn't work."

"When someone gets a lump sum of money like this," I offered, "it immediately makes me think that she was involved in some consulting business. Or was a writer, or artist. Any of those jibe with what you know about her?"

"Nope. I asked her mother what Ms. Warren did for a living. She said she wasn't sure. I guess they didn't talk much."

"Chief, would you be willing to come with me to the bank where this was deposited?"

"I suppose so."

"I don't think the bank would release a photocopy of the check to me. But they might to you as part of your official investigation."

"Happy to oblige, Mrs. Fletcher."

It was a few minutes past three when we arrived at the bank. The door was locked. McPartland banged on it. A young man inside recognized the chief and opened the door. "Hello, Chief McPartland," he said. "What can I do for you?"

"This is Mrs. Jessica Fletcher, the famous mystery writer," McPartland said.

The young man broke into a grin. "Yes, I've seen you on television, and I've read some of your books. You're terrific."

"Thank you. You're very kind."

McPartland said, "I have a deposit slip from Ms. Warren's house. Ten thousand dollars, deposited here the day before she was murdered."

"What a terrible thing. You move to someplace like the Cape and you just don't expect things like this to happen. Not like in the city, anyway." He took the slip from McPartland and examined it. "She deposited a check," he said. "Not cash."

"I assume you photocopy checks that are deposited," I said.

"Yes, we do. Are you asking to see a copy of this particular check?"

I looked to Chief McPartland, who nodded.

"Come in," the young man said. "By the way, I'm Joe Richer. I'm the manager."

"Pleased to meet you," I said.

He led us through the bank to his office in the rear, invited us to sit, and said he would be gone for just a minute.

When he returned, he carried with him a sheet of paper on which both sides of the check had been copied. He handed it to McPartland, who in turn handed it to me.

The check had been made out to cash. On the back of the check, Cynthia Warren had written "For Deposit Only," and had signed it. The front of the check had the word "Cash" on it, the amount, and the signature of the person issuing it to her. That person, according to the printed name and address in the top left corner, was Harry LeClaire. The address was a street in Boston.

I stared at the photocopy long enough to cause

McPartland to ask, "Anything wrong, Mrs. Fletcher?"

"Yes, I think there might be." To Mr. Richer: "May I take this photocopy with me?"

"Yes, ma'am."

"Thank you very much. You've been very helpful."

Once outside the bank, McPartland asked what I'd reacted to in the manager's office.

I responded lightly, "Oh, nothing, really. I thought I recognized the name on the top of the check, but I now realize I don't."

"Well, glad I could be of help. Can I buy you a cup of coffee?"

"That's very kind of you, Chief, but I really must get back to Boston."

"Okay," he said, "but I do have a favor to ask."

"What is that?" I asked.

"Would you take a minute to stop back at my office and sign a book to me and the wife?"

"I'd be delighted. By the way, how's Ms. Warren's old dog?"

"Just fine. Gets along with my old-timer like they grew up together. I figured I might keep her, provided Ms. Warren's family agrees."

"I'm sure they will," I said. "And I'm glad she's found a good home."

I used the cellular phone in the Town Car to call Malcolm's office as we headed for Boston. This time, I connected with the answering machine, which informed me that no one was there to take my call.

"Where to?" Cathie asked as we entered the city.

"My hotel, if you don't mind."

"Hey, I'm at your disposal," she said, heading for the Ritz-Carlton.

"I'll wait," she said as I was getting out of the car.

"No need, Cathie. Get an early start on your evening. I won't need you until tomorrow morning."

"Sure?"

"Positive. And thank you. Two round trips to the Cape is quite enough for one day."

I freshened up in my suite, then tried Malcolm McLoon at home. No luck. Rachel Cohen answered her phone on the first ring.

"Rachel, it's Jessica."

"Oh, good to hear from you," she said. I heard two children fighting in the background, and a dog barking. Rachel yelled for them to be quiet. "Jessica, Malcolm told us before he left the office that if we heard from you, you should join him at Jimmy's Harborside."

It was a good thing she couldn't see my facial reaction. It wasn't because Jimmy's Harborside isn't a splendid restaurant. But the thought of being present while Malcolm again pontificated was simply too painful to contemplate.

"I probably won't be able to do that, Rachel. I have plans this evening."

"I'm not going either. Ashley is in a school play tonight."

"Tell her to break a leg," I said. "No, don't tell her that. You know how children can take things literally. What's the schedule for tomorrow?"

"Court convenes at nine."

"I'll see you there," I said.

"Malcolm said you went back to the Cape this afternoon to check up on something. Anything new?"

"No. A wasted trip. Enjoy the play, Rachel. I'll see you in the morning."

I was about to leave when the phone rang. It was Seth Hazlitt calling from Cabot Cove. "Jessica, how are you?"

"Just fine, Seth. How are you?"

"I'd be a lot better if I didn't read reports about jurors on that trial of yours being run down."

"A terrible accident."

"Comin' on the heels of that young lady down on Cape Cod being murdered—the one who was supposed to provide an alibi for your client—I'd say there's a good possibility it wasn't an accident."

"Well, Seth, I must admit I've been wondering the same thing."

"My suggestion would be for you to pack your bags and get back home here. You already helped select the jury. Nothing else for you to do there, it seems to me."

"Oh, no, Malcolm McLoon has me doing other things. It's exciting being part of the defense team."

"Exciting, and maybe a little dangerous."

"Don't be silly. I'm just fine. Enjoying Boston, and making lots of notes for my next book. I really do have to run. Thanks for calling."

"I thought I might head over to Boston in a day or two. Could use some shirts and ties from Filene's. Got a sale going on this week."

"Well, then, I think you should come. Be sure and let me know ahead of time so I can clear my schedule."

"Ayuh, I'll do that. You said you had to run. Where to?"

"I'm going to see the family of that woman from the jury who was killed by the hit-and-run driver."

"Doesn't sound like a very pleasant thing to do."

"No, it isn't, but I feel I must. Hate to be rude, Seth, but I have to go. Call me when you're coming to Boston. We'll have lunch, or dinner."

I hung up the phone and went to the window, looked down over the splendor of the Public Garden.

Should I go? Was it my place to visit the grieving family of Ms. Montrone? Would I be violating Judge Wilson's admonition about not contacting jurors?

For a moment, I considered scrapping the idea and enjoying some quiet time by myself in the suite, perhaps have dinner sent up to the room, or seek out a pleasant restaurant I hadn't enjoyed before.

But once the idea of visiting Ms. Montrone's family had entered my mind, there was no way of making it go away. I made sure I had the slip of paper in my pocket with her address, and left.

Chapter Seventeen

Marie Montrone, known to the world on Court TV as Juror Number Seven, had been an attractively plain thirty-four-year-old woman with two children, a sickly mother-in-law for whom she cared, and a husband who worked as a construction foreman. She enjoyed painting-by-the-numbers, baking, and collecting seashells. I remember liking her the moment she started answering questions during voir dire, that phase of the trial where the attorneys from each side questioned prospective jurors to ferret out hidden prejudices, veiled biases, or life circumstances creating a conflict of interest. She'd been straightforward in her answers, someone who would take her duties as a juror seriously, especially where the accused faced the rest of his life in prison. I hadn't hesitated in telling Malcolm that in my judgment, she was the sort of fair-minded person we wanted on the jury.

Marie Montrone and her family lived in Boston's North End, home to Boston's sizable Italian-American population.

When I arrived at their modest row house, her husband had just returned from the church and funeral home where he'd made arrangements for the service and burial. Gino Montrone was a broad, beefy man with a workman's hands and large, sad brown eyes. His suit was too small for him, probably bought many pounds ago, and he appeared to be distinctly uncomfortable wearing it. His mother sat stoically in a wheelchair, rosary beads clutched tightly in her gnarled fingers.

"I'm sorry to intrude at such a sad time," I said to Mr. Montrone when he responded to my knocking at their front door. "My name is Jessica Fletcher."

He cocked his head and narrowed his eyes. "The mystery writer?"

"Yes. I'm also a consultant to Billy Brannigan's defense team."

"I know that," he said. He had the slightest trace of an Italian accent. "We read about you. My wife said . . ." He turned away as his eyes moistened.

"I'm so sorry about what happened," I said. "I didn't know your wife, but I liked her the minute she started answering questions from the lawyers. I knew she'd make a fine and fair juror."

He wiped his cheek with the back of his hand. "Maybe if she hadn't been on that damn jury, she'd still be alive," he said.

"Do you think her death had something to do with being a juror?" I asked.

"All I know, Mrs. Fletcher, is that she was alive before the trial started. Now, she's laid out, about to be put in the ground."

"That's why I've come," I said. "I know she was killed by a hit-and-run driver. Is there anything to lead you to believe it was deliberate?"

"Seems to me it was," he replied. "She was up on the curb when it happened. She'd gone to the convenience store down the block for milk, and ice cream for my mother. My mother likes a kind of ice cream they carry there. Marie was always doing things like that for her." He looked down at his mother and smiled, then added, "Seems to me he had to aim for her to hit her on the curb."

"Yes," I said. "It does seem that way. Did you have any indication how she was leaning as a juror?"

He became angry. "Is that why you're here, trying to find out whether she thought that Brannigan brat is guilty of murdering his own brother?"

"Only to see if what I'm thinking about your wife's death might be true. If it was connected with her serving as a juror—if it wasn't an accident—steps must be taken to get to the bottom of it, find who's responsible."

Gino Montrone said nothing.

"I take from what you said before that your wife thought Mr. Brannigan was probably guilty."

"Jurors aren't supposed to talk about the case with anybody, including family."

"I know, but it's human nature to—"

"Yes, she talked about it."

"And?"

"She didn't think he did it. Killed his brother. I tried to talk sense to her but—I don't suppose I should be telling you this, but it doesn't seem to make any difference anymore. The judge can't do anything to hurt her now."

"So your wife *was* leaning in favor of the defendant," I said.

"Yeah. She was that way, a soft heart. What do they say, a knee-jerk something or other. Always taking the side of the accused, the underdog. Brannigan will get off. We all know that. People with money always do."

Ms. Montrone's mother-in-law had sat silently during my conversation with her son. Now, she looked up and said, "She was a good woman. Like my own daughter. May God shine His light on her."

I swallowed the lump in my throat, thanked them for allowing me to intrude in their time of grief, and quickly left the house.

The last place I intended to go was Jimmy's Harborside, where Malcolm said he would be that evening. But I had to talk to someone.

I hailed a cab and went directly to the pier-side restaurant. The dining room and bar were packed. I squeezed through knots of people in search of Malcolm, but his instantly recognizable hulk didn't seem to be there.

I sought out an assistant manager, who was taking reservations at a podium. "Excuse me," I said, "I'm looking for—"

"Jessica Fletcher," he said.

"Yes. I'm Jessica—I'm looking for Mr. McLoon. The attorney."

"Will you be having dinner? I can give you a nice window table."

"Thank you, but I'm here looking for—"

"I think Mr. McLoon is over there." He pointed to a far corner of the large bar area.

"Yes. There he is. Thank you."

Malcolm sat hunched over a tiny table, a drink surrounded by both hands. His usually neatly combed hair was unruly. His gaze was on the glass. I came up behind him and placed my hand on his shoulder. He slowly turned and looked up.

"Hello, Malcolm," I said.

"Ah, Jessica." His speech was slurred. He tried to stand but didn't make it.

"Please, don't get up," I said, settling in a chair across from him.

"How was Cape Cod, Jessica?"

"Interesting. That's why I came here tonight." A waiter asked if I wanted a drink. "No, thank you," I said. "I'm only staying a few minutes."

"Why?" Malcolm asked after ordering a refill.

"Because I'm very tired," I replied. I wondered whether I should have even bothered seeking him out. He was obviously inebriated, and probably wouldn't understand the significance of what I was about to show him.

"Stay for dinner," he said. "Best fish chowder in Boston. The old man, the original Jimmy, used to bring his chowder down to Washington for President Kennedy."

"That's very interesting, Malcolm, but I'll have to enjoy the chowder another time. I visited Ms. Montrone's home this afternoon."

"You did? Don't say it too loud."

"She was leaning in favor of an acquittal."

"You and Jill already figured that out."

"But I confirmed it."

I pulled the photocopy of Cynthia Warren's deposit slip from my purse and placed it in front of him.

"What's this?"

I explained, and watched him put on his half-glasses and struggle to read what was on the paper. My earlier question of whether I should have bothered coming here loomed larger. The man was in no condition to understand the ramifications of what I was showing him.

But then Malcolm McLoon drew a deep breath, sat up straight, and said, "Do you realize what this means?" His eyes had cleared; they now shone brightly.

"I think I do," I said.

"Harry LeClaire gave Cynthia Warren a check for ten thousand dollars the day before she was killed."

"Looks that way."

"Harry LeClaire."

"Yes. Harry LeClaire. What will you do with this?"

"Sit on it for a day or two, think about it."

"I suppose that's wise. Do you think—"

"What do *you* think, Jessica?"

"I think I won't have to plot my next novel. I think it's being plotted for me."

"Why would one of the alternate jurors, Mr. Harry LeClaire to be precise, be giving the defendant's alibi witness ten thousand dollars—and the day before she's murdered in cold blood?"

"A good question."

"There must be good money to be made in the tweezers business, Jessica."

"Must be." The man's recuperative powers were amazing. He was stone-cold sober, his mind working at a pace that was almost audible.

A waiter delivered two bowls of fish chowder to an adjacent table. It smelled and looked heavenly.

"I've changed my mind," I said.

"About what?"

"About fish chowder. If it was good enough for JFK, it's good enough for me."

Chapter Eighteen

Malcolm had become wide awake, and talkative once I showed him the photocopy of the check Cynthia Warren had deposited. After finishing off the chowder, which was as good as Malcolm had claimed, he dropped me off at the Ritz. As I was about to leave the car, he said in a conspiratorial tone, "Let's keep this between us, Jessica, this business of LeClaire giving Cynthia Warren money. Not another soul."

"Rachel? Georgia?"

"*No one*, until I've decided what to do with the information."

"But shouldn't we report this to the police? At least to Judge Wilson?"

"I'll do what's right, when the time is right. In the meantime, get yourself some sleep. I see why you write bestselling murder mysteries, Jessica. The police never noticed that deposit slip, but you did. Good night, fair lady. See you in court."

I arrived at the courthouse early the next morning expecting to take my place at the defense table. But Malcolm took me aside before Judge Wilson gaveled the proceedings to order. "Jess, it occurred to me last night that you could make better use of this day by doing some checking into Mr. LeClaire."

"I thought Ritchie did that before jury selection began."

"He did. But he obviously missed something. Besides, he didn't have any reason to suspect a connection between Cynthia Warren and LeClaire. Now that we know there was, you might have better success."

"All right," I said. "I'm not sure how to start, but I'll do my best."

"That's all I can ask. I don't intend to mention what you came up with on the Cape until we learn a little more."

"Sure that's smart?" I asked.

He broke into a wide grin. "Trust me, Jessica. Between us, we'll see justice served for Billy Brannigan, and maybe turn up a *real* murderer in the bargain."

I left the courthouse with conflicting thoughts.

On the one hand, I had serious reservations about expanding my reason for being in Boston. I'd come there only to learn about how a murder trial works for my next novel. Although in addition to writing about crimes, I'd ended up over the years solving a few, I don't consider myself a qualified detective. Those incidents had just happened.

On the other hand, once I'd discovered the deposit slip (that had just happened, too), and had linked it to one of the six alternate jurors in the Billy Brannigan trial, businessman Harry LeClaire, owner of a company that manufactured tweezers and scissors, it would have been constitutionally hard—no, make that almost impossible—for me to simply walk away, no matter what Malcolm decided to do with the information.

I returned to the hotel and changed into more comfortable clothing. It had blown up cool that morning in Boston, and the forecast was for rain later in the day. I wore slacks, a comfortable pullover shirt, sneakers, and carried a lightweight windbreaker. And I took with me a printout of information Ritchie Fleigler had dug up on Harry LeClaire.

Cathie was waiting outside. "No court today?" she asked.

"No, no court today. Does your company have a different car we could use?"

"A different car? A bigger one?"

"A smaller one, less conspicuous than this vehicle."

"Sure."

A half hour later we pulled out of the limousine company's parking lot in a plain blue Chevy sedan.

"Where to?" Cathie asked.

"Let's head here first." I handed her the address of Harry LeClaire's corporate headquarters, located in Dorchester, literally a part of the city of Boston but almost a city in its own right.

LeClaire Metals was in an old warehouse that had been renovated to house the company's manufacturing operations, and offices. A sign read: TWEEZERS YOU CAN COUNT ON.

"What's here?" Cathie asked as we parked across the street.

"Tweezers."

"That's why we're here? You want to buy a pair of tweezers?"

"Maybe. LeClaire tweezers are supposed to be the best." I noted the puzzled expression on her face. "Wait here," I said.

Although it was overcast, I put on an oversized pair of sunglasses before leaving the car. I waited for traffic to thin, then crossed the street and entered the front door of LeClaire Metals where I was confronted by a receptionist, and a uniformed security guard. "May I help you?" the receptionist asked.

"Perhaps," I said. "I'm a high school teacher in Dorchester. I'm teaching a section on local businesses, and wondered whether you schedule tours."

"Tours?" She smiled, then laughed. The guard laughed, too.

"Did I say something funny?" I asked.

"Who'd want a tour of this place?" the receptionist asked. "It's just a dirty old factory back there."

"But it's obviously a successful business," I said. "My students would—"

"Wait just a moment, Ms.—"

"Ah, Jennifer Flechter."

She called someone on the phone. A few minutes later a young man emerged from a door behind the reception desk. "Can I help you?" he asked, introducing himself as Paul Molloy, the company's manufacturing supervisor.

"I hope so," I said. I repeated my lie.

"I suppose we could accommodate you," he said. "When would you want to have this tour?"

"Oh, in a few weeks. Whatever would be convenient with you. May I see what my students will see?"

Twenty minutes later I was back in the lobby with Molloy and the receptionist. "Thank you so much," I said. "It's more interesting than one might imagine. Oh, by the way, a friend of mine did some consulting work for LeClaire Metals. At least I think she did. Her name is Cynthia Warren."

Molloy and the receptionist looked at each other.

"Did you know her?"

"She was—"

"Yes?" I said, hoping to encourage the receptionist to say more.

"I don't remember anyone working here by that name," Molloy said.

"Do you?" I asked the receptionist.

"No."

They were both lying, and I knew it.

"Give a call when you want to set up the tour," Molloy said. "Sorry, but I'm late for a meeting." He left the lobby.

"Is there a LeClaire at LeClaire Metals?" I asked the receptionist.

"Yes. Harry LeClaire. He's the son of the founder. He's on jury duty."

"Really?"

"The Brannigan trial. Excuse me. I have work to do."

"Of course. Thanks again."

I left the building and walked up the street. Once I was sure no one in LeClaire Metals could see me, I waved for Cathie to pick me up at the corner.

"I hate to be nosy, Mrs. Fletcher, but what's going on with the sunglasses, and visiting a factory?" she asked after I'd gotten in beside her.

"A hobby of mine," I said. "Touring local businesses."

"A hobby."

"Let's go here next." I gave her Harry LeClaire's home address.

LeClaire's house was modest in size, and not particularly well-kept, a house very much lived in. I told Cathie to park a few houses down, on the opposite side of the street. Her expression said confusion, curiosity, and amusement.

We were there only a few minutes when a

woman came out the front door, followed by a teenage girl, and a boy I judged to be about ten. I knew from his jury questionnaire that Harry LeClaire had two children. He was forty-two years old, and had been married to his wife, Susan, for seventeen years. It was the first marriage for both.

Susan LeClaire and her children got into a Volvo station wagon, backed out of the driveway, and passed us. I jotted down the plate number.

"Are we just going to sit here?" Cathie asked.

"Just give me a moment," I said, pulling out LeClaire's questionnaire and reading it again.

"Can I ask a dumb question, Mrs. Fletcher?" Cathie asked.

I looked up and smiled. "Of course."

"Are you trying to disguise yourself with those sunglasses?"

"No, I—yes, I am."

"Why?"

"Because I'm not being entirely truthful about who I am when I talk with certain people."

"Can I make a suggestion?"

"Sure."

"It doesn't work."

"My disguise?"

"Yup. Here."

She handed me a floppy canvas hat. "This should do it," she said.

I put on the hat and checked myself in the mirror. "I like it," I said.

"Good. Okay, where to now, Sherlock?"

"Am I that obvious?" I said, laughing.

"Worse than that. But driving you is more fun than most of the people I get stuck with."

"Thank you, Cathie. And may I call you Watson?"

"Absolutely."

"Then let's continue—Watson."

We swung by Malcolm's office where I asked Linda to dig out the file of clippings about Billy Brannigan's alleged rape of a girl on Cape Cod, which had prompted Jack Brannigan to cut Billy out of the family trust. Although the rape had supposedly taken place on the Cape, Billy's accuser was from Dorchester.

"Mind if I take this with me for the day?" I asked.

"Please do," Linda said. "Why aren't you at the trial?"

"Day off, compliments of Mr. McLoon."

"Lucky you."

"Why do you say that?"

"Georgia called a few minutes ago. Judge Wilson has revoked Billy's bail."

"I'm sorry to hear that. Did she say who replaced Ms. Montrone on the jury?"

"A woman. She didn't tell me what number alternate she was."

"You're sure it was a woman?"

"That's what she said."

The phone rang. Linda picked it up. I started to leave but she motioned for me to stay. "Yes, I understand," she said to the caller. "Of course. That's terrible. She's right here." She extended the phone to me.

"Hello?"

"Jessica. It's Malcolm. Glad I caught you there."

"What's going on?"

"Many things, none of them good. We're in a recess. Can you come to the courthouse right away?"

"Yes, of course. But why?"

"I'll tell you when you get here."

I handed the phone back to Linda. "What's this all about?" I asked. She'd obviously been told something by McLoon that had prompted her to say, "that's terrible."

"Malcolm said Billy's alibi has gone up in smoke."

"His alibi went up in smoke the day Cynthia Warren was murdered."

"I don't know what he meant. He sounded very upset."

"I'd better get down there, Linda. Thanks for the file. It's safe with me."

When I arrived, Malcolm, Rachel, Georgia, Jill Farkas, and Ritchie Fleigler were in a conference room set aside for use by the defense team. Their faces were decidedly grim. If I didn't know better, I would have looked for a casket and corpse.

"What's happened?" I asked.

"This," Malcolm said, tossing a photocopy of a letter on the table in front of me.

The letter was written on Cynthia Warren's letterhead, and was dated the day of her murder. It consisted of three typewritten paragraphs:

To Whom it May Concern:

The burden of lying for someone who has done a terrible thing is too heavy for me, and I can no longer do it, even the man I once considered marrying, William Brannigan.

I agreed to say that Billy was with me the night of his brother's murder because I loved him, and did not want to see him hurt. But when I consider the horrible hurt he has inflicted upon his family, I must violate my promise to him.

He was here that day, but earlier. We did buy lobsters to cook that night, but he left before dinner after receiving a phone call from his brother, Jack, that angered him. I begged him not to go, but he went. And, as sad as it is, he went to meet his brother at the Swan Boats in the Public Garden. And then—only he, and God knows.

It was signed "Cynthia Warren."

"How did this surface?" I asked.

"The DA proffered it in court this morning," Rachel said.

"How did they get it?" I asked.

There were shrugs around the table.

"Judge Wilson has the original," Malcolm said.

"A postmark?" I asked.

"Harwichport, Cape Cod," Georgia Bobley said.

"She must have mailed it that morning, just before she was murdered," Ritchie offered.

"I don't think so," I said.

They all looked at me.

"She was dressed in pajamas and a robe," I said. "Remember, Ritchie?"

He nodded.

"And her hair wasn't combed. I doubt if she'd showered yet. Ms. Warren was an extremely attractive girl. Every picture shows her neat as a pin, perfect in every way."

"Maybe she threw on some clothes to mail it, then returned home and got back into her pj's and robe," said Malcolm.

"No," I said. "She would not have gone to the post office, or anywhere else for that matter, without first making herself look good. I think someone else mailed that letter."

"Someone she asked?" Georgia said.

"Or someone who wanted that letter mailed," I said. "Is it her signature?"

"I have a call in to the best handwriting expert in New England," Malcolm replied.

"I didn't see a typewriter or a computer when I was there," I said. "Did you, Ritchie?"

He thought for a moment. "No, I don't think I did."

"Doesn't mean she didn't have one in a closet, or in some sort of cabinet," Jill Farkas said.

"No, it doesn't," I agreed. "Just an observation."

"What happens now?" Georgia asked Malcolm.

"Wilson has scheduled arguments at one on allowing the letter into evidence. I'll offer a motion to suppress it on discovery grounds, at least request a continuance until we've had the handwriting expert examine it. Whitney claims they just received it this morning. My instincts tell me they've had it longer than that, and were holding it as their trump card in the event things were going poorly for them—which they have been."

I wondered as I sat there whether Malcolm had shared with the others the evident link between Cynthia Warren and one of our alternate jurors, Harry LeClaire. I assumed not, since no one brought it up. I certainly wasn't about to.

Malcolm changed the subject by asking Jill Farkas for a reading on the alternate juror who'd taken Marie Montrone's place on the jury. She reported that according to her analysis, the new juror was not as likely to be in our camp as Ms. Montrone had been, but wasn't a threat, either. She was older than Ms. Montrone, a retired travel editor who'd worked for the *Boston Globe* for twenty-five years.

"She's likely to view young people with some disdain," Jill said. "Her choice in clothing is old-fashioned and proper. Remember when she answered the questions? Precise in her use of language, which is to be expected from an editor. I'd try to work in any material on how Billy wasn't like most of his peers, dressed nicely, respected his parents, did well in school. Those things will impact favorably upon her."

"Good suggestion," said Malcolm.

Jill looked at me. "Do you agree, Jessica?"

"Yes."

"I'm pleased to hear that," Jill said.

Ritchie checked his watch. "Time for lunch," he said. "I'm starved."

"Yes, go to lunch. Make it a quick one," Malcolm said.

"Do you want me here this afternoon?" I asked.

"Let's talk about that," Malcolm said. "Go on, the rest of you get lunch. Georgia, bring me back the usual."

They filed from the room. When Malcolm and I were alone, he said, "What do you think?"

"About the possibility that Harry LeClaire might have had something to do with that letter?"

"Exactly."

"But why would he want to buy such a letter from Cynthia Warren?"

"Because for some reason, he wants to see Billy convicted."

"But if she was paid ten thousand dollars by him, and *did* write the letter, he wouldn't have any reason to kill her. Would he?"

"I figured I'd leave that for you to find out, Jessica."

I filled him in on having visited LeClaire Metals, and Harry LeClaire's home.

"Learn anything?"

"Only that the two people I spoke with at LeClaire Metals knew who Cynthia Warren was."

"Maybe read about her murder in the papers."

I shook my head. "No, Malcolm, I had the feeling—and that's all it was, a gut feeling—that the mention of her name triggered a reaction in them that goes beyond knowing Cynthia simply as a murder victim who made the papers."

"Uh-huh. So what do you intend to do now?"

"First, I want to speak with Jill about the rest of the jurors. Which one, if any, feels the way Ms. Montrone did about Billy's innocence. Speaking of him, I heard Judge Wilson revoked his bail."

"That's right. Pure political decision. Billy's devastated by it. He'll call a cell his home until this is over."

"Poor thing."

"There's one advantage."

"What's that?"

"As long as he's behind bars, no one can accuse him of murdering anybody else. I take it you don't want to be here this afternoon."

"I had some other things I thought I might do."

"Then do them. I'll call you in the car if I need you."

"Not in this car, Malcolm. I'm being driven around town in a plain old Chevy sedan."

"Then check in with Linda on a regular basis."

"That I'll do. Do you know what, Malcolm?"

"What?"

"I don't believe that letter for a minute."

Chapter Nineteen

The change in Jill Farkas's attitude toward me over the past few days was unmistakable.

When I'd first met her, she was extremely cordial, and certainly helpful. The dinner at my hotel, during which she'd so generously shared her expert knowledge about jury selection, remained a highlight of my courtroom adventure.

But the warm and giving Jill Farkas was now cold and standoffish, which was why I was hesitant to ask her for her latest jury analysis. But I didn't let that stop me.

I cornered her when she returned from lunch. "Jill, could we spend a few minutes together before you go back into the courtroom?" I asked.

She looked at her watch. "I suppose."

"Just a few minutes. I promise."

She sighed, rolled her eyes, and followed me into the empty conference room. "What is it?" she asked the moment we were inside.

"I'm working on a project for Malcolm, which I'm sure he'll explain to you at some point. But right now, I need to know whether you've identified any of the jurors who might be leaning in the same direction that Juror Number Seven had been. Someone you think might have already decided that Billy is innocent."

She pulled a computer printout from her briefcase and scanned it. "If I had to choose one person on that jury we can count on, it would be Juror Number Ten."

I had my notes in front of me, and found the biographical section dealing with Juror Number Ten. He was a black man named Karl Jerome, who worked as a chef at Grendel's Den, on Winthrop Street, in Cambridge. He was thirty-seven years old, divorced, and lived in Cambridge.

"What about the analysis you ran on the alternates?" I asked.

She answered by shoving the papers back in her briefcase and standing. "I'm still working on it." With that she was gone.

I was hungry as I left the courthouse (Malcolm had delivered to him a hero piled high with liverwurst, and smeared with mayonnaise), but I decided to grab a quick bite on my way. I got in the Chevy sedan and gave Cathie an address in Somerville, a community northeast of Cambridge. We drove along the Charles River on Storrow Drive until crossing the river at the Charles River Dam. That put us on Somerville Avenue, also known as the Monsignor O'Brien Highway. Eventually, we came to a stop in front of a pretty two-story house on Walnut Street.

"Did you follow the news accounts of the alleged rape attempt by Billy Brannigan of a young lady named Gina Simone?" I asked.

"Sure," she replied. "There was a lot of controversy over her name being made public, wasn't there?"

"That's right, according to what I've read. Her name was withheld until she waived her right to privacy. That's when it became public."

"It was a big story here in Boston because of the Brannigan family. I remember when she dropped the charges."

"What was the prevailing public opinion about that, Cathie?"

"I think most people figured the Brannigan family had bought her off. But then it came out that because of the charge, the trust fund the Brannigan family had set up for Billy was going to be canceled, if that's what you do with a trust fund."

"Strange, wasn't it, that the trust said only that if Billy Brannigan were *charged* with a crime involving moral turpitude, his older brother, Jack, could cut Billy off."

"I guess so." Cathie looked to the two-story house. "Who lives here?"

"Gina Simone, according to my information."

"Why would you want to talk to her?"

"To try and put some pieces together. Where's my hat?"

Cathie laughed and handed it to me. I put it on, along with my sunglasses, got out of the car and went to one of two front doors. I checked the names over the buzzers. Gina Simone lived in the right-hand unit.

It took a few minutes for Ms. Simone to respond. She wore white shorts, a teal T-shirt, and was barefoot. Her tan was deep and rich, as though she'd just returned from an extended vacation on some tropical island. But it wasn't the way she dressed that had my immediate attention. She was the same attractive young woman I'd seen in photographs at Cynthia Warren's home the day of her murder.

"May I help you?" she asked.

"Yes. You are Gina Simone?"

"Yes."

I started to introduce myself with the same false name I'd used at LeClaire Metals, but decided that was silly. I was under no court restriction when it came to talking to anyone other than jurors. I removed the floppy canvas hat and sunglasses and said, "My name is Jessica Fletcher."

Ms. Simone's large brown eyes opened wide. "Yes, I can see that," she said. "You're the famous mystery writer."

"Well, I am a mystery writer. May I come in?"

"Why?" she asked, frowning. "I don't mean to

be rude, Mrs. Fletcher, but why would you be visiting me?"

I started to answer but she cut me off. "You're working with Billy Brannigan's defense team." There was an edge to her voice.

"Yes, I am. But I was also the one who discovered the body of—"

"Cynthia."

"Yes, Cynthia. Your friend."

"Why do you say my *friend*?"

"Because when I was inside Cynthia's house, I saw pictures of you with her."

"So what?"

"Well, I suppose I'm wondering why the young man with whom she was involved, Billy Brannigan, would have attempted to rape someone who was obviously her good friend."

"I dropped the charges, Mrs. Fletcher."

"Yes, I know you did, and I'm sure you had good reason. But you also know that simply by charging him with rape, you caused a violation of the trust fund of which he was a beneficiary."

"I don't have to talk to you," she said. "Excuse me."

"Ms. Simone, do you know Harry LeClaire?"

If my asking the receptionist and manufacturing supervisor at LeClaire Metals whether they knew Cynthia Warren caused a reaction, my mention of LeClaire's name to Gina Simone caused her to look as though I'd shoved a stake in her heart.

I followed up with, "Do you know of a relationship that existed between Harry LeClaire and Cynthia Warren?"

She answered by slamming the door in my face.

I returned to the car, got in the front seat, and looked back at the house. Ms. Simone was peering down at me through a second-story window.

"I get the feeling you weren't welcome," Cathie said.

"I would say that's an understatement."

"Would I be out of place asking you some questions, Mrs. Fletcher?"

"No one is ever out of place *asking* questions. Whether I'll answer them is another matter. Shoot."

"I have a feeling you're doing a lot more than acting as a jury consultant."

"I would say that's a fair assumption. But let me ask *you* a question."

"What?"

"Can I can trust you to keep everything that I say, and do, between us? And I really mean *between us.*"

"Discretion is my middle name. You should see some of the situations I end up observing as a limo driver."

"Good. Then let's keep going."

"Okay. Next stop?"

"Around the corner."

"What?"

"Find a place to park where we can keep an eye on Ms. Simone's house. If she leaves, we'll—"

"Go in the same direction," Cathie said, laughing.

"Exactly."

After we'd found a good spot, and had parked, I said, "I wonder how the trial is going?"

"Let's see," Cathie said, turning on the radio. "This station has been carrying a lot of it."

After a series of loud commercials, a newscaster said:

"As I reported before the break, the Billy Brannigan trial has taken an unexpected early recess until tomorrow morning. It's expected that Judge Walter Wilson will render his decision then on the admissibility of a letter, allegedly written by Billy Brannigan's girlfriend, Cynthia Warren, recanting her claim that they were together the night of Jack Brannigan's murder. Cynthia Warren, you will recall, was recently found murdered in her Cape Cod home. We'll continue our coverage when court resumes tomorrow."

"Does that change your plans, Mrs. Fletcher?" Cathie asked.

"Not at all. It could even hasten things along."

When Gina Simone hadn't left after we'd waited for a half hour, I considered giving it up. But just as I was about to announce this to Cathie, a black Cadillac passed us and pulled up in front of the house. I leaned closer to the window and narrowed my eyes. No doubt about it. It was alternate juror Harry LeClaire behind the wheel.

He beeped the horn. Moments later Ms. Simone, now dressed in black slacks and a tan blazer, and carrying a large overnight bag, bounded down the steps and got in the Cadillac.

"Do we?" Cathie asked, having already started the engine.

"Absolutely. But keep your distance. I don't want them to know we're following."

Cathie giggled. "This is exciting," she said. "I've never followed anyone before. Like cops and robbers."

I didn't say what I was thinking—that this was no game.

Harry LeClaire had given Cynthia Warren ten thousand dollars the day before she was murdered. And he obviously had a relationship of some sort with Cynthia's friend, Gina Simone, the young lady who'd accused Cynthia's boyfriend, Billy Brannigan, of rape, potentially depriving him of his trust benefits.

We followed them as they headed out of Somerville and in the direction of Logan Airport.

"Looks like somebody's taking a flight," Cathie said as they turned on to the airport access road.

"Looks like it," I said, my eyes trained on the back of the Caddy.

They pulled into the American Airlines departure area and stopped. Cathie came up behind, maintaining a three-car gap between us. Gina Simone got out with her bag and walked away from the car, but returned and started talking to LeClaire through the open front door. I couldn't hear what she was saying, but her body language and facial expression said she was angry. She confirmed that by slamming the door and stomping through the terminal doors.

LeClaire reached across the seat, closed the door, and prepared to join the traffic flow.

"Do we go with him?" Cathie asked.

"No. But how about following Ms. Simone in the terminal, Cathie? See if you can determine where she's headed. I'd go, but she'll recognize me."

"Just like a private eye," she said.

"Robert Parker would be proud of you," I said, referring to the best-selling Boston-based crime writer.

She got out of the car and disappeared inside the terminal.

A uniformed security guard came to where I waited and told me to move.

"My driver is inside," I said. "She'll only be a minute."

"You can't sit here," he said.

"Just one minute," I said. "I'd move it, but I don't drive."

He walked away to instruct another driver to move, and I was relieved when Cathie came running through the doors and got behind the wheel.

"We almost got a ticket," I said.

"Wouldn't be my first, Mrs. Fletcher. She's taking a flight to Florida."

"Miami?"

"Fort Lauderdale. Leaves in a half hour."

"Good work," I said. "Thanks."

"I'm enjoying this," she said. "Beats driving boring business moguls to board meetings. What's next?"

The digital clock on the dashboard read four-thirty.

"I think I'll head back to the hotel."

"I'm available this evening."

"What about my nighttime driver?"

"You haven't been using him," Cathie said as we pulled away from the curb.

"I know. No need for a driver tonight. I need a quiet night by myself."

"Whatever you say. What time do I pick you up tomorrow?"

"Eight. Court convenes at nine."

"Have a nice evening, Mrs. Fletcher," Cathie said when we arrived at the Ritz-Carlton.

"You, too, Cathie. See you in the morning."

"I just want you to know, Mrs. Fletcher, that you can trust me to keep my mouth shut. I mean, they could torture me and I wouldn't say anything, burn me with cigarettes, shove bamboo shoots under my nails, no matter what. My lips are sealed."

I smiled and patted her arm. "Hopefully," I said, "you won't be put to such a severe test. But it's nice to know I can trust you. Good night."

She'd obviously watched a lot of World War II movies.

Chapter Twenty

I'd promised to keep in touch with Malcolm's office, but hadn't, and called the moment I reached my suite. Rachel Cohen answered.

"Hello, Rachel, It's Jessica."

"Malcolm was asking about you. Court broke early."

"So I heard. Is he there?"

"No. He's at a Bar Association dinner at the Copley Plaza. How was your day?"

"Good. Yours?"

"Okay. Judge Wilson says he'll rule on the Warren letter tomorrow morning."

"I heard that, too. Any inkling of which way he'll go?"

"No. He's a good poker player. By the way, are you free for dinner?"

"Free? Yes. Willing? No."

She laughed. "Joe has the night off from the hospital and is taking care of the kids. So I have this one night of liberation—and not the slightest idea what to do with it."

"Sounds like a pleasant dilemma. Sorry, Rachel, but I'm not up to much more than a long, hot soak and a good night's sleep."

"I understand."

"I'll be here at the hotel if anyone needs me."

"I'll pass the word. See you in court in the morning?"

"Yes. I'll be there."

I followed through on my intentions for the evening, luxuriating in a hot tub filled with aromatic bath gel, then ordering up a variety of appetizers from room service. My phone didn't ring once: I wondered if I might have died and gone to heaven.

But once I'd settled down to start reading a new book I'd brought with me, my mind began to wander. I couldn't get off the first page.

I went to the window and looked down over the Public Garden. There was still some daylight left, although darkness was closing in. The weather forecast was for rain that night. I decided it was nonproductive to stay in the suite and try to achieve the calm I'd sought. I left the hotel and took a taxi to Boston's dramatically revived and rejuvenated waterfront. The city's approach to turning a dreary waterfront area into a handsome amalgamation of apartment and office buildings, restaurants and shops had become a model for other cities around the country.

Many shops were closed, but a few remained open. As I browsed windows, taking in the displays of designer clothing, glittering jewelry, and supple leather goods, I felt the tickle of mist on my cheeks. It was now clouded over; rain wasn't far away.

I crossed a street and stopped in front of an art gallery called FIRE & ICE. The name struck a bell. Of course. It was the name of the gallery owned by the pottery maker, Thomas McEnroe, one of the six alternate jurors.

One window of Fire and Ice was dominated by two modern paintings on easels. The other window featured small pieces of wire sculpture, and ceramic pottery. One pot immediately grabbed my attention. It had a pre-Columbian look to it, yet the artist's use of metallic green and yellow were distinctly modern in concept and execution. It instantly appealed to me. It was also markedly similar to one of the ceramic pieces I'd seen in Cynthia Warren's home the day she was killed.

I stepped inside the well-lighted gallery, where dozens of interesting paintings on the walls, and artifacts on pedestals provided a feast for the eyes.

A tiny bell attached to the door sounded, bringing from a back room a short, slender woman wearing a flowered artist's smock. Her dull brown hair was pulled back into a severe chignon. Oversized glasses rendered her eyes twice as large as they actually were. The term "mousy" came to mind.

"Hello," she said in a voice as small as she was. "May I help you?"

"I'm just browsing," I said. "It's starting to rain."

"Yes, it is."

"You have a beautiful gallery."

"Thank you. Is there anything you're especially interested in?"

"That pot in the window. The one with the metallic green-and-yellow highlights."

"That's one of my favorites," she said, going to the window, removing the pot, and handing it to me. I turned it over in my hands, and held it up to catch the light. As I did, I glanced at the woman. She was watching me with intense interest, face screwed up in deep thought, arms crossed on her chest.

"It's lovely," I said. "How much is it?"

"You're Jessica Fletcher," she said flatly.

I lowered the pot and smiled. "That's right. Are you the owner?"

"Part owner. You know my partner, Thom. He's on the jury."

"That's right."

"Is that why you came, because of him? Or because you want to buy a ceramic pot?"

"I came here only because I happened to be passing by. It looked like it was about to rain, and I saw this lovely work of art in the window. But yes, I did realize before entering the gallery that Thomas McEnroe owned it."

Her expression said she was debating whether to believe me.

"You know who *I* am," I said. "You are?"

"Patty Zeltner."

"Pleased to meet you. Do you and Mr. McEnroe work together on the pottery?"

"No. Thom is the artist. I manage the gallery."

"It's a beautiful space."

"Beautiful, and expensive. Very expensive."

"I imagine. It's always that way when an area gentrifies. It must be difficult with him away on jury duty."

"Worse than that. He's not creating anything new. It also helps to have him here to sell. Buyers like to meet the artist."

"I always do. Is Mr. McEnroe here? I understand the trial recessed early today."

I asked not because I wanted to see him, but because I *didn't* want to see him. I wasn't anxious to violate Judge Wilson's stern admonition to stay away from jurors.

I examined the pot again. "How much is it?" I asked.

"Two-hundred and fifty dollars."

"It's worth it," I said. "I recently saw a similar pot."

"We've sold a few like this one," Ms. Zeltner said. "Where did you see it?"

"On the Cape. And under unfortunate circumstances, I'm afraid."

"Oh?" Her face went to stone.

"It was in the home of a young woman who was murdered."

"Cynthia Warren."

"Yes. I'm sure you've been reading about her."

She said nothing as she took the pot from me and returned it to the window.

"I'd like to buy it," I said.

She responded by going behind a counter and pretending to straighten things that didn't need straightening. Her abrupt dismissal of me was off-putting. I didn't know whether to leave, or to force further conversation. She resolved my dilemma by saying, "You'll have to excuse me, Mrs. Fletcher. It's just that—"

I said as I approached the counter, "I'm sorry if I said something to upset you. Did you know Cynthia Warren? Did she buy her pot from you?"

She looked as though she might break into tears, biting her thin lip and taking a deep breath.

"Ms. Zeltner, let me be completely honest with you. I didn't intend to come here this evening. It never crossed my mind to do that. But now that I'm here, and now that my mention of Cynthia Warren has caused an obvious reaction in you, I have to ask, why?"

She stared at the countertop for what seemed a very long time. Then she placed her hands on it and muttered, "Bitch."

I thought she meant me.

Realizing what I was thinking, she looked up and said, "Please, I'm sorry. I didn't mean you."

"I'm relieved," I said. "You meant Cynthia Warren."

"I shouldn't have said it. It's just that—"

"Ms. Zeltner, I said I'd be honest with you. I've been investigating Ms. Warren's murder. Not in any official capacity, of course, but because I'm beginning to believe that others might be in jeopardy. You read, I assume, about one of the jurors, a Mrs. Montrone, being run down."

"It was a hit-and-run, wasn't it? An accident."

"Perhaps. Perhaps not. Why did you react so visibly when I mentioned Cynthia Warren?"

"Because—look, Mrs. Fletcher, things are very tense here between Thom and me."

"I'm sorry. Has being tied up with the Brannigan trial contributed to that?"

"I suppose so." She looked up at a clock. "Thom will be here any minute."

"Which means I'd better leave. I'm an official part of the Brannigan defense team. And *that* means no contact with jurors or alternates."

"It's all money, isn't it?" she said.

"What is?"

"Everything. It is with us. With Thom and me."

"You're having money problems?"

"Yes. Serious money problems. Cynthia was going to—"

She now had my total interest. "You say her name as though you knew her quite well," I said.

She silently dusted an already pristine countertop. It occurred to me as I processed what she'd said that if Thomas McEnroe personally knew Cynthia Warren, he should have made that known when he was questioned by the attorneys during voir dire. Cynthia Warren was to be Billy Brannigan's prime alibi witness. Not indicating he knew her was as egregious an omission as Harry LeClaire not admitting he knew Gina Simone, Brannigan's accuser as a rapist, *and* Cynthia Warren.

But that was a matter to take up with Malcolm and Rachel Cohen. Fortunately, neither McEnroe nor LeClaire had joined the twelve-person jury, and would not be voting on Billy Brannigan's guilt or innocence. Not yet, anyway. If my supposition was correct—and that's all it was at that juncture, a supposition—then any other juror likely to acquit Billy might face the same sort of danger as Marie Montrone.

I wasn't sure whether Patty Zeltner would welcome further questions. She appeared poised for flight. But since she'd offered what she had, I felt there was nothing to be lost by pressing on.

"How well did Thom know Cynthia Warren?" I asked.

"I really have things to do in the back before Thom arrives, Mrs. Fletcher. You'll have to excuse me."

"What about the pot in the window? I'd like to buy it."

"It will have to be another time. Sorry, Mrs. Fletcher. The shop is closed."

She went to the front door and opened it for me.

"May I come back?" I asked.

"Yes. Another time. I'll put the pot aside."

"Thank you. It is lovely. I'd like to take it home with me as a souvenir of my Boston trip."

I crossed the street and entered a small coffee shop, took a table by the window that afforded me a view of the gallery, and ordered a cappuccino. As the waitress placed the steaming cup in front of me, Thomas McEnroe pulled up in front of Fire and Ice in a white convertible. He fairly leaped from it, entered the gallery, appeared to lock the door behind him, turned off the lights in the showroom, and disappeared, presumably into the back room.

I finished my coffee, paid, and stepped outside. It was now dark, and rain had begun to fall with serious purpose.

I crossed the street and stood in front of the gallery. A hint of light spilled into the showroom through a crack in the door to the rear room.

I stepped closer to McEnroe's car. It was a Mercedes. I have no interest in cars, and don't know one from the other. But I did know a Mercedes was expensive. If the gallery was having money problems, as indicated by Patty Zeltner, Thomas McEnroe didn't seem to be suffering them personally.

I spotted a cab and waved it down. As I was about to step into the taxi, my eye went to the license plate on Thom McEnroe's convertible. SUMRLVN 2.

The plate on Cynthia Warren's car that was

parked in her driveway on the Cape the day her
body was discovered was SUMRLOVN.

Evidently, Thomas McEnroe and Cynthia Warren knew each other pretty well.

Chapter Twenty-one

My sojourn to Boston's gentrified waterfront, and my conversation with Patty Zeltner, hadn't taken more than a couple of hours. But in that brief time away from my suite, I received seven phone calls.

Four were from media people; my respite from them evidently had ended.

Seth Hazlitt called from Cabot Cove to say he was coming to Boston the next day to do some shopping, would be staying at the Ritz-Carlton, and would get in touch when he arrived.

Another call from Cabot Cove was from Mort Metzger, our sheriff and my good friend. The only message he left was that he would call again.

Rachel Cohen's message was that she was having dinner with a friend at Terramia, and if I changed my mind, I could join them there.

I decided not to return any of the calls, and tried to resurrect my quiet evening alone. I got into my nightgown and robe, finished the appetizer platter I'd ordered earlier in the evening, and settled in to start reading, once again, the book I'd given up on. My second attempt was no more successful than my first; the events of that day kept intruding upon my concentration.

I pulled a yellow legal pad from my briefcase, sat in an overstuffed chair by the window and wrote down what I knew up to this point.

> > William Brannigan, from a wealthy family, benefited from a trust. His older brother, Jack, was trustee.

> > The trust called for Billy Brannigan to be cut out of the trust if he was ever charged with a crime involving moral turpitude.

> > A stunning young woman, Gina Simone, accused Billy of attempting to rape her.

> > Although Gina Simone eventually withdrew her charge of rape, Billy's brother, Jack, threatened to invoke the moral turpitude clause of the trust.

> > Jack Brannigan was found stabbed to death in one of the famous Swan Boats in Boston's Public Garden.

> > Billy Brannigan was indicted for Jack's murder, and hired flamboyant defense attorney, Malcolm McLoon.

> > Billy's Cape Cod girlfriend, Cynthia Warren, claimed she was with Billy on the Cape the night Jack Brannigan was murdered, and would testify to that at his trial.

> > McLoon's investigator, Ritchie Fleigler, and

I went to Cape Cod to bring Ms. Warren to Boston in advance of her testimony. We found her dead in her home, also a stabbing victim.

> > A ten-thousand-dollar deposit slip found in Warren's home turned out to have been money given her the day before her murder by one of six alternate jurors on the Brannigan case, Harry LeClaire, a businessman and owner of LeClaire Metals, manufacturer of tweezers and scissors.

> > The reaction of two employees of LeClaire Metals when I mentioned Cynthia Warren's name said to me that they knew her.

> > A letter, allegedly written by Cynthia Warren, Billy Brannigan's dead alibi witness, arrived at the office of Billy's prosecutors. In it, Ms. Warren recanted her claim that she was with Billy the night of his brother's murder. A handwriting expert had been called in by Malcolm McLoon to evaluate the letter's authenticity.

> > Question: Had Harry LeClaire paid Warren the ten thousand dollars to have her write that letter?

> > I visited Gina Simone, who seemed to panic when I mentioned Harry LeClaire's name. Shortly after my visit, she was picked up by LeClaire and dropped at the airport for a flight to Fort Lauderdale.

> > Harry LeClaire knew both Cynthia Warren and Gina Simone.

> > Gina Simone and Cynthia Warren were

friends. Yet, Gina charged Cynthia's boyfriend, Billy Brannigan, with attempted rape.

> > Another alternate juror, pottery maker Thomas McEnroe, evidently created a piece of ceramic art found in Cynthia Warren's home. His "partner," Patty Zeltner, demonstrated a distinct change of attitude when I mentioned Cynthia Warren's name, and called her a "bitch."

> > Thomas McEnroe drives an expensive automobile, with a license plate, SUMRLVN 2. Cynthia Warren's plate was, SUMRLOVN. Like matching shorts and shirts. Like two people who knew each other very well.

> > According to Patty Zeltner, she and McEnroe were having financial problems at the gallery.

I returned the pad to my briefcase and was heading for bed when the phone rang. It was Malcolm's investigator, Ritchie Fleigler. "Hope I didn't wake you," he said.

"Almost. What can I do for you, Ritchie?"

"I figured you might want to hear the latest information I've come up with on the jurors."

I knew Malcolm had instructed Ritchie to continue digging into the background of the jurors, both the twelve sitting members and the six alternates. But I'd forgotten he was actually doing it.

"Sure," I said. "Go ahead."

He ran through some names. While I was inherently interested in learning more about the lives of the jurors, nothing he said caught my attention, until he mentioned Harry LeClaire.

"This LeClaire is a high-roller. He—"

"What's a high-roller?" I asked.

"Big gambler. Well known in Las Vegas and Atlantic City."

"I see."

"Problem is he seems to have run out of money to throw away at the craps table. He owes big bucks to a few casinos, at least according to my source."

"What constitutes 'big bucks'?" I asked.

"Thousands. Tens of thousands."

"I'd say that's big. Any idea why he's gone into such large gambling debts? He has a business, which I assume is successful."

"Maybe it isn't, Jessica. Then again, maybe the business is successful, but he blows all the profits in Vegas."

As he talked, I wondered how someone who owed so much money to casinos could come up with ten thousand dollars to give to Cynthia Warren.

"Anything else on Mr. LeClaire?" I asked.

"Just scuttlebutt. I know this waitress who knows LeClaire. She says he's a swinger, a big man with the ladies."

"He's married," I said. "Two children."

Ritchie laughed. "Doesn't mean much these days, Mrs. Fletcher."

"No, I suppose it doesn't. Well, Ritchie, I appreciate your sharing this with me. Have you told Malcolm yet?"

"No. He's at some Bar Association dinner. Probably passed out by now."

I winced at his callous, albeit probably accurate description of the esteemed counselor.

"See you in court?" he asked.

"Yes, you will. Good night."

I'd been sleepy before the call. Now, I was wide awake. I turned on TV just in time to see the end of a local newscast in which Malcolm was being interviewed at the conclusion of the Bar Association dinner. He wore a tuxedo, and contrary to what Ritchie assumed, appeared to be sober and alert.

"The People haven't proved a thing," he boomed. "All you have to do is look into the faces of the jury. *They* know he's innocent, and that's the way they'll vote. Excuse me. I have a trial to prepare for."

A reporter shouted, "What about the Warren letter?"

"All smoke and no fire," Malcolm said. "Sorry, but I have to go."

I stayed up until midnight chewing on everything that had occurred to date. It was when I finally got to bed, and was about to fall asleep, that an old and wise adage came to mind. It said that if you want to solve a mystery—personal, political, or business—follow the money trail.

That's what I decided I'd do the next day. There was plenty of trail to follow.

Chapter Twenty-two

"Malcolm, can I see you for a moment?" I asked at the courthouse the following morning. I caught him coming through the front door, and kept pace as he headed for the courtroom.

"Not now, Jessica. The judge wants to hear more arguments on the letter. I have to get in there."

"Did your handwriting expert examine it?"

"Yes. Says it's Cynthia Warren's signature."

"Sorry to hear that."

"No damage. We won't use him. We'll get another expert."

"Malcolm, I found out things yesterday I think you should—"

"Tell me at lunch," he said, pushing open the swinging doors and disappearing through them, leaving me standing in the hallway.

I debated following him inside but decided not to. If the morning was to be taken up with legal arguments, I had nothing to contribute.

I left the building and got into the Chevy with Cathie. "Where to?" she asked.

"Not quite sure. Give me a few minutes."

Despite Malcolm's downplaying of the hand-writing expert's finding, it struck me as a serious blow to the defense. But I'd learned in my brief exposure to the legal system that things weren't always as they seemed to be. Lawyers have a way of taking black and turning it into white, and vice versa.

Follow the money.

I pulled out my Boston guidebook and went to the section that recommended Boston's better stores. The guide listed two shops under the cut-lery heading.

The first was located in Copley Place, a ten-acre complex built above the Massachusetts Turn-pike that includes hotels, movie theaters, apart-ments, restaurants, and a hundred upscale shops.

The shop had just opened when I arrived, and a distinguished looking gentleman asked if I needed help.

"Yes," I said. "I'm looking for a pair of scissors, and tweezers as a gift for a friend."

"I'm sure we have what you want," he said, opening the back of a glass-topped counter and removing a pair of scissors.

I examined them, paying particular attention to the engraved manufacturer's name. I handed them back. "Actually," I said, "I wanted to buy LeClaire scissors and tweezers."

He made a face as though a mildly unpleasant odor had been released.

"Do you carry them?" I asked.

"No, we don't. They aren't up to our standards."

"Really? I thought they were of especially high quality."

"I'm afraid not. LeClaire has always produced inferior scissors. Low-end. And lately—well, that doesn't help you make a purchase."

"You started to say."

"LeClaire is about to go out of business. At least that's what I hear. If you insist upon buying their scissors and tweezers, I suggest you check out—"

"No, I'm not committed to their products. I must have been misinformed about them. I'll be back after I do some other shopping. Thank you so much."

"My pleasure, madam."

The second shop was on Newbury Street, and was considerably larger than the one in Copley Place. A young woman helped me.

"Do you carry LeClaire scissors?" I asked.

"No. We haven't in more than a year."

"Oh. I was interested in buying a pair."

"Sorry, but we can't help you. I'm not even sure they still make them."

"That's interesting," I said.

"Is LeClaire even *in* business?" she asked a colleague.

"I don't know," he replied.

"Well, thank you very much," I said.

"We have a wonderful selection of scissors," she said.

"Yes, I can certainly see that. I'll be back."

Obviously, LeClaire Metals was not what you'd term a going business. Going *out* of business, maybe.

But its owner had given Cynthia Warren a check for ten thousand dollars the day before her murder.

And Harry LeClaire was, according to Ritchie Fleigler, an inveterate gambler, who'd suffered large losses. Which could explain, of course, why his business was failing.

Follow the money.

I intended to return to the courthouse before the morning session broke because I wanted to tell Malcolm that a second alternate juror, Thomas McEnroe, had what appeared to be a previous relationship with Cynthia Warren, and that Harry LeClaire not only gave Ms. Warren money the day before she died, but he knew Gina Simone, too. What Malcolm would do with the information was conjecture on my part. But he had to know.

I had an hour before returning to the court, and decided to run back to the hotel where I'd left the Gina Simone file of clippings. I'd meant to read it earlier, and to return it to Malcolm's office, as I'd promised Linda I would. I'd failed on both counts.

I'd no sooner stepped out of the Chevy in front

of the Ritz-Carlton than I heard someone call "Jessica." Seth Hazlitt had just paid his taxi driver and was instructing a uniformed bellhop what to do with his luggage.

We hugged.

"What good timing," Seth said, grinning. "I thought you'd probably be sitting in that musty old courtroom all day."

"Not today," I said. "But I do have to get over there before the noon recess. There's something I have to talk to Malcolm McLoon about."

"How is the bigger-than-life counselor?"

"Fine. I have to get something from my room. Come with me."

When I opened the door to allow him to enter, he laughed and said, " 'Room' you call it? It's a princely suite."

"I know. Compliments of Malcolm."

I found the file and shoved it into my briefcase. "Are you going to Filene's now?" I asked.

"Maybe later. Sale's on for two days. Since I caught up with you so easy, Jessica, how about my accompanying you to court, see what you've been up to since comin' to Boston?"

"I'd love that, Seth, but I won't be able to stay with you all the time. I have to meet with Malcolm about something important. He suggested lunch together. I'm sure you're welcome to join us."

"Wouldn't want to intrude," he said.

"And you wouldn't be. Come on. I can't be late. I have a car at my disposal."

"Also courtesy of the great McLoon?"

"Seth, I have the distinct impression that you dislike him."

"Ayuh."

"But you've never met him."

"I know enough about him from what I've read, and seen on the television. Let's go. Can't wait to make his acquaintance in the flesh."

We arrived only minutes before Judge Wilson called the noon recess. As Seth and I walked into the courthouse, Malcolm came through the swinging doors leading to the courtroom, followed by Rachel Cohen, Georgia Bobley, Jill Farkas, and Ritchie Fleigler. Judging from their expressions, things hadn't gone well.

"Malcolm," I said. "This is my friend, Dr. Seth Hazlitt, from Cabot Cove."

Malcolm stopped, scowled at Seth, and muttered, "Excuse me."

Seth and I fell in behind the entourage. "What's happened?" I asked Georgia.

"Judge Wilson ruled the letter could be introduced by the DA. They had a police department handwriting expert examine it, too. He agrees with our expert. Cynthia Warren wrote the letter. Or at least signed it."

"Where are we going?" I asked anyone who would listen.

"Malcolm wants lunch at Clarke's," Rachel said.

Malcolm's limo, and the Chevy driven by Cathie were at the curb. We all waited for Malcolm's next move.

"Maybe I'll just go on to Filene's," Seth said to me.

With that, Malcolm placed his hand on Seth's back and virtually pushed him into the limousine's backseat. Rachel and Georgia followed, and Malcolm squeezed his bulk into the front seat beside the driver. That left Jill Farkas, Ritchie Fleigler, and me on the sidewalk.

"Clarke's," Malcolm said through the open window. He told his driver to go.

I went to the Chevy. "Do you know where Clarke's is?" I asked Cathie.

"Sure. Everybody knows Clarke's."

"That's where we're going," I said, holding open the door for Jill and Ritchie.

Clarke's, according to Cathie, was one of the city's most popular saloons. Her use of that descriptive word caused my stomach to knot. Was Malcolm about to go on a binge in the middle of the day?

"Is court in session this afternoon?" I asked Jill Farkas.

"No. Judge Wilson has a toothache. He's seeing a dentist this afternoon."

My stomach flip-flopped again. Poor Seth, captive in a limousine with a man for whom his dis-

like was palpable. He should have gone to
Filene's.

We walked into a crowded Clarke's and found
Malcolm and the others at a large table in the bar
area. I couldn't help but smile at seeing Seth, who
was at Malcolm's right. He sat ramrod straight,
his eyes focused straight ahead, a man about to
be given his last meal before the execution.

"Jessica, sit here," Malcolm commanded, indicating an empty chair to his left. I took it, leaned
across him, and asked, "How are you holding
up, Seth?"

"Fair to middlin'."

"Your doctor friend doesn't say much," Malcolm
said as a waitress took our drink orders.

"He's a man of few words," I said.

"Doesn't seem to be much room for anyone else
to speak around here," Seth said haughtily.

"If doctors said less, and did more for their pa-
tients, everyone would be better off," Malcolm
said, downing his drink and getting in his order
for a second before the waitress departed.

"And if lawyers weren't so greedy," Seth said,
"we wouldn't have all the trumped-up malpractice
cases cloggin' our courts."

Malcolm started to respond but I stepped in.
"Malcolm, do you think we could find a few minutes alone? Over there?" I pointed to a spot by a
window that hadn't been occupied yet by other
patrons.

"What is it, Jessica?" he asked as we went to it.

"Without going into detail," I said, "you should know that Harry LeClaire not only knew Cynthia Warren well enough to give her ten thousand dollars the day before she died, he knows Gina Simone as well."

"The young woman who charged Billy with attempted rape?"

"Exactly. I visited her. When I mentioned LeClaire's name, she froze, slammed the door in my face. A half hour later, LeClaire picked her up and drove her to the airport for a flight to Fort Lauderdale."

"You've been busy," he said.

"Yes, I have. There's more. A second alternate juror, the pottery maker, Thomas McEnroe, also knew Cynthia Warren."

"He did?"

"According to his partner in his gallery, a woman named Patty Zeltner. I spoke with her last night."

He broke into a grin. "You've been more than busy, I'd say. Sure about McEnroe?"

"Yes."

"What else has our distaff Sherlock turned up?"

"Only that LeClaire's business is in trouble. According to Ritchie, he's a heavy gambler, and owes casinos a great deal of money."

"But he had enough to give Cynthia Warren ten grand."

"Right. The court should know all this, shouldn't it?"

"Oh, yes, Jessica, it certainly should know that two of its alternate jurors lied."

"To get on the jury?"

"Could be. But I don't want to spring it on Judge Wilson just yet."

"Why not?"

"Poor man has a toothache. No sense making it worse."

"Malcolm, I appreciate the humor but—"

"Not a word to anyone about this, Jessica."

"But—"

He whispered now. "Neither LeClaire nor McEnroe have made the sitting jury. They won't be voting on Billy's innocence or guilt unless another juror drops out."

"Or dies."

"Or dies. The reason I want to keep this under wraps, Jessica, is that it's good to have it in our pocket in the event Billy is convicted. Grounds for appeal no judge can ignore. And if he's acquitted, I'll bring it to the attention of the DA. No, let's just keep it between us for now."

"I still don't think that's a good idea, Malcolm. But you're the attorney."

"And you're the mystery writer and detective. Keep digging."

"Why?"

"Because things aren't going as good as they were before with our case. That damn letter will pack a powerful punch with the jury. We'll need everything we can come up with."

I glanced back at the table, where Seth was looking in our direction, the same pained expression on his face. "We'd better get back," I said.

"I suppose we should. Your doctor friend is an opinionated gentleman."

I laughed. "He's a sweetheart."

"If you like doctors. My rule is to stay as far away from them as possible."

"Unless you need them. Like lawyers."

"That's right. Unless you need them. Come on. They serve up decent scrod here, and the fries can't be beat. We'll be meeting all afternoon back at the office. You go on with your sleuthing, give me a call later in the day."

Malcolm was right. The scrod and fries were good.

As we prepared to leave the restaurant, a familiar face came to the table. It was Warren Parker, the proverbial man-about-town to whom I'd been introduced by Malcolm during our first lunch together at the Seaside. As at our first meeting, he was impeccably dressed, and carried himself with the casual air of a man supremely sure of himself.

"Mrs. Fletcher," he said, extending his hand limply. "Still slumming with the eminent counselor, I see."

"Hello, Mr. Parker. This is Dr. Seth Hazlitt, my friend from back home."

"A pleasure," Parker said.

"Whitney James here with you?" Malcolm asked

without looking up from the check he was mentally going over.

"Not with me," Parker said, flashing a smile. "Ms. James and I are not—how shall I say it—we no longer share tables at lunch, or philosophical thoughts."

He said it directly to me.

"Nice seeing you again, Mr. Parker," I said as Malcolm tossed cash on the check and stood. As we headed for the door, Parker stopped me. "Would you be free for dinner this evening, Mrs. Fletcher?"

"I—no, I'm not. Dr. Hazlitt and I will be having dinner."

"Then let the three of us dine together. My treat."

Seth had been standing next to me and heard the invitation. "Seth?" I said.

"If you wish, Jessica."

"All right," I said. "Where and when?"

"Jasper's, of course. Commercial Street at Atlantic. Shall we say seven?"

"All right."

"Pretentious fella, isn't he?" Seth said as we joined the others outside.

"Extremely. Mind having dinner with him?"

"Better than wasting a meal with that insufferable McLoon."

I laughed and patted him on the back. "He's really very nice once you get to know him. Malcolm grows on you."

"So does fungus. What's on your agenda this afternoon, Jessica?"

"First, to help you pick out some shirts and ties at Filene's."

"Appreciate the help. You always did have a good eye."

"And after that, I have a few places to visit for the case. You're welcome to join me."

As we waited for the cars to pull up, I asked Malcolm how Billy Brannigan was faring in jail.

"Not too good," he replied. "Very depressed. We've got him on a suicide watch."

"How awful. I thought I might visit him, if that's all right with you."

"Fine with me. You're on the approved visitors list." He turned to Seth. "What kind of medicine do you practice, Doc?"

"Sound medicine—chum."

The arrival of the Chevy was in time, and welcome.

Chapter Twenty-three

"Sure that tie with all the yellow and red is right for me?" Seth asked as we left the famed Filene's Basement, the country's first discount store and still going strong.

"It will go wonderfully with that blue blazer you're so fond of wearing."

"If you say so. Well, what does the rest of the afternoon hold for us?"

"While you were trying on that suit—I wish you'd bought it—I called the jail where Billy Brannigan is being held. I have an appointment to visit him there at four. But you won't be allowed in with me."

"Not a disappointment, Jessica. Treating inmates at the Maine correctional facility once a month is enough jail time for me. Think I'll head back to the hotel and unpack my bags, maybe take a nap before dinner with your pompous friend."

"He's not my friend, Seth. Frankly, I accepted because I have the feeling I might learn something from him."

"How so?"

"When I first met him, he was—how shall I say it?—he was close with the district attorney in the Brannigan case. But from what he said today, that's no longer true. Besides, I'm looking forward to having dinner at Jasper's. It's supposed to be one of Boston's finest restaurants."

"Whatever you say, Jessica."

"Come on," I said. "Cathie can drop you off at the hotel."

"No. You go on ahead. Not much of a walk, as I recollect, and I can use it. Go visit your client, Mr. Brannigan. We'll meet at six-thirty?"

"Sounds fine. In the lobby. And wear your blue blazer and new tie. You'll look smashing."

I watched my friend walk away and was glad he was there. As much as I liked the people I'd met since signing on to the Brannigan defense team, I didn't feel close to them. But Seth was like a comfortable pair of slippers, a link with my roots, roots that had anchored me in Cabot Cove for so many years.

"Your friend is nice," Cathie said.

"Yes, he is. Well, let's head for jail."

"Got your 'Get Out of Jail' card?"

"Like 'Pass Go'? Afraid not, Watson. You'll visit me if they lock me up?"

"Sure. I'll hide a file in pound cake. The way I make pound cake, they'd never find anything in it, let alone be able to eat it."

Billy Brannigan's few days behind bars had aged

him years. His eyes were sunken, and his lip twitched as he said hello and sat across a scarred wooden table in a room reserved for attorney-client meetings. A guard stood just outside the door, which had a small glass insert covered with close-mesh wire.

"How are you holding up?" I asked, knowing that the answer was written all over his handsome, youthful face.

"Not too good, Mrs. Fletcher. I hate it here. Why did the judge revoke my bail? I didn't go anywhere, run away when I was out on bail."

"Because of Cynthia Warren's murder, as I understand it."

His laugh was rueful, more of an editorial grunt.

"Billy, I asked to see you because I'm trying to piece together some things I've learned that might help you."

"I don't think there's anything anybody can do. Mr. McLoon told me about Cynthia's letter saying we weren't together the night Jack was killed. That's a lie. I was there with her."

"I'm sure you were. Any idea why she might have written it?"

"I don't think she did," he said.

"Why?"

"Why would she? Cynthia had a lot of faults, Mrs. Fletcher, but she wasn't a liar."

"Do you think someone might have gotten her to write the letter? Coerced her into doing it? Paid her to do it?"

"Who?"

"That's what I'm trying to find out. Did she ever mention a Mr. Harry LeClaire to you?"

He shook his head.

"Name doesn't ring a bell?"

"No."

He obviously hadn't bothered to learn the names of the jurors and alternates for his own trial. He'd made the point from the first day I met him that he wasn't interested in reading about the trial in the papers, or watching it on television. I certainly wasn't about to reveal that Harry LeClaire was one of those alternates because it might cause him to do something that ran contrary to Malcolm's strategy. I'd promised Malcolm I'd tell no one, and intended to keep my pledge.

"Billy, tell me about Gina Simone."

"That bitch? Sorry. I didn't mean to curse in front of you."

"That's quite all right. I've heard the term before." I didn't add that my most recent exposure was when it was directed at his deceased girlfriend, Cynthia Warren.

Because he hadn't indicated any knowledge that Harry LeClaire was on the jury, I felt safe mentioning Thomas McEnroe. I received the same response, a shaking of the head.

"Billy, when I mentioned Gina Simone's name, you reacted with anger, and I can understand why. Tell me more about her."

"Why?"

"Just one of the pieces I'm trying to fit into a larger puzzle. What does she do for a living?"

"Lives off men."

"Oh? You make it sound as though she's a prostitute."

"She is, but not the way you usually think of prostitutes. She's a great-looking girl. Woman. Knows how to play guys to get what she wants. She says she's an actress, but she's never acted in anything that I know of. A wannabe actress. But maybe she is a good actress, the way she always gets her way."

"I read in newspaper clippings that she claimed to be an actress. I was reading them while waiting to see you. You said she lives off men. How?"

"Gina only runs with guys with money. Doesn't matter if they're married. In fact, maybe she prefers that they are. Makes it easier to blackmail them into keeping her, paying her bills, her rent, buying her clothes and jewelry."

"I see."

"I hated that she and Cynthia were such good friends. Cynthia and I used to fight about that a lot. Gina was a bad influence on Cynthia."

"Are you saying that Cynthia used men, too."

"No. Well, sometimes. Before I met her. She and Gina used to run together, always with high-rollers, big shots, party girls I guess you could call them."

"High-rollers. Gamblers?"

"I don't know. Guys with money. Jet-set types."

"What did Cynthia do for a living? Her home on the Cape is beautiful."

"Some uncle left it to her. Caused a big stink in the family. It was her mother's brother, and her mother thought the house was being left to her. Surprise, Mom. Cynthia got it."

"But keeping up a house like that costs money. And she had a nice car sitting in the driveway. How did she earn money?"

"She said she was a design consultant to businesses in Boston and New York."

"Did you know who her clients were?"

"No. I asked a few times but she said it was confidential. Like a lawyer and client. Didn't make any sense to me, so I stopped asking."

The guard opened the door. "Ten minutes, ma'am," he said.

"Yes. All right."

I waited for him to close the door before saying to Billy, "You come from quite a family."

He smiled genuinely for the first time. "I guess I do," he said. "Sure is a rich one."

"Your brother, Jack, ran the business as I understand it."

"Maybe ran it into the ground is more like it."

I hadn't expected that response, and was speechless for a moment.

"Maybe you'd better explain, Billy. I thought Brannigan's Bean Pot was an extremely successful business. I see the product everywhere I go."

"Oh, sure. It's a success. A big success. Always

has been since my grandfather started it. Secret recipe and all."

"I've tasted Brannigan's baked beans. Very good—almost as good as the ones I make."

"Yeah. It's good. Jack was a good businessman, I suppose, only some of the other family members involved in the business thought he played too loose and easy with the money."

"How so?"

"He gambled."

"Did he? Big stakes?"

"Sometimes. Every once in a while he'd come back from the Bahamas and tell me how much he lost. Big bucks. But I guess when you have it, it doesn't mean much."

Follow the money.

I asked, "Did your brother have business dealings with others outside Brannigan's Bean Pot?"

"Like who?"

"Oh, I don't know, Billy. Investments in other businesses."

"Sure."

"Any names?"

"Not that I remember. Jack didn't talk much about those things to me, I guess because I didn't want anything to do with business. I was content to live off the trust."

"But I thought you said that on the morning of his murder, you got up and went to work."

"I did. I have a friend on the Cape who makes a living clamming. I went out with him that day.

I bought some lobsters, went back to Cynthia's house, took a shower and—well, then the next morning I heard about Jack. I never had to work a steady job, not with the trust. So I did odd jobs, for friends, things I enjoyed doing. I didn't want to just sit around like some spoiled rich kid."

"If your brother had gone through with his threat to cut you out of the trust's proceeds, your lifestyle would have changed dramatically."

"Yeah, I guess it would have."

"Billy, I know I have to leave. Before I do, can you think of anyone who might have hated your brother enough to kill him?"

"No. I mean, he wasn't the nicest guy in the world. Like any businessman, he struck hard deals and made enemies. But—"

"Other members of your family? You said some of them didn't approve of how Jack handled the company's funds."

"Nobody in the family would get that mad at him. Had to be somebody outside the family, somebody who got screwed by Jack in a business deal."

"Any suggestions? Did he owe people money?"

"No. People owed *him* money. It was like a hobby with Jack, lending money to people at big interest rates."

"You make him sound like a loan shark."

"He was, like Gina Simone was a prostitute. Not literally in either case, but doing basically the same thing."

"Who owed Jack money?"

"I don't know. As I said, Mrs. Fletcher, Jack didn't discuss details with me. But he'd brag when he'd make a score, either gambling or lending money. I remember once he laughed and said he had somebody by the—had them in a tough position because he'd loaned money to them."

"But he didn't say who it was."

"No. I think he called him the tweezer guy."

"The tweezer guy?"

"Yeah, whatever that means. Jack always talked that way. The car guy. The bank guy. The meat guy. The tweezer guy."

The door opened.

"I'm leaving," I told the guard. "Billy, before I go, do you know anyone who had a specific, obvious reason for killing your brother?"

"No. But I bet whoever killed him killed Cynthia."

"Anything to back that up?" I asked.

"Makes sense, doesn't it? I mean, they were killed the same way, knife to the chest and all. And she was going to testify that I was with her the night Jack was killed. Whoever killed Jack wants me convicted of the crime so he can go free."

"I suppose it does make sense. Well, I have to leave." I stood and shook his hand. "Thanks for sharing these things with me," I said. "And don't lose faith."

Chapter Twenty-four

". . . and so, Mr. Parker, you say that the district attorney, Ms. James, is confident that with the letter from Cynthia Warren introduced into evidence, Billy Brannigan's conviction is a sure thing."

I asked the question in the spacious, muted splendor of Jasper's, where we'd feasted on grilled lobster sausage, pork and clams *Alentejo* (with garlic and tomatoes), Maine rock crab cakes, and a grilled duck salad with papaya and spiced pecans.

"Yes," he replied. "In her usual arrogant way, Whitney thinks she can't lose. And in convicting Billy Brannigan, she launches herself into higher office, attorney general, perhaps even governor."

"An ambitious lady," Seth offered, finishing his dessert.

Parker laughed. " 'Ambitious' is too mild, Dr. Hazlitt. Whitney James will stop at nothing to rise above her level of incompetence." He chuckled.

"Seems to me you don't like the lady much,"

Seth said, removing his linen napkin from where he'd tucked it into his shirt collar, and wiping his mouth.

"Another understatement," said Parker.

It had been a pleasant dinner. Warren Parker was a man with a sizable ego and sneering charm, yet he seemed to know when to defer to Seth or myself, when to lecture and when to listen. I was surprised at Seth's acceptance of our host. Usually, the good doctor from Cabot Cove was quick to let people like Parker know what he thought of them. But he was on his best behavior this night, and went along with the conversation without challenging him.

"You'll excuse me," Seth said. "Nature calls."

The moment he left the table, Parker placed his hand on mine and said, "Your friend seems tired, Jessica. How about dropping him at the Ritz, and you and I continuing the evening in more intimate surroundings?"

I slid my hand from beneath his and laughed. "I think you're mistaken," I said, "in judging who's the tired one. As lovely as this evening has been, I'm the one who needs to go straight to bed."

I knew the moment I said it that he would turn it into a double entendre. He sought my hand again and smiled.

"I'm tired, Warren, and—"

"I think we should have a talk, Jessica. Just the two of us."

"Oh?"

"You might have gathered that Whitney James and I have had a close relationship in the past."

"I assumed that."

"And that I enjoy a certain status in the community. I know many important people, Jessica, who confide in me."

"I don't doubt that."

"Truth is, Jessica, I can hand you and Malcolm McLoon what you need to ensure Brannigan's acquittal."

I sat up straight and stared at him. "I'm not quite sure I understand," I said.

"You will once we shuck your friend for the evening and head for a quiet, private spot where I can explain."

"I'm sorry, Mr. Parker, but—"

"It's Warren. Remember?"

"Don't spoil an otherwise nice evening," I said. "If you have something that would clear Billy Brannigan, you have a legal and moral obligation to come forward with it, publicly and openly. No need for a quiet, private spot."

He sat back, his expression exaggerated shock. "Are you suggesting that I'm not a good citizen, Jessica?"

"I'm suggesting that—"

Seth returned to the table. "Did I miss anything?" he asked.

"Yes," I said.

"What was it I missed?"

I looked Warren Parker in the eye and said,

"Mr. Parker—Warren—knows something that will help free Billy Brannigan."

Parker's eyes narrowed, and his mouth formed a straight line.

"Isn't that true, Warren?"

His smile returned. "Your friend here drives a hard bargain," he said.

Seth smiled, too. "She always has. Beneath that pleasant exterior is a woman made of steel. What is it you know, Warren, that would help Mr. Brannigan?"

I read Parker's face. He knew I'd put him in an awkward spot, and was trying to decide how to slip out of it smoothly, and without loss of face. He examined his fingernails for a moment before saying, "It's hardly the sort of thing to be discussed in so public a place. But I will tell you this, Jessica. The rape charge brought against your client was false."

"Gina Simone lied?"

"Oh, yes."

"That's hardly a revelation," I said. "She withdrew the charge, ostensibly because she didn't want to go through the rigors of a trial. I've always wondered whether she withdrew because she knew she was lying, and was afraid someone could prove it."

Parker's smile was smug as he said, "And you are looking at that person," he said.

"That's interesting, Warren. Perhaps you'd like to elaborate."

"Oh, I would very much. But at another time. Free for lunch tomorrow?"

"No."

"Pity. Well, time to call it a night. I've thoroughly enjoyed the evening, Jessica. Seth."

"Fine meal," Seth said. "Sure I can't help with the bill?"

"Absolutely not. My treat. We'll do it again another time. In the meantime, Jessica, you might think about who benefited most from having Billy Brannigan charged with rape."

I said it instantly: "His brother, Jack, of course. Billy's share of the trust would go to him."

Parker laughed. "You're as astute in person as you are in your books."

"Are you saying Jack Brannigan *arranged* for Gina Simone to claim Billy attempted to rape her?"

"Give me a call when you're free," Parker said, handing me his business card. "Safe home. Good night, Doctor. Always a pleasure to be with a physician when you don't need one. By the way, that's a striking tie. Italian?"

"Filene's Basement."

"Ah, yes. Filene's. Excuse me. I see someone I've been trying to catch up with all week." He joined another table.

It wasn't until we were in the Ritz-Carlton lobby that Seth brought up the conversation between Parker and me. "What was that all about?" he asked.

"The Brannigan trial," I replied.

"I gathered that," he said as we waited for the elevator. "Sounded to me like Parker was sayin' that your client's brother deliberately set him up."

"That's exactly what he was saying."

"Not a very brotherly thing to do."

"No, it's not. Nightcap in my suite?"

"Only if you'll fill me in a little about what's goin' on here. I've been following the trial on Court TV, know pretty much the basic story. But it looks like there's more than us television spectators are aware of."

"You are absolutely right, Seth. Come on. The mini-bar is always open to a visitor from Cabot Cove. And I need some good, old-fashioned, hardheaded Maine wisdom."

Chapter Twenty-five

Spending an hour with Seth in my suite was therapeutic.

I suppose I shared more with him than I should have, considering Malcolm's admonition to me to keep it strictly between us. But I'd reached the point of needing feedback. Besides, if there's anyone in the world I trust to keep confidences, it's Seth Hazlitt. In all the years we've been friends, I've never known him to betray anyone, especially me.

I didn't blame Malcolm for not having the time to fully discuss what I'd learned, or the ramifications of it. He was up to his neck in a trial that had started out promising for the defense, but had turned problematic.

I told Seth everything. I showed him the notes I'd made, and recounted my jailhouse visit to Billy Brannigan, including Billy's offhand comment that his brother, Jack, had loaned a large sum of money to "the tweezer guy," undoubtedly Harry LeClaire.

And now, according to Warren Parker, Jack Brannigan had arranged for Gina Simone's charge of rape against Billy in order to receive Billy's share of the trust set up by their father. I tended to believe Parker, even though it was obvious he was playing out some sort of vindictive behavior where DA Whitney James was concerned. Helping acquit Billy Brannigan would go a long way to satisfying that need for revenge.

"How do you think Jack Brannigan might have arranged with Gina Simone to bring a false charge?" I asked.

"Paid her." Seth seldom used more words than necessary to make his point.

"Which meant Jack Brannigan knew Gina well enough to offer her money," I said.

Seth finished a brandy he'd poured and placed the small snifter on the coffee table. "Not necessarily," he said. "Allow me to create a scenario?"

"Sure. I've run out of them."

"Let's say, Jessica, that this LeClaire fella, this 'tweezer guy,' couldn't pay Jack Brannigan the money he owed him."

"All right."

"And let's say Jack Brannigan offered him a way out."

"Yes?"

"Let's say Jack Brannigan suggested that if LeClaire could arrange for someone to charge Billy with rape, he'd forgive the debt LaClaire owed him."

"I buy that. Go on."

"You say LeClaire knew both Ms. Warren and Ms. Simone. He could have paid Ms. Simone—"

"But he paid Cynthia Warren," I interrupted.

"Perhaps she was supposed to share the money with her friend, Ms. Simone."

"Possible. That would mean Ms. Warren sold her boyfriend, Billy, down the river."

"From what you told me about Ms. Warren and her past, it wouldn't come as a shock. Billy told you that she and her friend, Ms. Simone, were sort of party girls."

"Yes, he did."

"Then again, Ms. Warren might have been paid for something entirely different."

"To deny she was with Billy the night of Jack's murder," I said.

"Could be."

"But who would have murdered Cynthia?"

"Could have been LeClaire to keep her quiet. Could have been Ms. Simone—to keep her quiet. Then again, it could have been someone not connected with the trial."

"I don't believe that," I said.

Seth stood and stretched. "Ayuh," he said. "You're probably right. Time for me to get to bed, Jessica. Shopping for clothes always tuckers me out."

I walked him to the door. "Your tie was a hit," I said.

"Thanks to you. Breakfast?"

"Sure. Seven-thirty downstairs?"

"I'll be there. We can continue this discussion over ham and eggs."

"Would you like to attend the trial today?" I asked Seth at breakfast.

"Ayuh," he replied, using that familiar Maine expression that means, generally, yes. "Can you arrange it?"

"I think so. Crowds have been big, but the prosecution and defense each have a number of seats assigned to them. I'll call right now."

We arrived at the courthouse a little before nine. Seth took a seat in the spectator section, and I joined Malcolm, Rachel, Georgia, and Jill Farkas at the defense table. Jill was surprisingly pleasant this particular morning. As we awaited Judge Wilson's arrival, she said, "Your doctor friend is charming, Jessica. And handsome, I might add."

"Yes, he is."

"Is he married?"

"Is he? No, he's not."

"Hmmm. Would you mind if I asked him for dinner tonight?"

"No. Why would I mind?"

"I just thought you and he might be—"

"Seth and I are good, old friends. If he wants to have dinner with you, then he should."

She squeezed my arm. "Thanks," she said. "You're terrific."

I was spared the need to reply when Judge Wilson entered the courtroom. We all stood until he'd taken his seat behind the bench, rapped his gavel, and announced that The People of Massachusetts versus William Brannigan was in session. I glanced over at Billy, who sat placidly—no, numb was a better description. I realized as I looked at him that I couldn't imagine anything worse than being locked up in jail, especially for a crime you hadn't committed. I shuddered at the thought, and wrapped my arms about myself. It was warm in the courtroom that morning, but I was chilled from within.

District Attorney Whitney James continued presenting the prosecution's case. I did what I'd previously done when in the courtroom, analyzed the reactions of each juror, and made notes of my observations.

Naturally, I spent a great deal of time looking at "the tweezer guy," Harry LeClaire, and the potter, Thomas McEnroe.

LeClaire was a handsome man in a smarmy way, thick-lipped and with a full head of black hair that had begun to show gray at the temples. He seemed to be bored most of the time.

Thom McEnroe was a different type, youthful and with an open and expressive face.

I also paid particular attention to Juror Number Ten, the African-American chef, Karl Jerome, who Jill had identified as the most likely of the twelve jurors to acquit Billy. His reactions to Whitney

James's presentation of witnesses, and Malcolm's cross-examination of them, did nothing to change that opinion for me. He paid keen attention to everything going on, and took more notes than any of the others.

But while it was comforting to have such a juror, it caused a parallel dread in me. What if my speculation was correct, that Juror Number Seven, Marie Montrone, had been run down because she seemed to be leaning in favor of acquittal? If so, did that place Juror Number Ten, Karl Jerome, in harm's way?

Seth declined to join us for lunch because he wanted to do some research at Harvard's medical library. "Might as well take advantage of that library while I'm here," he told me. "Are we havin' dinner together?"

I smiled, said, "That depends upon whether you're having dinner with Jill Farkas."

He gave me a puzzled look. "Jill Farkas? Oh, the jury selection lady. Didn't realize that was an option."

I started to explain when Jill came up to us. "Good morning, Dr. Hazlitt," she said, flashing a wide smile. "How nice to see you again."

"Likewise," he said.

"Jessica is tied up this evening, I believe, and I wondered if you'd like to have dinner together?"

Seth looked at me. "You're tied up?"

Jill didn't allow me to reply. She said quickly to Seth, "I have a favorite restaurant in Boston that very few people know about. I'd love for you to be my guest tonight."

"Well, I—"

"I think it's a wonderful idea, Seth," I said. "If it turns out to be as good as Jill claims, you can take me there another night."

"As long as you're not available this evening, Jessica, I think I might enjoy exploring this special restaurant."

"Splendid," said Jill. "You're staying at the Ritz?"

"Ayuh."

"I'll pick you up there at seven. Have to run an errand before the afternoon session. Bye."

"Charming lady," Seth said, standing a little straighter and adjusting the knot of his tie.

"A very nice person. Now you go on to your library. I have an errand to run, too."

"What are you tied up with tonight, Jessica?"

"Oh, nothing you'd be interested in. Call me when you get back from dinner. I'm dying to hear your reaction to this secret little restaurant—*and* to your evening with Ms. Farkas."

The Cynthia Warren letter was introduced into evidence that afternoon by the district attorney. The jurors read it carefully as it was passed among them. I noticed that Karl Jerome, Juror Number Ten, screwed up his face into a skeptical expression as he read it. He was holding true to form. He didn't buy it. And neither did I.

The DA put on as a witness the police depart-

ment handwriting expert, who testified that based
upon a comparison with samples of Cynthia Warren's signature on other documents, it was her
hand that signed the letter. Malcolm cross-exam-
ined him at length, with little impact. The expert
was a good witness, sure of himself and never
waivering from his opinion. Malcolm, I was told,
had arranged for another independent expert to
examine the letter that evening. If he disagreed
with the police witness, he would be put on early
in the defense case as a rebuttal witness.

The defense team had a brief meeting at the
end of the day to assess how things had gone.
Malcolm tried to put a positive spin on everything,
but he wasn't convincing. Because I was free for
the evening, I would have been hard-pressed to
decline a dinner invitation from him. But he
didn't offer one. "See everyone in the morning,"
he said, and lumbered from the conference room.

We all went our separate ways after the meeting. Once back in my suite, I began to wish I had
made dinner plans with someone. I was uncharac-
teristically restless, and decided to head for Cambridge, my favorite area of Boston in which to
take a walk and soak in the atmosphere.

After walking for an hour in Harvard Square
and enjoying its vibrant mix of students, professo-
rial types, foreigners, panhandlers, and protestors,
I took a table on Cafe Pamplona's outdoor terrace
and ordered a shrimp cocktail and a glass of spar-
kling water. It became crowded; people waited for

tables on the terrace. I paid my check and continued walking until I found myself standing in front
of Grendel's Den, the restaurant where Juror
Number Ten, Karl Jerome, worked as a chef. I
looked through the window into a large, wood
paneled room with a high ceiling. It was doing a
brisk business, mostly students occupying every
table. I glanced at a menu hanging outside. Cheap
eats, I thought, including an all-you-can-eat salad
bar. No wonder Grendel's Den was popular with
a young crowd. The salad bar alone had probably
sustained more than one student through a
semester.

I wondered if Mr. Jerome worked the night shift
after returning from his day as a juror, and peered
through the glass in search of him. Unlikely, I
told myself, that he would be in the dining area.
He was a chef, which meant being in the kitchen.

As I stood there on the busy sidewalk, I ration-
alized that ending up at Karl Jerome's place of
work had been an accident. I just happened to
be there.

But I knew that wasn't true. When I decided to
take my evening walk in Cambridge, he was very
much on my mind. So was Cynthia Warren, and
Marie Montrone. Two people connected with the
Billy Brannigan trial were dead, one the victim of
a brutal stabbing, the other run down on the sidewalk in front of her home.

The question was whether my supposition—
that Ms. Montrone was killed because she ap-

peared to be leaning toward an acquittal—was valid. I was, after all, a writer of murder mysteries, which called for a certain vivid imagination. Was I injecting that imagination into the reality of Juror Number Seven's death?

Possibly.

Then again—

I stepped into Grendel's Den and went to the salad bar from where I could see into the busy kitchen. My sight line kept being obscured by the swinging doors, but each time they opened, I could see inside. No sign of Karl Jerome.

"Like a table, ma'am?" a young man asked me. "Should be one opening up in a minute."

"No, thank you. I was dropping something off for one of your chefs, Karl Jerome."

"Not here. He's on jury duty."

"I thought he might work nights."

"Not this week. Give it to me. I'll see that he gets it."

"Thank you, but I'll come back."

Once outside, I checked Jerome's home address from the notebook I carried in my oversized purse, then consulted my pocket map. He lived only a few blocks away, and I slowly walked in that direction. Darkness had fallen; lights came to life in shops and the area's many university buildings.

I paused at the corner. Last chance to change your mind, Jess. You've been lucky so far that no one's reported you to the court. Let it go. You're probably wrong anyway. Just a coincidence that two people so intimately associated with the Brannigan trial were dead. You're in Boston as a jury consultant, I reminded myself, not to prove a conspiracy. You came here because an old friend, attorney Malcolm McLoon, asked you to come, and because you wanted to soak up the atmosphere of a real murder trial to use in your next novel.

Give it up. Go back to your lovely hotel suite, take a Jacuzzi, read a good book and—

I stood opposite Karl Jerome's six-story apartment building, drew a deep breath, and looked up the one-way street. A car was approaching; plenty of time to make it across the street.

But as I stepped off the curb, the sudden roar of the car's engine froze me in my tracks. I turned. It was bearing down on me at racetrack speed.

I twisted and hurled myself back in the direction of the curb, landing with a thud on the pavement, my cheek making painful contact with the concrete. The car, large and dark in color—brown? black? blue?—flashed by in a blur, its left tire missing my foot by an inch.

I didn't give Karl Jerome another thought until the smiling young doctor in Harvard University Hospital's emergency room assured me my face was only scraped and bruised, nothing broken. By then, I wanted only to get back to the Ritz-Carlton, lock the door and shut the drapes against the outside world and all its potential violence. Before I could, however, the police questioned me about the incident.

I told them everything I could remember, which wasn't much. One thing I was sure of, I said. The driver of that dark car deliberately tried to run me down.

"What were you doing on that particular street, Mrs. Fletcher?" one officer asked.

"I was—just sightseeing."

"That's a residential street," he said. "Nothing touristy."

"A pretty street," I said. "I sort of wandered down it."

"You're on the Brannigan defense team," his partner said as they prepared to drive me back to the hotel.

"That's right."

"My wife's been watching the trial on Court TV."

"Oh? I'm not sure I agree with allowing television cameras into the courtroom," I said, gingerly touching fingertips to my stinging cheekbone. "But then again, there is the public's right to know what goes on in its justice system."

"Shame how that juror died," he said, holding open the rear door of the marked police car.

"Terrible," I agreed.

He and his partner got in the front seat. The engine came to life and we pulled into Boston traffic. "Yeah," the officer said, turning his head to speak directly to me. "Really strange, that juror run down like you almost were, and that alibi witness from the Cape being murdered. Then another juror getting it."

It took a moment for his words to sink in. When they did, I sprang forward and placed my hands on his shoulders. "Did you say another juror 'got it'?"

"Yes, ma'am. That's why I was interested in how come you were on that street when you were. Another juror died there tonight. A black fellow, a chef here in Cambridge. Grendel's Den. Name was Jerome. Karl Jerome. Fell off his roof just a little before you almost got run down."

"Fell—off—his—roof?"

"Or got pushed."

I slumped back in the seat and pressed my fingers to my temples. The stinging on my cheek had been replaced by a pounding, pulsating pain deep inside my head. I'd been right. It was no longer just a theory. Two members of the Billy Brannigan jury had died in less than a week.

I believe in coincidence. I think it happens more than we realize.

But there's coincidence, and then there's coincidence.

This was no coincidence.

Somebody was killing off the jurors, and it looked like only those who were sympathetic to the defense were marked for death.

Then it dawned on me that it wasn't only jurors who were in jeopardy. This jury consultant had almost become coincidence number three. No, make it four. Let's not forget Cynthia Warren.

"Could you drive a little faster," I said. "I have some very important phone calls to make."

Chapter Twenty-six

The full impact of my near brush with death didn't hit me until I was in my suite. I looked at my face in the mirror and winced at seeing the injury to my cheek, which had grown darker and angrier since leaving the hospital.

The police had asked if I wanted protection that night, but I declined their offer. The way I processed it, whoever had tried to run me over was probably the same person who'd killed Marie Montrone. If so, his, or her M.O.—*modus operandi*—was to use a vehicle as a weapon. Little chance of being run over in my suite.

My nerves were on edge, frayed, uninsulated wires crossing and sparking. I took a miniature bottle of brandy from the mini-bar and poured it into a snifter. It went down hot and hard, but immediately caused a welcome calm, a fire extinguisher for my sizzling nerve ends.

The phone rang. I picked it up and said, "Hello?"

"Mrs. Fletcher?"

"Yes. Who is this?"

"Patty Zeltner. From Fire and Ice."

"The gallery. Of course. How are you?"

"Mrs. Fletcher, I—"

"Yes?"

"Are you buying the pot? The one from the window?"

"I'd forgotten about that. Is that why you're calling?"

"Yes. Well, no. I tried to call you before. Two or three times."

I noticed for the first time that the red message light on the phone was blinking. "I'm sorry," I said. "I didn't check for messages. About the pot."

"Mrs. Fletcher, I need to talk to you."

"All right."

"Not now. Not on the phone. Can you—would you come to the gallery?"

"Now?"

"Yes. Please."

"Is this about the Brannigan trial? Cynthia Warren?"

"Yes. Could you come right away?"

"I suppose so. I've had an accident tonight, but if you give me a half hour, I can leave by then."

"An accident?"

"Minor bruises. I'll be there as soon as I can."

I checked my messages. There were the two from Patty Zeltner, one from Seth to tell me he would call when he returned from dinner with Jill Farkas, a reporter from a radio station wanting to interview me, Regina Wells of Court TV wanting the same thing, and Mort Metzger, sheriff of Cabot Cove, who complained that I hadn't returned his last message.

After applying makeup in a futile attempt to cover the spreading bruise on my cheek, and debating taking a fast Jacuzzi to ease pains that had developed in every joint and limb, I left the hotel and took a cab to Fire and Ice where Ms. Zeltner was waiting. She'd locked the door; the interior was illuminated by a single low wattage bulb in a lamp behind the counter.

She was overtly nervous as she let me in, and locked the door behind us. As we walked to the counter, the light caught the injury to my cheek. "What happened to you?" she asked.

"I was almost run over."

She gasped, pressed the knuckles of her right fist to her mouth, and grabbed the counter for support. I put my hands on her arms and helped her onto a high stool. "What's wrong, Ms. Zeltner? Are you ill?"

"No. It's just that—" Her teary eyes met mine.

"It's just that *what*, Ms. Zeltner?"

"I'm afraid I'm going to be killed, too."

"You? Why?"

She pulled herself up straight, wiped her tears with the back of a hand, and said, "Because Thom killed Cynthia Warren, and I think he'll do the same to me."

"Wait a minute," I said, sitting on a second stool behind the counter. "Run that by me again."

"Thom killed her."

"Why?"

"Because she was a bitch."

"You said that the first time I was here."

"She was going to give him the money to keep the gallery going."

"She knew him that well?"

She guffawed. "You bet she did. They were lovers. No, let me put it this way. He was one of many lovers. She was a slut."

"You say she was going to give Thom money for the gallery. That doesn't seem to be a motive for him to kill her. You don't go around killing those who are about to give you something."

"That was the problem. Cynthia reneged on the money. Without it, the gallery was going to go under."

"How much money had she promised Thom?"

"Fifty thousand dollars, I think."

"That's a lot of money. What did she expect in return?"

"Half ownership in the business."

I leaned back and thought for a moment. "Ms. Zeltner, if Cynthia had become half owner of this gallery, what would that have done to you?"

Her face turned hard. "It meant I was out. I couldn't believe Thom would do that to me. I'd put up my life savings to open the gallery."

"That must have been extremely hurtful to you," I said.

"I wanted to die."

"May I call you Patty?" I asked.

"Of course."

"Patty, if Thom is a murderer—if he has it in him to so brutally murder a young woman, no matter what the reason—do you think he might have killed Jack Brannigan, too?"

"I wouldn't know about that."

"Where is Thom tonight?" I asked.

"He's meeting with someone who might be interested in representing his work on a national basis."

"That sounds exciting. Are you sure he's with this person?"

"Yes. I called him at the man's office twice a few hours ago."

I got off the stool and walked to the gallery's front window. The street was empty. My cheek and head hurt. So did my stomach. The shrimp cocktail at Cafe Pamplona seemed years ago, and I hadn't eaten since. Some people can't eat under stress. I'm not one of them.

I turned and faced her. She was still sitting on the stool. "Patty," I said, "you must go to the police with this information."

"I can't. If Thom found out, he'd—"

"What would it matter what he thinks? You're afraid he's out to kill you now. The police can protect you until this is sorted out."

She lowered her head; I assumed she was thinking. I didn't intrude. Eventually, she looked up and said, "I'm willing to tell the police what I know."

"Good," I said. "Here's what I suggest. Come back to my hotel with me. I can arrange for a room there, or you can stay in my suite. I'll call Malcolm McLoon, the attorney, and get his advice about how to proceed."

"All right." She sounded defeated, out of energy and air. She slipped on a green raincoat, turned off the lamp, locked the door, and walked with me to a busier corner where we found a cab.

As we rode back to the Ritz, I was consumed with sympathy for her, and concern for her safety. If what she'd told me was true, the seemingly mild-mannered and creative Thomas McEnroe had within him the capacity to wantonly kill.

"You're a very kind person," she said after we'd settled into the suite, and I was about to call Malcolm.

"Thank you," I said.

"Would you mind if I made myself a drink from the mini-bar?"

"No, of course not."

"This is a beautiful suite," she said, removing two miniature bottles of vodka from the bar and pouring them into a glass. She also took a bag of peanuts, and potato chips. The transformation in her was marked. She was no longer the frightened, vulnerable woman she'd been at the gallery.

She looked calm, contented, even smug. She smiled and raised her glass to me in a toast.

"I'll try to reach Malcolm," I said, sitting in an easy chair next to a phone in the living room.

I reached for the phone, but it rang before I had a chance to pick it up. I quickly lifted the receiver.

"Hello," I said.

"Jessica? It's Seth."

"Where are you?" I asked.

"In my room. I thought we could meet up at the bar for a nightcap."

"I have a better idea," I said, taking a deep breath and checking Ms. Zeltner again. "Let's have a nightcap here, in my suite."

"But I thought it might be nice to—"

"Please, Seth. Come now."

Chapter Twenty-seven

Seth arrived within minutes.

"Gorry, Jess, what happened to your face?" he asked the minute he stepped into the suite.

"A long story, Seth. Wait for the others to arrive so I don't have to repeat it."

I introduced him to Patty Zeltner, whose previous calm had disappeared at having this stranger enter the picture. But after I explained who Seth was, and he'd chatted pleasantly with her for a few minutes, she visibly relaxed again, enough to make herself another drink from the last miniature bottle of vodka.

"You say you reached McLoon at home," Seth said.

"Yes. He's on his way. I think he's bringing some others from the defense team with him."

"What's all this about, Jessica?"

"Again, let's wait for the others. Tell me about dinner with Jill Farkas."

"Charming lady. Extremely intelligent. Pretty, too, wouldn't you say?"

"Oh, yes. Very pretty. Was it a nice restaurant?"

"Ayuh. Unusual. We started with—"

"Would you like me to go into the next room?" Patty asked.

"No need," I said. "Just personal gossip."

The desk called to say Mr. McLoon and two others were there to see me.

"Send them up," I said.

Malcolm, Georgia Bobley, and Rachel Cohen came in together. "Ritchie will be along shortly," Malcolm said. "Now, why are we here?"

"You remember Dr. Hazlitt," I said.

"Certainly do. How are you this fine evening, Doctor?"

"Just fine, Mr. McLoon. And you?"

"Curious," Malcolm replied.

"Jessica!" Rachel said. "What happened to your face?"

"Looks like it's storytelling time." They listened with shock and horror to the play-by-play of my near miss on the streets of Cambridge. Patty Zeltner sat quietly in a corner, her drink in hand. When I'd finished, all eyes went to her. I introduced her, and after cursory greetings were exchanged, I launched into what she'd told me at the gallery, and why I'd brought her to the hotel.

As Malcolm began questioning her, he became the trial attorney, the suite his courtroom. He started gently, and supportively. But then his questions sharpened, challenging much of what she said.

"I told Ms. Zeltner she should go to the police with this," I said during a break in Malcolm's unofficial cross-examination.

"No," he responded, shaking his large head and slowly pacing the room. "Not the police."

"Judge Wilson?" Rachel Cohen asked.

"Yes. But first I want to speak with our distinguished district attorney, Ms. James. I'm not quite sure how to approach her, but I'll have a strategy by morning."

"And what do I do?" Patty Zeltner asked.

"You just sit tight, little lady," Malcolm said. "Is she staying here with you tonight, Jessica?"

"I suppose so. I thought I might see if the hotel has a vacancy." I smiled at Patty: "I'm sure you'd prefer your own private space."

Malcolm indicated he wanted to speak privately, and ushered me into the bedroom.

"Yes?" I asked once the door was closed.

"I'd rather she stay here," he said. "If her story holds up, this case is over and Billy Brannigan's a free man. I don't want happening to her what happened to Cynthia Warren."

"I understand," I said. "The only problem is that she sets me on edge."

"How so?"

"I don't know, her manner, personality, things she said."

"You're afraid of her, aren't you?"

"To be honest? Yes."

"Why? She says her boyfriend and partner did the killing. Not her."

"As I said, Malcolm, there's something about her. One minute she's a frightened and frail butterfly. The next minute she's calm, cool, and collected, and drinking vodka from my mini-bar."

He laughed. "You just don't want to pay for her drinks."

"You know me better than that."

"Why not have your fat physician friend, Hazlitt, stay with you?"

"Fat physician—?"

"Every other fat person is fat to me, Jessica. I'm a large man."

"Oh."

"Ritchie will be here any moment. He carries."

"A gun?"

"Yes. A perk of being a private investigator. I'll tell him to bunk in with you, sleep on the couch. Hell, he can sleep on the floor."

"No, Malcolm."

"Why not?"

"Because I wanted Ritchie to spend the night checking on a few things for me."

"What sort of things?"

"Just to put my mind at rest. I also have an assignment for Georgia, if it's all right with you. Nothing for you to be concerned about. You have enough on your mind. Based upon what you've learned here tonight, what do you intend to do besides approaching Ms. James?"

"Depends on how she reacts. I know this, Jessica. There won't be a court session tomorrow, unless it involves your Ms. Zeltner, and anybody else you come up with to support her story."

"Don't count on that."

"The way you've been going, I wouldn't be surprised if you walked into Wilson's chambers tomorrow with Jack Brannigan's murderer by one ear, Cynthia Warren's murderer by another, and whoever killed our two alternate jurors dragged behind you in chains."

"Maybe we should get back to the others," I said.

"Probably so."

"Malcolm."

"Yes?"

"Would it be possible to have an all-points bulletin put out on Gina Simone?"

"Why?"

"Because I think she's a crucial link to Jack Brannigan's murder. She's in Fort Lauderdale."

"I can call the DA's office and request she be brought back as a material witness. But I'll have to give a credible reason for a judge to get up in the middle of the night to issue a warrant."

"Motive. And opportunity."

"Are you saying Gina Simone killed Jack Brannigan?"

"I'm saying she had the motive, and the opportunity."

"What was her motive?"

"Money."

"How do you know that?"

"Because I've been following it."

"Following what?"

"The money trail. Let's get back. And don't worry about me. I'll take your advice and have Dr. Hazlitt keep an eye on us tonight. So? Can I use Ritchie and Georgia tonight to look into a few things for me?"

"They're at your disposal, Jessica. We all are."

Chapter Twenty-eight

We met in Judge Walter Wilson's chambers at four the next afternoon. Because there were so many of us, one of the judge's clerks had to bring in additional chairs.

Present from the prosecution were District Attorney Whitney James and her assistant, Cliff Cecil.

The defense was represented by Malcolm McLoon, Rachel Cohen, Georgia Bobley, Jill Farkas, and me.

The two alternate jurors, Harry LeClaire and Thomas McEnroe, were there.

So was the accused, Billy Brannigan.

Judge Wilson entered the room and took his seat behind his large desk without as much as a nod at any of us. His face was grim, angry, serious. He glanced at the contents of a folder on the desk, looked up, and said, "In all my years as a prosecutor, and as a judge, I have never seen such a serious breach of the law as represented by the two jurors seated before me today."

He glared at LeClaire and McEnroe.

"Your Honor, I want a lawyer," LeClaire said.

"Yes, Mr. LeClaire, I would think you would. Both you and Mr. McEnroe lied to this court when you claimed to have no connection with any figure in this case."

LeClaire started to speak but Wilson cut him off.

"You, Mr. LeClaire, had borrowed large sums of money from the victim in this case, Jack Brannigan. You were intimately involved with who was to be a prime witness, Cynthia Warren, who was murdered. You were also intimately involved with her friend, a Miss Gina Simone, who had accused the defendant of having attempted to rape her, thus setting up what the prosecution proffered as the motive for the crime. You, sir—and I use that term very loosely—are a disgrace to the American system of jurisprudence!"

"I want a lawyer," LeClaire repeated.

Wilson ignored him. "And you, Mr. McEnroe, are no better. You intimately knew Ms. Warren, who was to be a witness in this case." The judge glanced down at his notes. "And according to information I've received as recently as early this morning—*very* early this morning—there is the strong possibility that you were responsible for Cynthia Warren's death."

McEnroe focused on his shoetops. When he looked up, he said in a soft voice, "That's not true, Your Honor. Who's accusing me of that. Patty?"

Malcolm stood. "Your Honor, this might be a good time to bring in Ms. Zeltner."

He'd no sooner said it than one of Judge Wilson's clerks opened the door to allow Ritchie Fleigler to enter. Malcolm quickly said, "Your Honor, this is my investigator, Mr. Fleigler. Excuse the interruption."

Ritchie sat between Malcolm and me.

"Well?" I whispered to him.

"She's back," he whispered in response.

"The other thing?"

"Bingo." He placed two rental car receipts on top of a one-page report Georgia Bobley had handed me before the judge's arrival.

I suppressed a smile because it would have been the only smile in the room.

"May we bring Ms. Zeltner in?" Malcolm asked.

"Yes," the judge growled.

Patty was escorted into the chambers and asked to sit in a chair in front of the judge. She was back in her nervous mode.

"Good afternoon, Ms. Zeltner," Wilson said icily.

"Hello," she said in a barely audible voice.

Wilson looked at Malcolm. "Care to explain this woman's relation to the Brannigan case, counselor?"

"No, Your Honor. I think Mrs. Fletcher is the one to do that."

I looked at Malcolm with wide eyes. I hadn't

expected this. I'd filled him in on everything I knew.

"Why?" the judge asked.

"Because she's the person who brought all this to light, Your Honor. She knows the details better than anyone, including me."

Judge Wilson looked at me and said, "Mrs. Fletcher, I'm anxious to hear what you have to say."

"I'd like this on the record, Judge," DA James said.

"Denied. I want to hear what's going on off the record before I decide how to proceed. Mrs. Fletcher."

I drew a deep breath, stood, and rested my hands on the table. "Your Honor, I am obviously not an attorney. I write books for a living."

"I'm well aware of that, Mrs. Fletcher. And very good ones, I might add."

"Thank you. Your Honor, Ms. Zeltner contacted me because she was frightened for her life. She told me that she was convinced that Mr. McEnroe here, her partner in their art gallery, had murdered Cynthia Warren. Mr. McEnroe had been one of Ms. Warren's many lovers, and she'd promised to invest a considerable sum of money in the gallery in order to force Ms. Zeltner out, and to become Mr. McEnroe's partner."

Thom McEnroe turned in his chair and stared at Patty. "Are you crazy?" he said.

She avoided his eyes.

"Go on, Mrs. Fletcher," the judge said. "You're doing fine, considering you're not a lawyer. Maybe *because* you're not a lawyer. Continue."

Malcolm grunted.

"I would like to ask Mr. Warren Parker to be present," I said.

"Warren Parker?" Judge Wilson said, his tone indicating he knew who he was. I looked to Whitney James, who appeared to be surprised, and uncomfortable. "For what purpose, Mrs. Fletcher?"

"Your Honor, I insist upon being represented by my lawyer," Harry LeClaire said.

"You'll have plenty of time for that, Mr. LeClaire. You aren't being asked to testify here this afternoon, to say anything. When you and Mr. McEnroe are charged with having lied to this court during voir dire, you can have all the lawyers you want. For now, be quiet. You might learn what your attorneys will face on your behalf."

"Your Honor," I said, "Mr. Warren Parker has evidence vital to this case, and we contend that this evidence will prove our defendant, Mr. William Brannigan, to be innocent." I couldn't believe I was saying such things as "we contend," and, "our defendant" with such ease in front of the judge. I glanced at Rachel Cohen, who smiled and gave me a little thumbs-up.

Warren Parker greeted Judge Wilson with a big smile, and did the same to District Attorney Whitney James, who turned away. Parker was the picture of a man at ease. He sat next to Patty Zeltner, crossed one leg over the other, ran his fingers along the razor crease of the top pant leg, and said, "Lovely room."

"Mr. Parker," Wilson said, "Mrs. Fletcher has asked that you be present during this hearing."

Whitney James stood. "Your Honor, that is exactly the point. This is a hearing, and should be on the record."

"I disagree, Ms. James. Go on, Mrs. Fletcher."

"Mr. Parker, did you tell me that a woman named Gina Simone lied in her claim that Billy Brannigan attempted to rape her?"

"Yes, I did."

"And did you tell our investigator last night that Ms. Simone had been paid to make that false charge?"

"Right again."

"You're sure of that?"

"Positive. Ms. Simone and I have been—" He flashed his dazzling smile again. "Let's just say that Ms. Simone and I have shared occasional pillow talk."

"And what was said on that pillow, Mr. Parker?" I asked.

"She admitted to me that she'd been paid to come up with the false charge against Billy Brannigan."

"And did she say *who* paid her?"

"Yes."

"And?"

"She was paid by this gentleman here." He turned and looked at Harry LeClaire.

LeClaire said nothing. No call for an attorney, no protest of any kind.

"True, Mr. LeClaire?" Judge Wilson asked.

"Yes. I paid Gina to claim Brannigan tried to rape her. But it wasn't my money."

"Whose money was it?" I asked.

"His brother, Jack."

There was silence until Billy Brannigan stood. "My own brother arranged that?"

"You bet he did," said LeClaire.

"Why?" Billy asked.

"To get ahold of your share of the trust. Your brother was broke. He owed money to everybody."

"Sit down, Mr. Brannigan," Judge Wilson said. Billy took his seat.

I said, "But you owed *him* money, Mr. LeClaire."

"That's right. He told me that if I could get somebody to claim Billy had tried to rape her, he'd write off my debt to him. What he stood to make from the trust was a hell of a lot more than what I owed him."

District Attorney James stood. "Your Honor, the issue of the rape charge against the defendant is irrelevant. What is at issue is the *murder* of Jack Brannigan."

"And Cynthia Warren," I said. "And Juror Number Seven, Marie Montrone, and Juror Number Ten, Karl Jerome. They are inextricably linked."

"I'm going to let you continue, Mrs. Fletcher," Wilson said, "because I find what you've brought out so far to be compelling. Based upon Mr. LeClaire's admission, a charge of attempted rape against the defendant has been debunked."

"Just remember, Judge," LeClaire said, "that it was Jack Brannigan's idea, and money, to phoney up the charge against his own brother. Not me. All I did was ask Cynthia whether she could get Gina to make the charge and—" He stopped abruptly when he realized he'd mentioned Cynthia Warren.

"What's next, Mrs. Fletcher?" Judge Wilson asked.

"Gina Simone, Your Honor. She was returned from Florida today, based upon the warrant you so graciously granted Mr. McLoon in the early hours of this morning. I must say the law enforcement authorities did a remarkable job. She was located almost immediately by the Florida police and put on a plane."

"Mr. McLoon was impressively persuasive this morning," Wilson said. "And I was tired, having been awakened at such an ungodly hour." To his clerk: "Bring in Ms. Simone."

Gina Simone looked exactly as she should have looked. Her beautiful face was drawn from fatigue. Her hair reflected a night without sleep, and a long plane ride. Her overriding expression was one of sadness. I felt sorry for her. On the other hand—

"Please take a seat, Ms. Simone," Judge Wilson said.

She sat next to Warren Parker, hands folded in her lap, eyes focused on the floor.

"Mrs. Fletcher," Wilson said.

"Hello again, Ms. Simone," I said.

She looked at me; tears began to roll down her cheeks.

I took in Malcolm, Rachel, Georgia, Jill, and Ritchie before saying to Harry LeClaire, "I have a special interest in you, Mr. LeClaire, because I was almost run down last night, the way juror Marie Montrone was."

LeClaire looked at Gina Simone, who was now sobbing.

"You became a juror, Mr. LeClaire, because you were determined to see Billy Brannigan found guilty of his brother's murder."

LeClaire said, "I don't have to sit here and listen to this. I want my attorney present now."

The judge ignored him and instructed me to continue. I picked up the two rental car receipts. "Your Honor, may I give these to you?" He nodded and I handed them to him. "Mr. LeClaire drives a very nice automobile, Your Honor. A black Cadillac of recent vintage, to be precise."

"So what?" LeClaire said.

"Despite owning such a vehicle," I said, "he found it necessary to rent a less expensive and very basic car on the night Juror Number Seven was run down, and last night, when I almost suffered the same fate."

Judge Wilson tossed the receipts on his desk and looked at Harry LeClaire. "Anything to say, Mr. LeClaire?" he asked.

Malcolm couldn't contain himself. He stood and said in his usual stentorian voice, "The only motive Mr. LeClaire would have, Your Honor, to rent these cars, was to kill off members of the regular jury so that he might be seated, and see that my client, William Brannigan, was convicted. And *that*, Your Honor, was because *he* killed Jack Brannigan."

LeClaire got to his feet and started for the door. But then I said, "Mr. LeClaire did *not* kill Jack Brannigan." He stopped, turned, and stared at me.

"I think Mr. LeClaire did what he did—take advantage of being called for jury duty for the Brannigan trial—in order to help Ms. Simone. He killed Marie Montrone and Karl Jerome because they were leaning toward acquittal in this case."

Before LeClaire could again attempt to leave, Judge Wilson said to two bailiffs flanking the door, "Detain him."

He said to District Attorney James: "I want you to prepare charges against Mr. LeClaire—and against you, Mr. McEnroe—for perjury. I'm sure there will be additional charges in the near future."

LeClaire exploded with mock indignation. "This is outrageous," he shouted. "I'll sue you and everybody else in this room for defamation. For libel. For false arrest."

"Stop it, Harry," Gina Simone said, standing.

All eyes went to her.

"Everything you say is true," she said to me. "Jack Brannigan paid to have me lie about Billy. Cynthia asked me to do it, and we agreed to split the money. Ten thousand dollars. Harry gave Cynthia the money."

"Ms. Simone," I said, "why did you kill Jack Brannigan? You were paid. What had Jack Brannigan done to you to deserve being murdered?"

"He tried to blackmail me."

"*He* tried to blackmail *you*?" I said, not able to keep the tone of incredulity from my voice.

"Jack Brannigan was a bastard. He promised to share Billy's trust money with me. He lied. He tried to get me to give my body to men he owed money to. I refused. That's when he threatened to leak to the police that I'd lied about Billy—and that I"—she gulped to hold back another bout of crying—"that I've done other things I'm not very proud of."

"Why don't you shut up, Gina," Harry LeClaire said.

"I have nothing else to say. I killed Jack Brannigan. What else *is* there to say?"

"You'd better get some officers up here, Ms. James."

"Of course, Your Honor," she said, instructing her assistant to follow Wilson's order.

Minutes later, Harry LeClaire and Gina Simone were led from Judge Wilson's chambers.

"Mr. McEnroe," the judge said, "your partner and I assume someone with a personal relationship with you has accused you of having murdered Cynthia Warren. You have no obligation to respond to me in this setting, and you are legally entitled to be represented by counsel."

McEnroe turned to Patty and said, "How could you say that about me, that I killed Cynthia?"

"Isn't it true?" she replied. She had that smug, contented expression again.

"No, it's not, and you know it. All you are, Patty, is an angry woman. What's the saying? 'Hell has no wrath like a woman spurned'? Sure, Cynthia and I had an affair. And Cynthia was going to put up money for the gallery. Since this seems to be true confession time, I admit that I persuaded Cynthia to write the letter about Billy Brannigan. He wasn't with her the night his brother was murdered. Cynthia only agreed to testify—to lie for Billy—because she was afraid of him. She confided that in me, and I urged her not to lie for him, not lie for anyone."

"Hold on a second," Judge Wilson said. "If Ms. Zeltner's charge is accurate, that Mr. McEnroe murdered Ms. Warren, that can be investigated by the proper authorities. In the meantime, Mr. McEnroe, you'll be charged with perjury for your statements during jury selection."

"Before you leave, Mr. McEnroe, why did you lie to get on the jury?" I asked.

"To try and make sure that Billy Brannigan was found guilty. Just like LeClaire, except for different reasons. I was sure he'd killed his brother, based upon Cynthia telling me that Billy was lying about having been with her that night. I didn't want to see him get off and hurt her." He looked squarely into Patty Zeltner's eyes. "I loved Cynthia, Patty. I loved her more than I ever loved you."

Patty went for his face with nails like talons, but Warren Parker grabbed her from behind and held her until a bailiff took over.

Thom McEnroe was led from the room, and Patty chose to leave. Her final words were directed at me: "I don't care what anyone believes, Mrs. Fletcher. Thom killed Cynthia Warren."

When she was gone, Judge Wilson said to District Attorney Whitney James, "Based upon Ms. Simone's confession, I presume you'll be dropping charges against Mr. Brannigan."

"Of course, Your Honor," she replied.

"For the murder of his brother, Jack," I said.

Everyone looked at me.

"Obviously," I said, "Billy didn't kill his brother."

"We know that, thanks to you, Mrs. Fletcher," said Judge Wilson.

"But I believe he isn't innocent of murder."

Malcolm stood. "Jessica," he said, "you've done

a remarkable job of unraveling things. Now I suggest that—"

"Malcolm," I said, "I know you had total belief in Billy's innocence, and it was well-placed faith. Your client is free of guilt. But only where his brother's murder is involved."

I turned and looked at Billy, whose happy mood a few moments ago had been replaced with fear and confusion.

"Billy," I said, "I'm sorry to have to do this. But I must. You murdered Cynthia Warren. You told me when I visited you in jail that you assumed the same person killed your brother, and Cynthia. You based that upon the fact that both had been killed by a single stab wound to the chest."

"So?" he said, looking to Malcolm.

"So, Billy, I left the jail with a nagging feeling that no public account of Cynthia's murder indicated where she'd been stabbed. I had Georgia Bobley review all the newspaper and TV transcripts to be sure I was correct. I was. The only way you could have known was to have inflicted the fatal wound yourself."

Now, all eyes were on Billy.

"Why would I kill my only alibi?" he asked the room.

"Because, I assume, she changed her mind about lying for you. You'd coerced her into testifying she'd been with you the night Jack was killed. What did she do, Billy, demand money for her lie? Another case of greed? There's been so much of it in this case. There's an old Chinese proverb that says, 'There is no greater disaster than greed.' That certainly has been true here."

Follow the money.

Billy turned to Malcolm and said, "Tell them she's wrong, Mr. McLoon."

Malcolm didn't reply. He was slumped back in his chair, a blank expression on his round face. Then he pushed himself to his feet, cleared his throat, and said, "Your Honor, this court and county has no jurisdiction over the death of one Cynthia Warren. As the accused's attorney, I remind you, sir, that to ask any questions of my client without his having been formally charged represents a serious Constitutional breach."

"I said all along he never should have been out on bail," Whitney James said. "If he hadn't been—"

"File your charges, Ms. James," said the judge.

"I will, Your Honor, and I move that Mr. Brannigan be held until the proper charge can be brought."

"Get a court reporter in here," the judge commanded.

"I move that—"

"I object!"

"Overruled!"

I quietly left Judge Wilson's chambers, found a cab outside the courthouse, and returned to the

Ritz-Carlton where I immediately started packing. I was interrupted by the ringing of the phone.

"Jessica? Seth here. Thought you'd be at the courthouse."

"I was. I'm packing. I want to catch the first plane to Bangor."

"You sound upset."

"It will pass. I'm calling Jed Richardson to see if he can pick me up. Care to join me?"

"I would except—"

"Except what?"

"I made dinner plans with Ms. Farkas this evening."

I couldn't help but smile. "Then I suggest you follow through on those plans and come home later."

"What's happened to send you scurryin' back to Cabot Cove so fast?"

"Lawyers, Seth. And the law. I've had my fill. See you when you get back."

Chapter Twenty-nine

"Yes, Vaughan, it was an eye-opening experience," I said to my publisher, who'd called from New York.

"Remarkable ending to the Brannigan trial. How instrumental were you in its resolution?"

"Not very involved at all. After all, I was there just to learn about how a murder trial works."

"Then you'll be setting your next novel in a courtroom. I'm delighted to hear that."

"Sorry to disappoint you, Vaughan, but I thought my next novel would revolve around a small regional airline. Someone tampers with the planes to put the owner out of business. Jed Richardson has agreed to be my technical consultant."

"I see. Well, Jess, you know best. I would never try to tell you what to write about. Speaking of Richardson, has he said any more about writing a nonfiction book about his experiences in aviation?"

"He said he'd think about it."

"Thanks for considering my idea, Jess, and following through on the research. I'm sure Malcolm McLoon's sudden death was a great shock to you."

"Yes, it was. I had no idea he had such a serious heart problem. You'd never know it from the way he lived."

"I read that McLoon's assistant, Rachel Cohen, is handling Brannigan's defense in the murder of the Warren girl."

"That's right, Vaughan. And she'll do a fine job—provided she can find the right sitter for her children. Have to run. I'll be in touch."

I was about to spend an hour outlining my next book when the phone rang again. It was Seth Hazlitt.

"Are we still on for dinner tonight?" I asked.

"Ayuh. The three of us."

"Three?"

"Jill Farkas arrived this morning from Boston. I invited her to spend a few days in Cabot Cove, see the sights, get away from Boston. Thought the three of us could break bread and hash over everything that happened in Boston."

"Seth."

"What?"

"I just remembered an appointment I made for this evening. I completely forgot. You and Jill will just have to enjoy dinner together, without me."

"That's disappointing, Jessica."

"I know. Give me a call tomorrow. And my best to Jill."

I defrosted a container of homemade clam chowder, sliced a loaf of onion sourdough bread I'd bought that morning at Sassi's Bakery, and settled down at my computer.

OUTLINE
"Murder at 30,000 Feet"
By Jessica Fletcher

Life was good again.

Learn more about
the "art" of murder!

Don't miss the next
Murder, She Wrote
mystery novel:

A Palette for Murder

by Jessica Fletcher
& Donald Bain

Coming from Signet
in October, 1996

She was naked.

There wasn't a hint, an expression, a gesture to indicate that she was uneasy being nude in front of fifteen strangers, male and female.

She was a pretty young girl, in her early twenties perhaps, but not beautiful. At least not according to the prevailing standards set by the arbiters of beauty in Hollywood, or the modeling agencies. Her features were too coarse to be labeled classic. Sensuous, though, large brown heavy-lidded eyes; lips full and fleshy; and thick auburn hair, obviously washed that morning and catching the sun that poured through large windows on the studio's north wall.

Her body was firm and without blemish, breasts in proportion to her overall frame. I judged her to be only slightly over five feet tall, nothing willowy about her. She had somewhat thick, healthy legs that undoubtedly served her well in a gym, or when playing volleyball on a beach, and had an easy laugh as she bantered with the instructor, a middle-aged man trying desperately to appear twenty years younger. He wore his graying hair long in the back, secured by what looked to me to be a silver-and-turquoise clip of Zuni origin. He was bare-chested beneath a brown corduroy jacket that was, to be kind, well worn. His jeans had holes at the knees, although I suspected he'd cut them, rather than allowing them to have occurred naturally through wear and age. The jeans looked new. Leather sandals on large bare feet completed the "look."

I've always been more comfortable with people who simply get dressed in the morning, rather than costuming themselves. But I didn't let that cloud my judgment of Jorge, our teacher, who'd always been pleasant and courteous to me and the others in the class.

"Well, shall we begin?" he asked. He turned to the naked model. "Ready, Miki?"

"Sure," she replied, getting up from where she'd been perched on the edge of a battered desk and sitting on a tall stool in front of the room. She looked to Jorge for direction. I now noticed she wore white sweat socks, her only clothing. I felt a chill, and checked her for goose bumps. None. Evidently, she was used to being naked in cold rooms.

"All right, my budding Rembrandts and Caravaggios, pick up your pencils and go to work." To Miki: "Ten minutes, my dear. Profile. Sit up straight. Hair out of your eyes. That's it. A little to the left. Aha. Perfect. Hold that pose."

I glanced over at the easel to my immediate left. The artist, a pink-cheeked young man wearing thick glasses, began sketching with fervor, licking his lips as he did.

To my right, a painfully thin and pale young

woman kept cocking her head as she observed Miki, whose expression had settled into one of supreme boredom.

I made a curved line on the paper on my easel to represent Miki's back. No. It was wrong. Too curved. I muttered under my breath as I took an eraser to it. The woman to my right was still sizing up things. I reached into the oversized black leather portfolio I'd bought for the occasion and withdrew the sketches I'd made of the male model a few days earlier. Now *that* was a back. I felt I'd captured the curvature of his spine rather nicely, and went back to trying to achieve the same thing with Miki.

Ten minutes later, Jorge asked us to stop while Miki took a break. He should have called it a breather for her because she immediately slipped into a yellow terrycloth robe, opened a fire door at the rear of the white clapboard building and stepped outside to smoke a cigarette. So young, I thought, to be hooked on a nicotine habit. If I were her mother—which I wasn't, of course—but if I were, I'd try to convince her to quit before it became too ingrained and difficult.

Jorge strolled between easels, glancing at what we'd done during the first ten minutes. "Good start," he told me. The only thing on my paper was the redrawn curve of Miki's back.

"It's so difficult to get it just right," I said.

"You did better with Harold." Harold was the male model we'd sketched a few days earlier.

"I think you're right," I said. "Is it usually easier to draw men than women?"

"Depends entirely on your sexual orientation," he replied, a small smile on his lips.

"I didn't mean it that way," I said.

"Of course you didn't, Mrs. Jessup." He moved on to the next aspiring artist.

Mrs. Jessup. My *nom de plume* at the art studio. I'm not quite sure why I didn't want to use my real name while taking the course that summer in the Hamptons, on the east end of Long Island. For some reason—could it have been my embarrassment at sketching naked people, or at my amateurish results?—I didn't want anyone to know how I was spending my mornings. *Anyone*. Even my dear friends, Vaughan and Olga Buckley, my host and hostess for the two weeks. Vaughan had been my publisher for years, and he and his lovely wife had a splendid summer home there. But I wasn't staying with them because the house was undergoing massive renovations.

Which worked out better for me. It certainly made it easier to slip away early each morning from the charming inn where I was staying, and tote my portfolio, sketch pads, pens and pencils, and other tools of the artist to the studio. "What do I do each morning?" I repeated each evening to the Buckleys when turning down yet another invitation to join them for breakfast. "Oh, I'm just enjoying being by myself, watching the sun rise on the beach, feeling the sand between my toes. That's all."

Maybe some day I'd admit to them what I'd been doing. But maybe not. It depended upon whether I managed to turn out something decent enough to take credit for. That hadn't happened yet, although

I'd been playing out my closet passion back home in Cabot Cove for the past few years. Two of my "works" hung on the walls of my home there. No one ever asked who painted them, so I was spared having to lie to my Maine friends and neighbors, too.

Fortunately, no one in the class had recognized me as J. D. Fletcher, author of bestselling murder mysteries. I was Mrs. Jessup, who always came to class with her hair hidden under a brightly colored bandana, and who was partial to oversized sunglasses which seldom left her nose.

What fun!

"Let's go," Jorge said to Miki.

She snuffed out her second cigarette, came inside, dropped her robe, and again took her position on the stool. "We'll do fifteen this time," Jorge said. "Full frontal view."

Miki faced us. A wan smile came and went. She directed a stream of air at a lock of hair that had fallen over her forehead, hunched her shoulders, allowed them to relax, and settled in for another modeling session.

Time always went so quickly during these classes; I was surprised when that day's lesson was almost over. Miki had used each of her breaks to smoke outside. Now, she settled in for her final pose of the morning. Jorge instructed her to lean forward, with her head almost down between her legs, her hair skimming the floor.

"I hate this pose," she said.

"But it's a classic," Jorge said. "We'll do ten minutes and call it a day."

I'd loosened up as the morning progressed, my strokes with the pencil more free flowing now, less constricted. My chubby colleague next to me had filled his paper with odd shapes, mostly boxes and circles, his vision of Miki. I preferred mine, as imperfect as it might have been.

"Time," Jorge announced.

I started to pack away my materials. I looked up. Miki was still in her pose. Strange, I thought. Jorge noticed it, too. He tapped her shoulder, laughing as he did.

Instead of straightening up, she slowly continued in the direction in which she'd been leaning. Over she went, face first.

"Good Lord!" I said, getting up and going to where she was sprawled on the cold, bare floor. I knelt and placed my fingertips on her neck. There was no pulse.

The others had formed a tight circle around us. I looked up. "She's dead," I said.

There were screams, and muttered curses.

By the time I stood, Jorge had already called the local police. He asked for an ambulance, but I knew it was too late. I covered Miki's bare body with her robe.

Minutes later, the door opened and two uniformed officers entered, followed closely by a man and woman from the town's volunteer ambulance service.

"She's dead," the male medic said.

"I know," I said.

One of the officers looked at me. "Who are you?" he asked.

"I'm . . . I'm J. D. Fletcher. I'm a student here."

"Fletcher?" Jorge said. "I thought you were Mrs. Jessup."

"Well, you see, I—"

The older of the two policemen narrowed his eyes. "You're that famous mystery writer."

"I really—"

"It is," one of my fellow students said loudly. "It's Jessica Fletcher. I've read some of your books."

I held up my hands and said, "I really think who I am is beside the point. Our lovely model is dead."

An hour later, after Miki Dorsey's body had been removed and we'd all given statements to the police, I packed up my things, left the studio and started walking back to the inn. There was no way, of course, that I could have discerned that my portfolio was slightly lighter than when I'd arrived that morning. A couple of sketches don't weigh much.

It wasn't until later in the day that I discovered they were missing.

⍟ SIGNET　　　　　　　　　　　　　　　　　　　Ⓔ ONYX

MURDER MYSTERIES

☐ **MURDER BY PRESCRIPTION A Cal & Plato Marley Mystery by Bill Pomidor.** When Dr. Callista Marley and her brilliant family physician husband, Dr. Plato Marley's fellow M.D.s start dying mysteriously, they risk their careers and their lives to uncover the cause, means, motive—and perpetrator of what looks like an epidemic of foul play.
(184165—$4.99)

☐ **POISONED PINS A Claire Malloy Mystery by Joan Hess.** When a sorority sister is killed, Claire refuses to believe it was a simple hit-and-run accident and decides to investigate herself.
(403908—$5.99)

☐ **THE WOMAN WHO MARRIED A BEAR by John Straley.** A bitingly vivid and suspenseful journey that will take you from the gritty Alaskan urban lower depths to the dark heart of the northern wilderness, and from a sordid tangle of sex and greed to primitive myth and magic.
(404211—$4.99)

☐ **BLOOD AND THUNDER A Nathan Heller Novel by Max Allan Collins.** Nate Heller finds himself defying the authorities, battling local riff-raff, and schmoozing with the political elite when he's lured to New York to deliver a bullet-proof vest to Huey Long, former governor of Louisiana. But someone wants to do away with the controversial presidential candidate—permanently. "A masterful job."—*Richmond Times Dispatch*
(179765—$5.99)

☐ **CARNAL HOURS by Max Allan Collins.** No sooner is Chicago detective Nathan Heller in the Bahamas when a billionaire turns up murdedred. With his client—and meal-ticket—suddenly gone up in smoke, Nate's left without a case. Until Sir Harry's beautiful daughter convinces him to take on her problem. Her husband has just been accused of murder.
(179757—$5.99)

*Prices slightly higher in Canada

Buy them at your local bookstore or use this convenient coupon for ordering.

PENGUIN USA
P.O. Box 999 — Dept. #17109
Bergenfield, New Jersey 07621

Please send me the books I have checked above.
I am enclosing $＿＿＿＿＿＿＿＿ (please add $2.00 to cover postage and handling). Send check or money order (no cash or C.O.D.'s) or charge by Mastercard or VISA (with a $15.00 minimum). Prices and numbers are subject to change without notice.

Card #＿＿＿＿＿＿＿＿＿＿＿＿＿＿ Exp. Date ＿＿＿＿＿＿＿＿＿＿＿＿
Signature＿＿＿＿＿＿＿＿＿＿＿＿＿＿＿＿＿＿＿＿＿＿＿＿＿＿＿＿＿＿
Name＿＿＿＿＿＿＿＿＿＿＿＿＿＿＿＿＿＿＿＿＿＿＿＿＿＿＿＿＿＿＿＿
Address＿＿＿＿＿＿＿＿＿＿＿＿＿＿＿＿＿＿＿＿＿＿＿＿＿＿＿＿＿＿
City ＿＿＿＿＿＿＿＿＿＿＿＿ State ＿＿＿＿＿＿＿＿ Zip Code ＿＿＿＿＿＿

For faster service when ordering by credit card call **1-800-253-6476**

Allow a minimum of 4-6 weeks for delivery. This offer is subject to change without notice.

Ø SIGNET   Ⓑ ONYX   (0451)

MYSTERY FAVORITES

☐ **MIDNIGHT BABY A Maggie MacGowen Mystery by Wendy Hornsby.** When Maggie MacGowen, an investigative filmmaker and a razor-sharp sleuth, comes across "Pisces," a fourteen-year-old hooker, she sees beneath the garish makeup to a child with a dangerous secret. Maggie wants to help this girl—but it's too late. Pisces is found the following night with her throat slashed. Now, Maggie must find her murderer.
(181360—$5.99)

☐ **THE BURGLAR WHO TRADED TED WILLIAMS A Bernie Rhodenbarr Mystery by Lawrence Block.** Bernie Rhodenbarr is trying to make an honest living, but when his new landlord raises the rent to an astronomical sum, there's only one thing left for a reformed burglar to do. But on his first night back on the job, Bernie finds not only a stash of cash but a very dead body. "Exceptional."—*Washington Post Book World*
(184262—$5.99)

☐ **ANNA'S BOOK Ruth Rendell writing as Barbara Vine.** Anna is a young woman living in turn-of-the-century London, confiding her rebellious thoughts and well-guarded secrets only to her diary. Years later, her granddaughter discovers that a single entry has been cut out—an entry that may forge a link between her mother's birth and a gory, unsolved murder in the long, hot summer of 1905. "A captivating story within a story."—*Washington Post Book World*   (405498—$5.99)

Price slightly higher in Canada   **FA2X**

Buy them at your local bookstore or use this convenient coupon for ordering.

PENGUIN USA
P.O. Box 999 — Dept. #17109
Bergenfield, New Jersey 07621

Please send me the books I have checked above.
I am enclosing $_____ (please add $2.00 to cover postage and handling). Send check or money order (no cash or C.O.D.'s) or charge by Mastercard or VISA (with a $15.00 minimum). Prices and numbers are subject to change without notice.

Card #_____ Exp. Date _____
Signature_____
Name_____
Address_____
City _____ State _____ Zip Code _____

For faster service when ordering by credit card call **1-800-253-6476**

Allow a minimum of 4-6 weeks for delivery. This offer is subject to change without notice.

Ⓞ SIGNET

MYSTERIES TO DIE FOR . . .

☐ **SOMEBODY ELSE'S CHILD by Terris McMahan Grimes.** Theresa Galloway, size sixteen, married mother of two, is a buppie—a black urban professional, but walking around the 'hood she is soon trading in her classic pumps for gumshoes, following a deadly killer in the shadow land between black and white, where the point of intersection is red. Blood-red. . . . (186729—$4.99)

☐ **A KILLIING IN REAL ESTATE, A Schuyler Ridgway Mystery, by Tierney McClellan.** Schuyler Ridgway, Kentucky realtor and amateur sleuth, hopes to sell an expensive brick colonial, but blonde, beautiful Trudi Vittitoe, the cutthroat new agent in the office, has beat her to it—again. But Trudi's appointment to show the house turns out to be murder when Schuyler finds Trudi's corpse in the basement and is sure that she, not Trudi, was the killer's real target. (187652—$5.50)

☐ **BUSY BODIES by Joan Hess.** Leave it to Claire Malloy, a devoted amateur sleuth, to start out having tea and end up investigating a murder When Zeno Gorgias, an avant-garde artist who's just moved into town, is arrested for murder after a dead body is found inside a coffin in his front yard, Claire starts snooping where she doesn't belong to become the busybody who finds the real killer. (405609—$5.50)

Prices slightly higher in Canada

Buy them at your local bookstore or use this convenient coupon for ordering.

PENGUIN USA
P.O. Box 999 — Dept. #17109
Bergenfield, New Jersey 07621

Please send me the books I have checked above.
I am enclosing $_____ (please add $2.00 to cover postage and handling). Send check or money order (no cash or C.O.D.'s) or charge by Mastercard or VISA (with a $15.00 minimum). Prices and numbers are subject to change without notice.

Card #_____ Exp. Date _____
Signature_____
Name_____
Address_____
City _____ State _____ Zip Code _____

For faster service when ordering by credit card call **1-800-253-6476**

Allow a minimum of 4-6 weeks for delivery. This offer is subject to change without notice.

THE MURDER SHE WROTE
MYSTERY SERIES

☐ **MARTINIS & MAYHEM by Jessica Fletcher & Donald Bain.** Jessica can't wait for drinks and dinner on Fisherman's Wharf, a ride on the cable cars, and a romantic rendezvous with Scottish policeman George Sutherland in San Francisco. But what she doesn't know is that solving a murder may be penciled into her agenda.
(185129—$5.99)

☐ **BRANDY AND BULLETS by Jessica Fletcher and Donald Bain.** A posh retreat in cozy Cabot Cove, Maine, offers struggling artists a European spa, psychiatry, and even hypnotism. No one, however, expected a creative killer. And when an old friend mysteriously disappears, Jessica Fletcher fears a twisted genius is at work writing a scenario for murder—putting Jessica's own life on the line.
(184912—$5.99)

☐ **RUM AND RAZORS by Jessica Fletcher and Donald Bain.** From the moment Jessica Fletcher arrives at a four-star inn nestled by a beautiful lagoon, she senses trouble in paradise. She finds hotel owner Walter Marschalk's throat-slit-corpse at the edge of the lagoon. It's time for Jessica to unpack her talent for sleuthing and discover if the murderer is a slick business partner, a young travel writer, a rival hotelier, or even the lovely widow Laurie Marschalk. (183835—$4.99)

☐ **MANHATTANS AND MURDER by Jessica Fletcher and Donald Bain.** Promoting her latest book brings bestselling mystery writer, Jessica Fletcher to New York for Christmas. Her schedule includes book signings, *Larry King Live*, restaurants, department stores ... and murder? (181425—$5.99)

*Prices slightly higher in Canada   **FA63X**

Buy them at your local bookstore or use this convenient coupon for ordering.

PENGUIN USA
P.O. Box 999 — Dept. #17109
Bergenfield, New Jersey 07621

Please send me the books I have checked above.
I am enclosing $_____ (please add $2.00 to cover postage and handling). Send check or money order (no cash or C.O.D.'s) or charge by Mastercard or VISA (with a $15.00 minimum). Prices and numbers are subject to change without notice.

Card #_____ Exp. Date _____
Signature_____
Name_____
Address_____
City _____ State _____ Zip Code _____

For faster service when ordering by credit card call **1-800-253-6476**

Allow a minimum of 4-6 weeks for delivery. This offer is subject to change without notice.